He'd tried so hard not to care about Meghan

He'd tried to harden himself against her independent spirit that desperately needed someone to care. He'd tried to focus on the woman who worked overtime to pretend that she didn't need anyone at all, not the world-weary soul underneath who needed someone to love her more than she'd probably ever admit to herself.

He wouldn't deny the physical attraction that sparked like kinetic energy between them. But she wasn't the woman he'd loved two years ago. This Meghan was tougher, stronger—and yet more vulnerable.

He was her friend. Her protector. Nothing more.

Except he was dangerously close to becoming the man who loved her.

Again.

Dear Harlequin Intrigue Reader,

We have a thrilling summer lineup for this month and throughout the season to make your beach reading positively sizzle!

To start things off with a big splash, you won't want to miss the next installment in bestselling author Rebecca York's popular 43 LIGHT STREET series. An overturned conviction gives a hardened hero a new name, a new face and the means, motive and opportunity to close in on the real killer. But will his quest for revenge prevent him from becoming *Intimate Strangers* with the woman who fuels his every fantasy?

Reader favorite Debra Webb will leave you on the edge of your seat with the continuation of her ongoing series COLBY AGENCY. In *Her Secret Alibi*, a lethally sexy undercover agent will stop at nothing in the name of justice, only to fall under the mesmerizing spell of his prime suspect!

The heat wave continues with Julie Miller's next tantalizing tale in THE TAYLOR CLAN. When the one woman whom a smoldering arson investigator can't stop wanting becomes the target of a stalker, will *Kansas City's Bravest* battle an inferno of danger—and desire—in the name of love? And in *Sarah's Secrets* by Lisa Childs, shocking secret agendas ignite perilous sparks between a skittish single mom and a cynical tracker!

If you're in the mood for breathtaking romantic suspense, you'll be riveted by our selections this month!

Enjoy!

Denise O'Sullivan
Senior Editor
Harlequin Intrigue

KANSAS CITY'S BRAVEST
JULIE MILLER

HARLEQUIN®

TORONTO • NEW YORK • LONDON
AMSTERDAM • PARIS • SYDNEY • HAMBURG
STOCKHOLM • ATHENS • TOKYO • MILAN • MADRID
PRAGUE • WARSAW • BUDAPEST • AUCKLAND

ISBN 0-373-22719-1

KANSAS CITY'S BRAVEST

Copyright © 2003 by Julie Miller

ABOUT THE AUTHOR

Julie Miller attributes her passion for writing romance to all those fairy tales she read growing up, and to shyness. Encouragement from her family to write down all those feelings she couldn't express became a love for the written word. She gets continued support from her fellow members of the Prairieland Romance Writers, where she serves as the resident "grammar goddess." This award-winning author and teacher has published several paranormal romances. Inspired by the likes of Agatha Christie and Encyclopedia Brown, Ms. Miller believes the only thing better than a good mystery is a good romance.

Born and raised in Missouri, she now lives in Nebraska with her husband, son and smiling guard dog, Maxie. Write to Julie at P.O. Box 5162, Grand Island, NE 68802-5162.

Books by Julie Miller

THE TAYLOR CLAN

Sid and Martha Taylor:	butcher and homemaker ages 64 and 63 respectively
Brett Taylor:	contractor age 39 the protector
Mac Taylor:	forensic specialist age 37 the professor
Gideon Taylor:	firefighter/arson investigator age 36 the crusader
Cole Taylor:	the mysterious brother age 31 the lost soul
Jessica Taylor:	the lone daughter antiques dealer/buyer/restorer age 29 the survivor
Josh Taylor:	police officer age 28 at 6'3", he's still the baby of the family the charmer
Mitch Taylor:	Sid's nephew—raised like a son police captain age 40 the chief

CAST OF CHARACTERS

Gideon Taylor—It's up to this arson investigator to figure out who's burning down Kansas City one building at a time. But can he uncover the truth before the arsonist destroys a very special woman from his past?

Meghan Wright—Hot to the touch. Gideon once taught her about love and fighting fires. Now that a madman has her in his sights, she returns to the one place she feels safe—with Gideon.

Daniel Kelleher—The owner of four properties destroyed by fire is wondering if he made an unfortunate investment—or if the destruction is something personal.

Jack Quinton—Is the former convict back to his old tricks? Or is he passing on his fiery skills to an apprentice?

Saundra Ames—This reporter has the hottest story of the summer.

John Murdock—Is Meghan's partner watching her back just a little too closely?

Dorie Mesner—For years she has taken in troubled children.

Pete Preston—The memory of that monster just won't go away.

Alex—A former Westside Warrior. Who is a young man supposed to trust?

Edison—Just don't call him that. He's pretty darn smart for a ten-year-old.

Matthew and Mark—They are too young to understand the truth.

Crispy—Just like Meghan and her "boys," this pooch wants a real home.

With thanks to
Germane Friends and Michael "Fireplug" Jordan
of the Kansas City Fire Department for answering
all my questions and sending me the wonderful pictures
of real KCFD firefighters.

Any mistakes are mine.

Prologue

Too late. Too late.

The nightmare's fiery talons cut deep into Gideon Taylor's dreams.

The impact of raw, compressed air exploding into a ball of flame lifted him off his feet and dumped him on his backside.

"Luke!" The hoarse shout from Gideon's ravaged throat echoed inside his mask.

Trapped in the throes of the hideous dream that wouldn't die, Gideon twisted in his bed and struggled toward consciousness and peace. But the nightmare wouldn't release him.

He needed *her.*

The groans of the ancient rafters in the condemned apartment building matched the groans of mortal pain sifting through the hiss of static in Gideon's ear.

"Luke!" Gideon rolled onto his side, straining against his heavy gear, weighed down by a fearful extra burden of guilt.

It was alive now.

Ignition. Fuel to burn. Oxygen to live and breathe.

A simple yet deadly recipe for fire.

Gideon lurched to his feet. Stooping low, he closed his grit-filled eyes and concentrated on the sounds that could lead him to his partner. "Talk to me," he whispered, willing the collapsing fortress to reveal its secrets.

The mournful howl of iron girders buckling from the intense heat taunted him from above. An invitation.

The tornadic gasp of air currents, rising and gusting ahead of the flames hit his chest and pushed him back. A warning.

The wheezing rasp of his best friend, urging him away from the heart of the fire where he lay dying, cried in his ear.

His destiny.

Gideon's internal radar tuned in to that last, weak sound. He made the world go quiet inside his head. He forced his pounding heart and his own ragged breathing into silence.

He zeroed his horrible sixth sense in on Luke.

There.

Gideon plunged into the wall of smoke, lengthening his stride as much as he dared. He strode into the belly of the fiery beast to retrieve his friend.

"Taylor! Redding!" The order from the receiver inside his helmet went unheeded. "I said clear out!"

"Luke's down." Gideon's brief reply spoke volumes.

He didn't spare another breath to argue Deputy Chief Bridgerton's orders. The chief would understand. A firefighter wouldn't leave a man behind.

Feeling his way along the wall, Gideon tripped through the remnants of the blasted doorway into the boiler room and dropped to the floor. One knee hit concrete.

The other hit something softer.

Luke.

Gideon took his hand and squeezed it tight in his fist, offering a silent promise, trading an unspoken comfort. He stretched out beside his partner on the floor, peering through the six-inch window of clear air next to the floor. Luke was flat on his back. The burning bramble of rafters and twisted metal had pinned his right shoulder and chest to the floor.

"I'm here." Gideon barely heard the words himself. "You with me?"

Luke's helmet rolled back and forth as he tried to shake his head. "No good. Get— Sumbitch—"

"You insulting me?" Gideon crooked a smile as if Luke could somehow perceive it through his closed eyes and pain-filled delirium.

Gideon hooked his arms through Luke's elbow and around his knee and pulled. Trapped.

He needed a pickax. A crane. Two more men.

If God was listening, he needed a miracle.

"Honey?" Gideon moaned out loud, desperate to escape the certain doom that awaited him in his dream. He needed to hear that taut, sexy voice—full of spunk and sass one minute, full of vulnerable tenderness the next. He reached out for her.

Gideon pulled his hand away from the metal framework. Sticky strings of melted rubber glommed onto the tips of his gloves, snagging his fingers in a deadly web.

Gideon swore. One vivid word that gave voice to his frustration and alerted Deputy Chief Bridgerton to the deadly danger they were in.

"Taylor! I'm counting you down in seconds now. Get out!"

Feeling Luke's still form beneath him, Gideon resisted the urge to share the last breath of oxygen from his tank with him. He needed that air if either one of them stood a chance of getting out.

Gideon reached out and grasped the heavy metal bars, softened by molten heat, in both hands and rose to his feet. Spurred on by determination alone, he lifted the ceiling wreckage and shoved it off Luke into the ravenous mouth *of black smoke. As the debris disappeared and crashed to the floor, Gideon's glove went with it.*

He breathed in deeply, absorbing his tank's last hiss of clean air.

Then he was on his knees and lifting. Shoulder to gut. Hand behind knees. He pulled Luke's arm around his neck and rolled to his feet, staggering beneath the weight of a full-grown man dressed in heavy gear.

"Chief!"

He was up. He was moving.

Gideon lurched down the hall toward the busted-out hole through which he and Luke had first entered the blaze. He leaned against the wall and followed it with his elbow. And when that ran out he followed blind instinct and stumbled toward fresh air and freedom.

"Taylor!" Gideon's lungs fought for air, but there was none to be had. "Take him." His knees buckled.

Bridgerton's commands echoed through the blackness closing in on Gideon.

Before he hit the ground, the burden on his shoulders lifted. Hands were there to help him. To hold him up. To take Luke from his grasping arms.

Someone snatched off his helmet and his mask. His oxygen tank vanished. He was sucking clear, cold night air into his lungs, letting the oxygen pour like a cool compress through his throat. Then hands were lifting him, pushing a small plastic mask over his nose and mouth.

He saw flames—white and orange and laughing with victory—consume the midnight sky above him. The blackened skeleton of the condemned building was silhouetted against the blaze for one instant before another explosion rocked the earth and it crumpled into a heap of billowing smoke and flame.

"We're clear!"

Those were the last words Gideon heard before he surrendered to the darkness.

When he came to in the swaying ambulance minutes later, he knew all was lost. The silence of the paramedics told him the truth. Luke was gone.

Still, he reached across the gap between their guerneys to touch his friend. "Sorry, buddy. I was too late. Too late."

"Christ, Taylor. Your hand."

It took one endless moment for Gideon to pull his gaze from the peaceful expression on Luke's ashen face to focus on the blackened tips of the fingers on his left hand.

Shock gave way to pain as the flaking layers of seared skin registered with his brain. "No—"

"No—" The hoarse cry from his nightmare took shape and sound as a shard of phantom pain in his left hand woke him halfway toward consciousness.

He reached for comfort. Reached for solace. Reached for light and life and loving perfection.

"Meg?"

He held a cold pillow in his arms.

Full consciousness crashed in on Gideon with a cruel force as violent as the nightmare itself.

The bed was empty.

He stilled the needy grasp of his arms, breathing deeply to silence the pounding of his heart. He sat up and pushed the fingers of his right hand into the sweat-streaked hair at his temple. The damp sheet slipped down his naked chest and pooled around his hips.

The air-conditioning ran on high, and the humid city air of daytime had given way to a dark, moonless night outside. But his body was burning up beneath the twisted sheets.

He hadn't had the nightmare for a month. Why now?

He reached out and caressed the empty bed beside him.

The last two fingers on his left hand refused to curl into the pillow. But then, those two fingers hadn't been able to do much of anything for the past year. Not since the night of Luke's death.

Gideon snatched his hand back to his thigh and breathed deeply.

Meghan was gone.

She'd betrayed him by taking his heart and leaving him with nothing to hold in his crippled-up hands.

"Meghan." Whispering her name was a strident cry of discord to his ears. "What did I do wrong?"

She hadn't been there for him the night Luke died. She hadn't been in his bed for two long years.

When would he get it through his thick heart?

Gideon Taylor faced his nightmares alone.

Chapter One

Red and white lights swirled into the interior of the five-story warehouse, flashing in through broken windows and shattered doorways to glance off the walls of smoke and flame and imminent destruction.

A torrent of water rained down over the heads of firefighters in black pants and coats. Their thick, black boots splashed through the flood gathering at their feet.

Though the sirens had been killed, the cacophony of dry, brittle timbers snapping beneath the heat and the thunderous rush of water limited communication to the tiny microphones and receivers mounted inside their clear face masks. But a faint sound, high-pitched and more frantic than the rest of the chaos reached Meghan Wright's ears.

She handed off her hose to the giant of a man who stood behind her and dashed toward the sound.

"We don't have containment yet. Get your butt back here."

Meghan ignored her partner's warning and plunged into the thick, gray smoke. "I know I heard something, John. I'm checking it out."

The familiar rhythms of her equipment jangled against her back with each step, drowning out the faint, repetitive tapping sound she'd heard. Wearing more than forty pounds of protective gear didn't slow her down the way it once had. Though smoke was rapidly filling the open areas of the building, the fire itself hadn't yet reached the main floor. She trailed her hand along the cool wall and hurried down the corridor toward the tier of offices at the south end of the warehouse.

One choice expletive echoed in her ear. But she heard the relenting sigh in John Murdock's deep bass voice and knew he was already maneuvering to back her up as she took point on the search and rescue. "Report your twenty every minute."

"Roger." She butted up against a wall and halted, orienting herself before choosing which hallway to follow. "I'm heading left. That's east, going toward the outer wall."

"Copy. Be careful."

"You, too." The gray and black wall of smoke lightened into a misty, translucent haze, rewarding her choice of direction. "Good girl." She rubbed her gloved hands together at the small victory and moved on. She trusted her instincts now.

That hadn't always been the case.

Four years ago, at the age of twenty-two, she'd been too broke to finish college. Needing a job that required little more than her ability to pass a physical, she'd enrolled in firefighter training. But the work proved hard, the challenges grueling. The sniping put-downs from some of her classmates had sent her home in tears or temper more than once. She'd been all set to fail.

Just as she'd managed to fail the other big challenges in her life.

But then Gideon Taylor had stumbled into her life, literally, tripping over the hose she couldn't quite roll and carry on her own. He'd taken her under his wing and taught her confidence and patience. He'd taught her tricks to compensate for a lack of physical strength. He'd taught her to love the job.

He'd taught her to love, period.

Talons of flame shot up through the floorboards at Meghan's feet, calling her wandering thoughts back to the present. The fire that had started in the warehouse basement was slowly climbing its way up toward the rafters. Gideon would tell her to keep calm. To tune out everything but the fire itself.

Let the fire talk to you, he'd say. *It'll tell you what to do.*

Meghan tried to listen. The tapping sound had disappeared. She tried harder. She tried to remember everything he'd taught her.

Gideon.

She leaned against a wall and clutched her stomach, feeling an almost physical pain at the rush of memories that threatened to consume her.

She'd found a way to fail, after all.

"Meghan?" John's sharp warning reminded her of the time.

She gathered her wits and pushed away from the wall. "I'm okay." She scanned her surroundings and reported in. "I've gone about twenty paces. I've got flames up through the floor spaces, but it hasn't caught yet."

"Have you found the vic?"

"No victim yet." A sharp, high-pitched cry turned her attention to the wall above her. "Wait. I've got something."

It was the sound of fighting to survive against impossible odds. Meghan knew all about that kind of struggle. Staying alive was one of the few things she *had* managed to accomplish.

"I'm going up to the second floor," she reported, keeping John apprised of her location.

The twin beams of the flashlights mounted on her helmet shimmered in the distortion of overheated air that rose and filled the old building. She quickly eliminated the old freight elevator as a means of transportation to the upper levels. A zigzagging series of ramps and stairways that led up to various loading and storage platforms would lead her back into the heart of the smoke.

That left the wrought-iron ladder that had been mounted directly into the brick facade. She reached for the rung above her head and gave it a solid tug. Dust and mortar bits snowed down on her helmet. When the downpour stopped, she pulled herself up onto the first rung and felt the give of anchor bolts popping out of the wall above her head. She ducked and held her breath. But the ladder settled and clung fast to its shaky mounts, supporting her weight. For once her trim build would work to her advantage. "I'm climbing."

Hand over hand, foot over foot, she ascended the ladder. Though she was only a slender five-foot-five, she trained hard to maintain peak physical conditioning. What she lacked in strength, she made up for in speed and agility. As long as the fire cooperated and stayed below, she'd have no problem locating the victim and clearing the building with time to spare.

Meghan reached the second floor and swung her legs over onto the platform that ran the length of the dockside wall. Ages ago this building had been used as a storage and distribution facility for large bales of cotton to be shipped on the river. A giant iron hook and rigging attached to a support beam was still in place beside a boarded-up opening.

These days, though, the warehouse was nothing more than a hangout for teens with too much time on their hands and not enough direction in their lives. Or it served as a makeshift shelter for homeless vagrants looking to escape the dog days of August's summer heat when the local shelters were full.

During some of the blackest moments of her life, Meghan had been a teen in trouble *and* a homeless runaway. She knew that whoever had come up here to escape the fire was scared to begin with. "I'm here to help," she shouted, taking note of the smoke creeping into the open corridor below her. "Where are you?"

A plaintive cry answered and she drifted closer to the sound.

At the end of the platform was a boarded-up office. The door behind the crossed one-by-fours was closed. The window beside the door was boarded over. How could someone have gotten in?

She already had a suspicious feeling when she knocked.

The whine became a sharp, piercing bark.

"Oh, no."

The Kansas City Fire Department made every reasonable effort to save pets and livestock involved in a fire. But extreme means of rescue were reserved for people, not strays.

"John? It's a dog." She reported her location and situation. "I'm here. I might as well get him out."

She knew her partner wouldn't appreciate endangering herself on behalf of a stray. But he was an innocent victim of this blaze and she didn't intend to abandon him yet.

"Move it, Meghan. We've got fire on the main floor. We'll lay down water at your end to try to suppress it." He, too, knew it was too late to argue. "I'll notify Animal Rescue."

"You just lucked out, furball." She spoke through the door to the creature inside, hoping to calm him. "The cavalry's here."

Meghan made a quick scan of her escape route and noted the accuracy of John's report. The floorboards at the base of the ladder were burning now. And while brick didn't burn, it could become too hot to touch. And the metal itself would conduct heat and soften, making it impossible for the ladder to sustain its own weight, much less hers and a dog's. She needed to act fast.

"How'd you get in there, boy?" The answering cry from the other side cut straight through to Meghan's heart.

She squatted and reached beneath the bottom board. But the door had latched and couldn't be pushed open. "You closed it yourself after you crawled in, didn't you?" The dog called to her again. "I'll get you out. Don't worry."

Meghan reached behind her and lifted her ax from its shoulder carrier. She wedged the head between the door frame and the middle board and pulled back, using her own body weight as leverage to pry the board loose, then toss it aside.

She removed her insulated glove to check to make sure the door and knob were cool before she reached inside to open it.

A blur of tan and black shot out between her legs. "Whoa."

Meghan danced to one side as what looked like a pint-size German shepherd dashed toward the ramp he'd undoubtedly followed to get up here in the first place. "Hey, come back. Here, boy." She whistled. But the dog ignored her. Meghan shook her head. "There's gratitude for you."

It was time she made a hasty exit herself. She put on her glove and radioed in. "The pooch is on the loose, John. Let me know if he shows up outside. I don't want him to get caught in traffic after going through all this."

"I'll keep an eye out for him."

"I'm on my way down."

"Negative." John's order halted her from stepping onto the ladder. She shook it, testing its reliability. More mortar disintegrated and blew out in puffs of dust that vanished into the smoke clouds being pushed through the corridor ahead of the hoses. "Visibility is zero from our end. I can't tell if the floor's stable."

While she watched her escape route being gobbled up by the smoke, a sudden movement in the corridor below caught her eye.

"Damn dog."

Had she risked her life for nothing?

Her stomach clenched into a knot as she fought to control the instinctive response that boosted her pulse into overdrive. Meghan blinked and squinted through the haze. Something dark, darker than the smoke itself, darted back across the opening. "Did you see…?"

It was gone.

It had been little more than an after-image imprinted on her retinas. Had the pooch made it down the stairs that quickly? Though it seemed to have more mass to it than the dog she'd seen, the black shape hadn't been bulky enough to be a firefighter in full gear. And it had moved so quickly.

But then, the heated air could play tricks on a person's vision and depth perception. Maybe it had been a comrade-at-arms.

She spoke into her microphone. "Is the corridor clear?"

"Every man's accounted for," John replied. "Is there a problem?"

"I thought I saw someone below me." It had to be the dog. She hoped he found a safe way out. "Never mind. It's gone."

"You should be, too."

The memory of flames shooting up through the floorboards was impetus enough to send her toward the ramp. If the dog had gotten down that way, so could she. Maybe she could still find him down below and rescue him, after all. "I've got an alternate route."

She picked up her ax and trotted toward the billowing rise of smoke at the far end of the platform. She checked her gauge and breathed deeply, verifying her oxygen intake before plunging in.

Going in blind was risky. Though she trailed her hand along the wall to find her path, any misstep could send her flying over the edge of the platform or plummeting through a hole or...

The dog charged out of the smoke, plowing into her shin and knocking her back a step. "Whoa! How'd you do that?"

A loud crack thundered in her ears and the whole floor tipped.

"Meghan!"

She ignored John's call and braced her back against the wall to reverse course, zeroing in on the sound of the dog's whine.

What the hell was going on here?

"The secondary escape route's collapsing." She panted the words into her mike and started to pray.

The dog charged her legs again, then circled her feet. He barked as he followed his nose toward clear air. Meghan honed in on the sound as if it was an outstretched hand.

Three steps later she was clear.

She scooped up the dog. "Good boy. I don't know what miracle you just pulled, but you saved us both." As she petted the dog, trying to calm its fears and her own, a few things became obvious. She wasn't the only female fighting for her life in this building. "Sorry. Good girl. Let's get out of here. John?"

"It's no good." She could hear the effort it cost her partner to keep the fear out of his voice. "The floor's going. There's no way we can get a ladder to you."

No ladder. No ramp. No rescue.

The platform tilted another five degrees and Meghan

scrambled for balance. If this platform gave way they'd crash through the main floor into the basement. If the fall didn't kill them outright, the flames would consume them soon enough.

This was not how it was going to end.

When the world left her with no options, she made her own.

She'd coped with her mother's death and her father's abandonment.

She'd lived through aunts and uncles who cared and those who couldn't care less.

She'd cheated death in a car crash one fateful, foolish night.

And she'd survived walking away from the truest man in the whole world.

An image of Gideon Taylor's seal-brown hair and gentle smile blipped into her mind. She'd hurt him.

She'd never said how sorry she was for hurting him.

"Dammit!" she yelled, startling the dog into an answering bark. This was not her life flashing before her eyes! "We're not going down without a fight."

Galvanized by a fiery spirit that wasn't done living yet, she pushed everything from her mind but thoughts of escape.

The hook and wench. The boarded-up windows.

"Meghan, talk to me!"

She dropped the dog and picked up her ax. She struck the first blow against the rotting wood before responding. "I'm going out the back window, John."

"The foundation drops off to the river on that side. It's four stories down. There's no way to get a truck—"

She swung again. "I know how to swim."

The first board split in two. She was breathing hard now as she jammed the ax beneath the next board and pried it loose. Sweat lined her brow beneath the tight fit of the mask and dribbled down her face. She blinked the sting of it from her eyes and attacked the next board. The platform groaned and teetered toward the heart of the fire, costing her precious leverage.

The dog barked. "I know. I know." She scooted the mutt behind her and smashed the window. The sudden rush of shifting air pressures knocked her off balance. She scrambled back to her feet, climbing uphill now to reach the window.

Meghan cleared the glass around the frame, then pulled a rope from the gear on her back. She looped it around the bale rigging.

The floor pitched. The smoke crept up to the second floor and drifted toward her, as if just now discovering its two potential victims upstairs.

She said a nervous prayer while she knotted the ends around her hips and set up a rappelling line. "I gotta see my boys. They're all I've got." She scooped up the dog, unbuttoned her coat and slipped her inside. "You'd like them, too."

Lifting her helmet, she peeled off her mask and shrugged out of her gear harness, shedding every excess pound she could before replacing the helmet and hoisting herself up to the window. The platform sank to a forty-five-degree angle, ripping away from the wall and surrendering with a fiery crash to gravity, age and fire.

"Hang on."

Charcoal smoke gusted out around her head and shoulders.

Meghan held her breath and jumped.

FIRE CAPTAIN Gideon Taylor skirted the crowd in the aftermath of the fire, an unseen extra amid the swarm of uniformed professionals doing their best to secure the site, as well as to accommodate the press and curiosity seekers who had gathered to see the show play out on the long, cloudless afternoon.

He took note of several faces in the crowd, never ceasing to be amazed at how destruction brought people out of the woodwork. Some came to help, others to gawk, a few to give thanks that the tragedy wasn't happening to them.

An interstate highway carried most people past this old industrial area on the north bank of the Missouri River. But, whatever their reason, plenty of folks had pulled off and gathered around the border of yellow tape that cordoned off the ruins of the old textiles warehouse.

He headed toward the white-and-red SUV that indicated the chief of the fleet of yellow fire engines parked in front of the remaining shell of the old Meyer's Textile Company. He'd start with the official story from the scene commander, then see what the building itself had to say about the cause of the fire. He ducked beneath the yellow perimeter tape and paused. He'd bet this old girl had plenty to say about her demise.

Gideon adjusted the bill of his black K.C.F.D. cap and tipped his head back to study the outline of the 1920s brick skeleton. Wisps of steam and smoke still puffed up from its central core, though the flames themselves had been put out.

With care and money, this warehouse could have been renovated to its one-time glory and converted to office space or—God forbid—a casino, like the reclaimed-factory-turned-tourist-trap a half mile upriver. Silhouetted against the glare of the August sun, Gideon knew this old beauty would be torn down now. Its bricks would be sold for fireplaces and landscaping, and the land would be transformed into something with considerably less personality, such as a parking lot.

It was his third investigation in as many weeks.

Big fire. Gutted building.

Accidental? Natural? Intentional?

It was his job to determine the cause of the blaze. Now that the hydrants had been shut off and the paramedics had left the scene—now that the fire had died—it was his job to sort through the charred and water-soaked remains to determine its cause.

Arson investigator.

His job promotion following rehab put him in a safer position than life on the frontline had been. Better pay. Better title. A chance to carry a badge in his wallet and arrest the bad guys, just like his brothers who were cops.

He'd trade it all in a heartbeat for another chance to serve beside his comrades.

"Taylor?"

Gideon peered through his dark glasses at the short, muscular man striding toward him. "Chief."

"You can call me Tom now." Deputy Chief Bridgerton rested his forearms atop the rolled-down waist of his insulated fire pants and smiled like the grumpy old father figure he was.

"Some habits die hard." Gideon pulled off his sunglasses and shook hands with his former boss. "Good to see you again. What ya got?"

Old friend or not, Tom Bridgerton understood the urgency of the business at hand. Fire clues could be buried beneath rubble or blown away with the wind. The sooner the investigation started, the better chance Gideon had of pinpointing the cause of the blaze.

The chief turned toward the building and indicated areas with an inclination of his head. "The fire started in the basement. Don't know how long it was burning before we got a call this morning from Westin's casino up the road saying they noticed smoke. They knew the place was abandoned and called it in. A few of the casino workers drove over to check it out. They were the only ones on scene when we arrived. One of the police officers took their statement.''

''Any idea if the Meyer family had something stored in the basement?''

''Like a pile of rags?'' Bridgerton scratched at the silver hair beside his temple and frowned. ''This place hasn't been used to store textiles since the Meyers moved out in the early eighties. It's changed hands a couple of times since then. Now it's owned by a Daniel Kelleher. He's in real estate.''

''Has he been notified?''

Bridgerton nodded. ''I called him out of a meeting. He's on his way.''

Gideon made a mental note to speak to Kelleher when he arrived. Meanwhile, he'd start nosing around on his own. ''City hall says this place was out of use, but not condemned. Any ideas?''

''The boiler was out of commission, the gas line disconnected.'' The chief shrugged. ''Maybe one of the vagrants who camps out here was trying to keep warm and lost control of his fire.''

''In this heat?'' The summer drought left the air hazy with dust that filtered through the atmosphere from dried-up farms in neighboring counties. The moisture from the river and thick bands of trees caught in the haze, forming a canopy that pushed the heat index up past one hundred for the seventh day in a row. Maybe he should look at this a little less clinically and with a little more heart. ''There weren't any casualties, were there?''

''Just one.'' The chief grinned. ''She was treated for first-degree burns on her paws and tail and released.''

''A dog?''

''If she saw anything, she's not talking.''

His brief moment of concern eased and he joined the chief's laughter.

A round of applause from the crowd, punctuated by a couple of "Woo-hoo!'s," diverted Gideon's attention. He turned and noticed the bright lights of press cameras angled toward the gap at the center of the crowd. A crush of reporters, waving microphones and snapping pictures, blocked his view.

He glanced down at the chief. "How come they're not interviewing you? I count at least three news vans here."

Bridgerton laughed. "I gave my statement. But it seems they have a real celebrity today from over at Station 16. We had quite a rescue. Channel Ten and the others wanted shots of her instead of me."

Her? The reporters were interviewing a dog instead of a veteran, command-level firefighter?

The chief slapped him on the shoulder and backed away. "I'd better get back to cleanup duty. Good to see you, Gid."

"Same here, Ch—" He doffed a two-fingered salute and corrected himself. "Tom."

"Call us sometime. The guys over at the Twenty-third would love to see you."

"Yeah." The chief snagged a young man by the arm and pulled him along with him to take care of the next task at hand.

At thirty-five, Gideon wasn't—by normal standards—anywhere close to being over the hill. But he was out of touch. A young pup like the one jogging off to do Bridgerton's bidding probably considered himself invincible.

Gideon knew better. A hero like Luke Redding would be just a name in the wall of a memorial to that kid. And Gideon would be that old guy who used to fight fires. The one who couldn't cut it anymore. The one who couldn't save his partner.

He was top brass now. A desk jockey. Gideon stared down at the nearly lifeless fingers on his left hand. Yeah,

the new recruits could learn a lot from an old warhorse like
him. He tucked his hand into the pocket of his black chinos
and pushed the thought aside, not knowing if that was sarcasm or wishful thinking.

Maybe he'd do better to avoid a visit to his old station
house and the memories—both bitter and sweet—it held.

Gideon put his sunglasses back on and calmed his emotions on a slow exhale of breath.

He strolled toward the building, pulling out his notepad
and pen. He jotted a few particulars from his conversation
with Deputy Chief Bridgerton and walked the perimeter of
the fire scene before going inside.

A burst of laughter from the crowd caught his attention.
Pocketing the notebook, he altered his course and crossed
over to see this celebrity pooch that was causing such a
media stir. At a solid six-two, he was tall enough to stand
at the fringe of the audience and see over most of them.

A bulky television camera blocked his view of the dog,
but he recognized the tall, auburn-haired woman holding
the microphone from the evening news. She looked straight
into the light of the camera without blinking. "Saundra
Ames, Channel Ten news, at the scene of a devastating
warehouse fire in north Kansas City, between the Missouri
River and Levee Road."

Somehow she managed to relay the basic details of the
blaze while continuously showing off a perfect set of por-
celain-white teeth. He had to admire a woman who didn't
even pop a sweat when she was in the spotlight on a one-
hundred-degree day. The lady was a real pro.

"Now I'd like to introduce you to one of Kansas City's
bravest—the firefighter who saved the puppy we met earlier." The reporter thrust the microphone toward her inter-
viewee. The cameraman shifted positions.

Gideon's world froze for a heartbeat in time.

Meghan.

His heart lurched in his chest. His lungs constricted so tightly, for a moment he felt as if he were breathing in hot, toxic air.

She'd stripped her gear down to her royal-blue K.C.F.D. T-shirt and regulation black pants.

But her wholesome beauty was just as uncomplicated and straightforward as he remembered. She wore her hair pulled back in what she'd called a French braid. In shades of amber and wheat and champagne, a few wavy wisps clung to the damp sheen of her soft, honey-freckled skin.

She looked fresh and young, with no makeup except for the blush of color on her cheeks and the natural, peachy tint of her lips.

And though she smiled at the mutt that squiggled in her arms and licked her chin and sniffed the microphone, her big brown eyes still held the same guarded expression he'd come to know so well in the months they'd been together.

It was really her.

Time moved forward again as Saundra Ames asked her next question. "Are there a lot of women firefighters?"

Gideon drank in every nuance of Meg's expression, every detail of beauty that resonated through his body— waking dormant yet familiar desires.

He breathed in heavily, trying to dampen his body's incendiary response to the mere sight of her. He didn't want to feel anything. Not for her. Not anymore.

"There are a few of us," she answered. "More and more with each graduating class from the academy."

"How long have you been a firefighter?"

"About four years."

As the interview progressed, Gideon began to notice the way Meghan shifted on her feet, betraying the self-conscious tension she'd once tried to hide behind a tough-act facade. What had started as a physical awareness moved on to other parts of his body that were harder to control. His compassion. His curiosity. His heart.

"And yet you risked your life for a dog. Why?" the reporter asked, clearly not understanding the size of Meghan's heart.

Meghan's gaze went out of focus and she frowned. "She needed me."

Gideon shifted with a bit of tension himself.

If she pressed her lips together, then he'd know her emotions were getting the best of her. Meghan could handle anything if she set her mind to it. But she'd never really liked to call attention to herself.

She squinted against the bright light shining in her eyes.

"How does it feel to be a role model for young women in the Kansas City area?"

"Role model?" Meghan's lips flattened into a straight line. She stuttered to find her answer. "I—I'm…just doing my job. I'm not trying… Please don't set me up to be something…" She squeezed the dog in her arms.

Gideon pulled off his sunglasses and stepped forward, obeying an unspoken impulse to move in closer to protect her. To support her. To remind her she wasn't alone. The poor kid had always been so alone.

Meghan's gaze flew past the reporter, past the cameraman, past the crowd, and connected with his. As if somehow she had known he was there. As if she needed him.

Her eyes widened in startled recognition. Her lips parted in a silent gasp.

Their gazes locked. A familiar, dynamic energy flowed between them. Quickening his pulse. Filling him with want and need and questions and regrets.

Meghan blinked with the force of a slamming door, severing the connection and shutting him out.

Her downcast eyes refused to meet his again.

Stale air from a breath held too long rushed out of Gideon's lungs. Hell. What had he been thinking? As his heart hammered back to life in his chest, his compassionate instinct died and common sense took its place.

God. Two years. And he still hadn't gotten her out of his system.

These weren't old times.

Meghan no longer wanted his help. She'd made that abundantly clear. She'd turned down his proposal and walked out of his life.

And he'd walked straight into hell.

Throwing up a stoic wall of silence that was starting to fit him like a second skin, Gideon turned and walked into the rubble of the gutted building.

At least fire was a demon he could understand.

Chapter Two

"Yeah, yeah. Fifteen minutes of fame, my ass." Meghan chucked John Murdock's big shoulder to show the guys she worked with that she knew they were teasing and that she would give it right back. "You guys are just jealous that Saundra Ames didn't give any of *you* her card."

She endured their oohs and ahhs and manly remarks about prowess with women by rolling her eyes and clicking her tongue. It had taken her a long time to learn to take their flirty remarks in sisterly stride—to understand that their teasing was a means of inclusion, not criticism. Now that she was part of their team, the men usually curbed their locker room chatter around her. It also didn't hurt that the biggest man in the unit, John Murdock, had been assigned as her partner—to compensate for her smaller size, no doubt. She knew him to be a big teddy bear who preferred books to football, despite his pro-wrestler stature. But, intimidating by looks alone, nobody messed with John.

So, normally, the nine men who shared duty with her were on their best behavior. Tolerable, at least.

But right after battling a multialarm blaze, they needed to blow off some steam. And if giving her grief about her instant stardom was the way to do it, she'd let them.

"I keep telling you boys that women like men with a sensitive side." They paused in a circle around her, waiting for her insight into the secret ways of women. "Go get a puppy and the women will be knocking down your door to meet you."

Another round of hoots and laughter followed her as the crowd of onlookers began to disperse.

One of the rookies thumped his chest. "I get to rescue the mutt next time."

"My wife would shoot me if I brought home a dog."

"Hey, I put up with my girlfriend's cats. Isn't that sensitive enough?"

"Let's get back to work, guys." Meghan pocketed the number from the animal rescue worker who would be taking the dog to the shelter for a thorough check from a vet. Since the dog had been spayed, they also wanted to run the collarless pup's description through their database to see if she was someone's missing pet.

But if no one claimed her, Meghan had a pretty good idea where the miniature, German shepherd-marked mutt could find a home. She knew four boys who would benefit from the unconditional love a pet could bring them.

When she'd spotted her team heading toward the trucks to pack up their gear, it had given her the perfect excuse to escape the glare of the Channel Ten spotlight. The whole idea of girls looking up to her as some kind of role model had turned her stomach into knots.

You freak. I'll make you a real woman.

That degrading voice, slurred by booze and accusation, had suddenly bombarded Meghan's psyche from the hidden recesses of her memory, robbing her of her temporary confidence. Her skin crawled with the memory of cruel hands and a whiskey-soaked mouth.

She hadn't known whether to scream or to run or to faint—in front of a crowd, on television—as old wounds felt real again.

But then she'd seen Gideon.

Live. In the flesh. Not a memory.

Tall and perfectly proportioned.

Dark brown hair, trimmed short to control its tendency to curl, was half hidden beneath an omnipresent baseball-style cap. His sturdy shoulders tapered to a trim waist, and she knew his legs would be long and well-muscled. His eyes were as she remembered, rich and dark and as inviting as her strong morning coffee.

The strength of his quiet presence had calmed her like the soothing stroke of his hand or the gentler caress of his silky whisper in her ear. For one cherished moment she'd breathed easier. The remembered pain receded.

But then she'd noticed the changes in him.

His rugged features etched in unsmiling stone. New lines of strain marring the taut, tanned skin beside his eyes and mouth.

The cold shutters of distrust that suddenly dulled the warmth of his gaze.

And why should he smile at her?

She didn't deserve that kind of support from him. She had no right to ask. Not anymore.

So she'd blinked and turned away like a coward before she did something foolish such as run to him or call out his name or beg his forgiveness.

By then, Saundra Ames had been talking again. The camera rolling. Meghan had dug deep into the reserves of her composure and come up with a cogent answer. By the time she'd felt brave enough to look again, Gideon had disappeared.

Thank God she had her work. The physical and mental challenges, the sense of duty and purpose, had given her something to concentrate on besides questions about her past and what advice she could give young, career-minded women.

Her co-workers had gathered at the edge of the impromptu audience to egg her on about getting out of cleanup work. Nine men in K.C.F.D. T-shirts, each eye-catching in his own way, attracted their own sort of attention from the crowd, providing the distraction she'd needed to slip away from center stage to gather her wits and hide her wounds.

Some of the men were still talking about puppies and outrageous ways to impress the ladies as they reached the Station 16 trucks and went to work. There were hoses to fold and stack, ladders to mount on the engine, gear to stow.

Meghan didn't want to shirk her duties, or she'd never hear the end of it at the station house. She figured her TV interview would already earn her enough razzing to last a week. She picked up a wrench and two axes and opened a compartment door near the cab of Engine 31. Fitting together like a three-dimensional puzzle, each piece of equipment had its assigned place, making the most efficient use of the truck's limited space.

She slipped the wrench in first, then pressed each ax into its mounting clips. After latching the compartment door shut, she climbed up onto the running board beside the open cab to gather the rigging equipment that had been tossed inside. She plunked down onto the passenger side seat to rest while she rolled a nylon rope between her fist and elbow. She had the length of it tied into a bale before she noticed the conspicuously unofficial item resting in the folds of her black turnout coat on the floorboards at her feet.

"What the hell…?" Meghan stowed the rope beneath the seat and frowned as she bent to pluck a long-stemmed yellow rose from her coat. With the stem caught lightly between the thumb and forefinger of one hand, she rested the silky soft bud in the palm of the other. "Where did you come from?"

An unbidden urge of feminine curiosity made her lift the petals to her nose. Its sweet, fragrant scent tickled her sinuses and nearly gave her a headache. But it was soft to the touch, as gentle as a caress as she stroked it against her cheek. What a sentimental gesture. What a generous gift. Except...

Meghan looked through the windshield and scanned the scattering crowd for any indication of someone watching her reaction to the discovery. Everyone seemed to have a purpose to keep him or her busy that had nothing to do with Meghan. She hopped out of the cab and turned to sift through her coat. Where had it come from? Thirty minutes ago, she'd deposited her gear and had tried to tuck her hair back into its braid before talking to those reporters. It hadn't been here then. And there was no clue, no note of explanation, for its appearance now.

A giant shadow fell across her shoulders, diverting her attention. She looked over her shoulder into John Murdock's curious expression. "What's that?"

"I found it lying in the truck on my coat."

"You been holding out on me?" he teased. "Who's it from?"

"Do you really think it's for me?" She glanced down. *Wright* stared up at her, the name label clearly visible on the front left placket of her coat. "I don't want to assume."

"Since I'm not the rose type, that'd be my guess." She looked up to see his mouth curved in an indulgent smile. "You're the only lady on the crew. I'd take it and enjoy it."

"But it doesn't say whom it's from." She found the idea of an anonymous admirer unsettling rather than charming. Someone had to know something about it. "You didn't see anyone put it here? Anyone messing with the front of the truck in the last half hour or so?"

Those big shoulders shrugged and blocked out the sun.

"I was watching you on TV with the rest of the guys. I suppose anybody could have put it in here. Don't you like flowers?"

"Well, sure, but roses are a little fancy for—"

"Is Ms. Wright still on duty? I have a few follow-up items I'd like to clarify with her." Meghan froze, hearing the succinct, curious female voice on the other side of the truck. That damned reporter again.

Her stomach cramped right on cue as the tension set in. She tightened her fingers into a fist, forgetting all about the flower until a thorn pricked her palm. "Ow. Damn." She tossed the worrisome gift into the truck and pressed her lips against the tiny wound and muttered, "I'm not up for this again."

"Here." John pulled a blue bandanna from his pocket and pressed it into her hand. "Get out of here." He nudged her elbow and nodded toward the abandoned building. "Hide out for a few minutes. I'll cover for you."

Meghan breathed a deep sigh of relief. John might be built like a grizzly, but he was definitely a teddy bear. She squeezed his hand and mouthed her thanks. "I owe you one."

"You owe me a bunch. Now scoot."

She gladly did as ordered and quietly slipped away from the truck. She moved quickly and within a minute was leaning back against an interior wall of scorched brick, breathing deeply and trying to even out both her pulse and her nerves.

At last. She was alone.

She needed the quiet to regroup and to get her dealing-with-people facade back into place.

That rose had been a kind gesture from someone too shy to reveal himself. But on top of everything she'd gone through today, it felt like an invasion of her privacy. Saundra Ames's incisive reporting had already stripped her down to her most vulnerable fears. The rose was just the kicker that sent her over the edge into panic. There'd been a hundred or more onlookers in the parking lot watching her. It was probably a gift from one of those girls Ms. Ames had said she inspired.

Meghan breathed a little easier now that she was alone. She removed John's bandanna and inspected the puncture wound on her hand. The bleeding had stopped. Maybe she shouldn't read too much symbolism into the idea of being cut open to expose all her insecurities.

She'd always healed best when she was alone. For her, alone was the safest place to be. The only place where being imperfect didn't matter.

Tucking the bandanna into her belt, she tipped her chin up to study the empty shell of what had once been a magnificent building bustling with people and commerce. Now it echoed like a cavern.

Though the outer walls and most of the ceiling structure were basically undamaged, the interior was riddled with piles of blackened debris, some of it still steaming from the force of the fire and the heat of the day. The distinctive imprint of acrid smoke tingled her nostrils. Meghan pressed her knuckles to the tip of her nose to conquer the urge to sneeze.

Curiosity as well as a sense of mourning prompted her to push away from her hiding place and to take a walk over to where she had rescued the dog. She picked her way carefully across the wooden floorboards, knowing that even this far from the central source of the blaze, the support structures could be weakened.

Water still grouped in puddles in the sunken places on the main floor, and she could hear the steady drip of it working its way down to the basement level. The corridor where she'd first entered and followed the sounds of the dog's cries had been reduced to twin piles of ash and rubble.

She stopped near the edge of the last solid board and looked up at the back wall. The second-story platform was gone. The heavy beam and its iron rigging—with her rope still tied to it and hanging out the broken window—was the only structure left. She looked down into the exposed basement area. The rest of the support system had collapsed into a fiery pit.

She and the pooch had been damn lucky to survive.

"Revisiting the scene of the crime?"

Meghan sucked in a breath and clutched her hand at her waist, startled by the familiar voice. When she turned to face Gideon, the thudding of her heart still hadn't stopped. "I thought I was the only one in here."

His watchful eyes seemed to bore right through her. "I'm doing the preliminary walk-through on my investigation."

"That's right." Without the courage to meet the questions in his expression, she settled for talking to the center of his broad, streamlined chest. "I heard you got promoted to Investigator." Unexpectedly hungry to reacquaint herself with the strength and dimension of his body, she let her gaze drift up past the point of his chin to the classic male contours of his mouth. But she wasn't quite ready for eye contact. Gideon had always been able to read her emotions like a book. "Congratulations."

"Thanks."

A subtle movement at his waist dragged her gaze downward again. He'd tucked his hand into his pocket. He'd always had such wonderful hands. Nicked and calloused enough by life to give them character, with the strength and control that could soothe or arouse, by turn.

Sweet, tender memories flooded her, raising goose bumps of anticipation along her skin as she remembered his touch—so very different from the creepy sensations that had assaulted her earlier during the TV interview.

But then she realized he'd angled the left side of his body away from her. She'd been staring at his wrist above his pocket, wishing for things that could never be. Wanting something she had destroyed two years ago.

"Sorry." She mustered a smile and shrugged, not sure what she was apologizing for. Staring? Or breaking this good man's heart?

"So *you're* the one who made the great escape." Gideon was looking up at the rope and beam now. "You always were as agile as a monkey. Still, that must have been a close call."

"For once it paid to be scrawny." She wanted to thank him for changing the topic. Work was one thing she could talk about. It might be the only safe topic where Gideon was concerned. "I don't think that platform could have held a full-size man."

"Looks like it didn't hold you, either. You took a big risk."

For one brief instant Meghan's insides went all drizzly with warmth. Was that concern she heard? The smooth texture of his deep-pitched voice melted her momentary resolve into a pile of goo.

Though Gideon had always been the strong one in their relationship—the whole one, the one with his head on straight—he almost sounded as if *he* was the one who needed reassurance now.

"I'm okay. I know how to handle myself on the job now." Meghan looked around the angle of Gideon's shoulder and forced herself to make eye contact with him. It was impossible for her to look away from the raw hurt and hunger she saw there. "Really. I learned from the best. I'm fine."

"Scrawny, hmm?" A sudden blaze of heat shattered the

lingering walls of doubt and distrust in his expression. His warm brown gaze caressed the lines of her face and hair, then explored the subtle jut of her breasts, triggering a pebbling response at the tips as if he'd touched her with his hands. "As I recall, there were plenty of curves in all the right places on that body of yours."

Meghan crossed her arms and shivered at her body's wanton response to his hungry look and suggestive words.

She tried to come up with some kind of joke, some excuse to deny the powerful effect he still had on her. But she was trapped by desire, caught up in the memories of how good it felt to be close to this man, how exciting and scary it had been to have him want her. The meaning of this flood of heat eluded her, but she couldn't turn away.

When he reached up and traced the curve of her cheek with the tip of one finger, she closed her eyes and savored his touch. This was too good, too sweet, too wonderful to be real.

She tilted her face, urging him to repeat the caress along her jaw, her brow. He rested the weight of his finger against the arc of her lower lip.

A familiar coalescence, like warm, sweet syrup, gathered inside her and moved with nearly painful deliberation toward the juncture of her thighs. The pressure built with agonizing slowness. There. Deep in her belly.

Behind the scars.

Meghan flinched beneath the delicate stroke of his finger along the straight line of her nose, fighting the intrusion of memory. Fighting off the past that would rear its ugly head and destroy Gideon's magic.

"Meg?"

He caught the tip of her nose between his thumb and forefinger in a playful gesture one might use with a child.

A child.

She lost the fight. The spell was broken.

Meghan's eyes snapped open and she backed off a step, not sure whether to dredge up an apology or a thank-you.

"You had some soot on your nose." Gideon splayed his fingers in front of her face, showing her the greasy black residue.

"Oh." Embarrassment couldn't begin to describe the emotions trying to break through. She pressed her lips tightly together and waited for control to kick in. Gideon wouldn't want her to have any feelings for him—grateful or sexual or otherwise. She'd long ago killed any feelings he had for her. So she made a joke. "Well, you know me and makeup. I never get it quite right."

Gideon didn't laugh and neither did she. Instead he strode away from her and climbed down a ladder into the basement. It was an easy movement that betrayed no reaction to the heated moment they'd just shared. "I want you to have a look at something I found earlier."

If she was smart, she'd turn around and walk the other way. But then, she'd never been able to resist one of Gideon's challenges. And if it was work-related…

That was where their relationship had started in the first place. As a probationary recruit about to wash out of basic training, Gideon had taken her under his wing and turned her into a real firefighter. She'd learned her skills at the foot of a master. This was her career now. This was who she was and who she needed to be. She'd be foolish to turn down the opportunity to learn more.

Carefully watching her step and keeping her distance, she followed him down the ladder. "What is it?"

She stepped down into a half-inch slush of water and dirt and debris. While the muck oozed around the soles of her boots, Gideon directed his flashlight across the floor.

"There." He lifted one of the charred planks piled in the middle of the floor and tossed it aside. "You can hardly see it through this slime, but it's there."

She moved to help him clear more boards to prop them up in a makeshift dam until they'd exposed a four-foot square of old stone tile. He used the beam of his flashlight to point out crisscrossed markings burned into the floor that were a darker shade of black than the surrounding charcoal and ash.

Meghan squatted for a closer look. She wiped her hand clean on her pant leg and reached down to touch one of the charred lines. Her finger came back sticky. "What is it?"

Gideon hunkered down beside her, testing the tacky residue as she had, but bringing a sample up to his nose to sniff it. "My guess is a petroleum distillate, like kerosene or gasoline."

"A catalyst. Does that mean what I think it does?"

Gideon nodded. His serious expression left no room for doubt. "Arson. Someone set it deliberately."

A cold, cold feeling of alarm stilled the skittering pulse in her veins. The shadowy figure darting across the corridor before the platform collapse suddenly made sense. It hadn't been the dog at all.

"Gideon?" What she'd seen had been more hallucination than fact. Her description wouldn't give Gideon or the police much to go on. But it might be important. "You didn't find any trace of a body, did you?"

"No."

The quirk of his eyebrow told her he was interested in what she had to say.

"Then I think I saw who set the fire."

Chapter Three

Meghan didn't know which disturbed her more—her sudden notoriety or seeing Gideon again.

At least the congratulatory phone calls at the station and the bouquets of flowers from her battalion commander and three animal rights agencies would go away after a few days.

Memories of her time with Gideon Taylor would haunt her forever.

After she'd given her brief statement to Gideon, she returned with her team to the station house. Off duty for the next sixteen hours, Meghan had showered, changed into a pair of khaki shorts and a navy tank top, shoved her feet into a pair of slip-on tennis shoes and sped off in her pickup truck. She'd delivered all but the commander's bouquet to the Truman Medical Center, and stopped by the animal shelter.

She'd been efficient. An hour and a half later, she was pulling up to a house in the Kansas City suburb of Raytown, Missouri, not too far from Kauffman and Arrowhead stadiums. She parked her Ford Ranger in the long asphalt driveway in front of the white, two-story, barn-style house that felt more like home than her own apartment.

Meghan rolled down the window and killed the engine before leaning back into her seat and taking the first un-

fettered breath she'd enjoyed since the station dispatcher
had sounded the alarm that morning. She sat in the driveway and studied the house with its detached garage. The
gold shutters needed a new coat of paint and the shrubs out
front needed some pruning.

There was a normalcy about a house that was truly lived
in, which Meghan envied. But it wasn't the need to tend
something, or the towering pine trees, or even the massive
yard that brought her back here every evening and weekend
she was free. It was the people.

Her boys, to be more precise.

No. Dorie Mesner's boys. Or, most accurately, the four
boys who were orphaned or legal wards of the state who
had been assigned to live in Dorie's group home.

The same group home where Meghan had spent one relatively safe year of her life before turning eighteen and
moving out on her own.

She leaned across the bench seat and stuck her fingers
through the grate of the plastic pet carrier. She smiled at
the cold nose that butted her hand and laughed at the warm
tongue that licked her fingers. "Don't be nervous. I was at
my first visit, too. But Dorie's a nice lady. She comes on
all tough in the beginning, but by the end of the day she'll
be baking you cookies. Or, in your case, sneaking you dog
treats.''

The plaintive whine from the pooch, which the vet had
officially labeled a terrier mix, struck a familiar chord in
Meghan. The seven-month-old dog had been abandoned.
The dog's life as a runaway had left her traumatized by the
fire, with sore paws and two thumb-nail-size patches of bare
pink skin on her tail where she'd been singed by flying
embers.

Basically, Meghan had agreed to be the dog's foster parent. "Come here. We girls have to stick together around

here.'' She opened the carrier and let the dog climb into her lap so they could cuddle and trade comforts.

With the animal shelter full, she was to watch the dog until they could determine where she belonged. In the meantime, Meghan had to try to take care of her without becoming too attached—just in case the dog had to go away again. She scratched the base of the dog's ears, reassuring her of her good intentions without actually making the promise that she could stay.

Meghan had heard that promise and seen it broken more than once.

''Whatcha got, Meghan?''

Edison Pike. A gangly ten-year-old with a shock of two-toned blond hair stood at the open truck window. She should have known he'd spot the dog right away. His observant blue eyes didn't miss much. He was as smart as his namesake, but she knew better than to call him that.

''Hey, Eddie.'' The dog propped her two front paws on the door and sniffed at her potential playmate. Eddie, on the other hand, held himself perfectly still. ''It's okay.'' Meghan thought he might be leery of the dog's eager greeting. ''She's friendly. She doesn't bite, though she might try to lick you on the nose.''

''What's wrong with her? She's missing fur on her tail. What are the bandages on her paws for?'' Ah, yes. Asked with all the detachment of true scientific curiosity.

A nice cover for a boy who wasn't willing to risk his emotions. Meghan could relate.

''She was caught in a fire I worked today. The vet said the injuries aren't severe. No smoke inhalation to worry about, only a few minor burns. We just have to watch that she doesn't scratch or chew on the raw skin. We get to watch her for a few days.''

Eddie inched a step closer. ''Does she have a name?''

''Not yet.'' He lifted the back of his hand to within reach

of the dog's nose. The dog snuffled Eddie's hand, then twisted her neck to press the top of her head into his palm, demanding to be petted. "I think she likes you."

The dog was doing all the work, but Meghan was pleased to see that Eddie hadn't pulled his hand away. "I think we should call her Crispy."

"Yeah?"

"She's lucky she didn't get burned to a crisp," Eddie reasoned.

"Crispy it is, then. Here." She hooked a leash to Crispy's new red collar and handed her through the window to Eddie. "Keep a good hold on her. Why don't you run her to the backyard where the fence is? Make sure the gate's shut tight."

"Okay."

Pleased with his new friend and new responsibility, Eddie set the dog on the ground and took off toward the back of the house. Meghan moved at a much slower pace. As stress and adrenaline let down, fatigue set in. She picked up the carrier and a sack of pet supplies from the back of the truck, and hiked up to the front door. With her hands full, she nudged the doorbell with her elbow.

Seconds later the door sprang open. "Meghan."

Dorie Mesner, her cap of snow-white hair flying out in frizzy curls all around her head, uttered the robust greeting and pulled the grocery sack from her arms all at the same time. She stuck her nose inside the sack. "What have you done this time?"

Meghan grinned. "I'm fine, thanks. How are you?"

"Oh." Dorie grimaced and ushered Meghan inside. "Come in, come in."

Meghan followed the seventy-year-old woman through the house into the kitchen, then set up the carrier and bowls with food and water on the screened-in back porch. "Crispy is going to stay with us for a few days, until the humane society can verify whether she'll go up for adoption or not.''

''Just like those boys. It's a darn shame, living in limbo like that.'' Dorie picked up a wooden spoon and stirred something wonderfully spicy and aromatic on the stove. ''Don't mind my fussin'. She can stay. My Jim had huntin' dogs the whole thirty-six years I was married to him. That backyard was made for pets.'' She covered the pot and rinsed the spoon in the sink. ''I just hope those boys don't get too attached in case she does have a home to go to.''

''I know. It'd be hard on all of us. But we'll be there for each other, right?'' Meghan smiled, well aware of the other woman's penchant to helping anyone—or anything—in need. With shameless curiosity, Meghan opened the pot Dorie had just stirred. ''Mmm. Homemade spaghetti sauce. Mind if I stay for dinner?''

Dorie propped her hands on her ample hips. Her green eyes twinkled. ''Have I ever turned you away?''

Meghan crossed the room and traded hugs. ''Thankfully, no.''

''Oh, I almost forgot.'' Dorie dashed into the family room and Meghan stepped into double time to follow. ''You're going to be on TV. They showed a picture of you and that awful fire on the news teaser.'' She perched on the vinyl couch and picked up two remotes. ''I tried to program the VCR to record Channel Ten, but I never can tell if I got the right thing. Oh. There you are.''

Dorie's infectious excitement lost its appeal when the familiar image of the old Meyer's Textile warehouse flashed across the screen. The camera shot panned down across the crowd, as if drawn like a beacon to Saundra Ames's striking red hair.

''That Saundra Ames is a real looker, isn't she?''

Definitely, Meghan silently agreed. *She* looked like a small, pale shadow, by comparison, standing beside the statuesque reporter, clutching the dog. Meghan looked as if she'd been working a hard job on a hot day. A sheen of perspiration glistened on her forehead in the light of the camera, while Saundra commanded attention with the just-powdered perfection of her taut cheekbones and bright blue eyes. The reporter's soft blue silk suit looked stunning, while Meghan's sweat-marked T-shirt and slacks just looked tired. Like her.

What kind of woman are you, anyway, freak? You can't look the part, or act it, can you.

That was Uncle Pete's wretched voice taunting her inside her head. Meghan squeezed her eyes shut and tried to block the vile memory. She couldn't watch this. She could only see herself through Pete Preston's eyes, and the image wasn't very flattering.

She couldn't even remember what lame answers she'd given Ms. Ames, but she was sure she didn't want to listen to herself drone on about fire safety and her hopes that the young women of Kansas City would set goals and pursue them no matter what life threw at them.

Even if it threw you one doozy of a curve ball. Over and over again.

It was only in the past year or so that Meghan had learned to believe that a strikeout wasn't her only option. A few times, in fact, she'd managed to take one of those curve balls and turn it into a hit. Her therapist had advised her that her past didn't necessarily have to be a handicap. She could use it as a tool to help others.

That's when she'd called Dorie to ask if she needed an extra hand at her group home.

But healing was a long process. What had still been an open wound two years ago was now a thin scar that could withstand day-to-day encounters with her co-workers and a few close friends. But she still wasn't ready to see herself paraded in front of a camera as a potential object of ridicule. As a pariah who couldn't quite measure up. One who wasn't good enough or whole enough to be a success in a modern woman's world.

She might never be.

Let Dorie satisfy her curiosity. Meghan wanted no part of this. "Been there. Done that." She had already backed up to the open doorway. "I'll just go hang with Eddie in the backyard."

The older woman nodded without tearing her gaze from the television screen. "The little ones are outside, too. Would you mind checking on them?"

"Sure."

The evening air didn't feel any less scorching than this afternoon's. But Meghan inhaled a muggy breath, grateful for the chance to be outside, far away from the uncomfortable image of her freckled face plastered on the news for all of Kansas City to see.

She stood at the top of the stoop and let the worries of the day fade into the present. Crispy charged across the length of the yard, with Eddie and a tiny toddler in hot pursuit. Little Mark Grimes had just turned two. About the same size as the dog, Mark's dark brown curls bounced atop his head with each stiff-kneed waddle. His chubby fingers reached out for the dog, though he wasn't catching anything but air. And his delighted giggle as Crispy changed course and circled around him could only be described as a chortle.

So young, so innocent. Orphaned six months ago by a tragic house fire, all he wanted was someone to love him.

Meghan did.

As he toddled past, she dashed down the stairs and scooped him up into her arms. "Whee-ee!"

Mark laughed. He stuck his arms out like an airplane and she twirled him around, finally setting him down in the middle of the yard where Eddie and Crispy were wrestling.

Meghan plopped down onto the ground next to Mark and let him climb on her as if she were a jungle gym.

Mark was an adorable little tyke who would have been snatched up by adoptive parents in an instant if it wasn't for one not-so-small thing. His brother.

Speaking of which...

With Mark and Eddie occupied, she let her gaze slide around the perimeter of the yard. The swing set was empty, the sandbox unused. The remote-control car on the patio sat untouched.

A tight fist of unease gripped her stomach.

She plucked Mark from her shoulders and sent him toddling off after the dog again. "Eddie?" She rose to her knees, then purposely climbed to her feet. "Where's Matthew?"

Eddie's thin chest rose and fell as he panted for breath. He pointed to the garage. "Last I saw, he was in there."

Unlike his brother Mark, four-year-old Matthew Grimes remembered the night his home was destroyed and his parents were killed. The brothers were a matched set, legally and emotionally bonded to remain together. And Matthew was definitely a much harder sell to any prospective parent. Though child therapists had worked with him, he refused to talk about that night.

He refused to talk, period.

Feeling more than a twinge of concern tingling in her belly, Meghan hurried to the faded side door that opened onto the backyard. With the main door closed, the interior of the garage was dark and stale with humidity. She stood with her hand resting for a few moments on the peeling paint of the door frame, giving her vision a chance to adjust to the shadows. "Matthew?"

Not that she expected him to answer. She couldn't imagine the terror and grief that must have shocked the boy into such a sullen silence. She scanned the interior, much as she would a smoke-filled building, holding herself still and patiently waiting for some sound or smell to give away the location of any victims trapped inside.

Dorie must have mowed today. The air in the garage was pungent with the scents of cut grass and gasoline. But she detected no light, soap-water scent of boy. Until…

The creak of old wood and the rattle of metal on metal turned her attention to the workbench that had once belonged to Jim Mesner. Perched on top, with his short legs hanging over the edge, sat Matthew.

"Hey, big guy." Meghan greeted him with a smile and walked slowly toward him. The tension in her stomach eased a fraction at having located the boy, but the sadness in his eyes kept her from celebrating. "What are you doing out here? You know the garage is a 'no' place. Dorie wants you to play outside or in the basement or in your room. With the van and the tools—" not to mention the pesticides and can of gasoline for the lawnmower "—this isn't a safe place to play."

His gaze drifted over to her shoulder without really looking at her. Meghan climbed up beside him on the bench. Maybe he was making progress, after all—he didn't slide over or jump off to get away from her.

"I'll bet you didn't come here to play." She knew he hadn't. She could count on one hand the number of times she'd actually seen him holding a toy or chasing a ball or doing anything as carefree and therapeutic as letting loose and running through the yard with a child's energy and abandon. She tucked her hands between her knees and continued in a gentle voice. "Did you come in here to be alone?"

She'd almost given up hope of getting any kind of answer when he slowly nodded his head. Meghan pressed her lips together to keep herself from startling him with an effusive smile.

"I like to be alone sometimes, too." She shrugged her shoulders with an honest sigh. "Especially on a day like today." She skipped any talk about the fire. "Did you know I was on TV? Dorie's making a tape. I looked pretty silly holding that dog. Did you meet Crispy?"

Matthew was watching her face now. This was the kind of therapy his counselor had said he needed. Just keep talking to him. Keep interacting. Keep including him in day-to-day activities. Eventually, when he was ready, he'd join in. He'd start talking when he had something he wanted to say.

With his brown hair and brown eyes, Matthew was a miniature version of Gideon. Instantly the illusory pain in her belly returned.

Just keep talking. "I met an old friend of mine today."

Well, not exactly a friend. Not anymore.

"He looks a lot like you. Dark brown hair. Dark eyes." She offered him a gentle grin. "He's taller, though. I imagine you'll be just as tall one day."

Nothing.

"His name is Gideon Taylor." She'd steer away from his being a firefighter and wouldn't mention his big family. That left her with, "He's a very special man. Strong. Quiet, like you. Sometimes he communicates without using any words at all."

Matthew made eye contact.

Meghan's smile wavered. "I wish you could meet him." *He'd make a perfect daddy.* "He's patient." Matthew's eyebrows lifted into a questioning frown. "That means he takes his time to do things. He doesn't push anyone to go faster than they need to."

Her mind drifted back to all those evenings Gideon had worked with her after a training session to help her build her strength or to teach her a new skill. She thought of all those nights when he'd patiently shown her the way a man and woman could please each other. He hadn't minded the scars that showed on her belly. He'd treated her as if he thought she was beautiful. She remembered all the mornings after when they'd cuddled in bed and talked.

He'd made her feel as if she was a beautiful person— *almost.*

"He was a wonderful teacher." Her breath hitched on an unexpected gasp. Oh, God. Were those tears stinging her eyes? Meghan turned her head so Matthew couldn't see.

She was the one who had screwed things up. *She* was the one who had broken Gideon's heart without an explanation. He'd been willing to take a chance she couldn't allow him to take.

She didn't have the right to cry.

"The grass on that lawnmower must be getting to me." She'd never had an allergy in her life. Meghan wiped her hand across her eyes. "You'd like him."

On impulse, needing the human contact as much as she suspected Matthew did, she leaned over and hugged him. She squeezed him tight and pressed a kiss onto the crown of his silky fine hair.

Matthew didn't hug her back. But he didn't push her away, either.

This was as close as she'd ever come to having a child of her own. So she held him close a few moments longer, inhaling his sweet, clean scent and damning the fates for making her so flawed in the first place.

"Meghan!" Eddie's young tenor voice nabbed her attention before he appeared at the side door of the garage. Was there a problem with Mark? Crispy? She left a comforting hand on Matthew's shoulder and focused in on the rapid-fire delivery of Eddie's words. "Dorie says you have to come into the house right away. There's a phone call. It's Alex. I think he's in trouble again. She looks like she's gonna pass out. You gotta come."

Alexis Pitsaeli was the oldest boy who lived at the group home. He was all of sixteen and ready to take on the world. Unfortunately he didn't always choose the smartest way to conquer it.

Meghan jumped down off the workbench and took Matthew's hand. She never released him as he climbed down. Pulling him along behind her, she picked up Mark and followed Eddie into the house.

They found Dorie standing in the kitchen, grasping the disconnected phone in one hand and the counter in the other. Her skin had faded to an alarming shade of ash and her cheeks were splotched with color. This wasn't good.

"What's wrong?" Meghan asked, depositing Mark into Eddie's arms and sending the three boys down to the basement. She hung up the phone and guided Dorie to the table to make her sit.

"It's Alex. He's at a police station in downtown K.C. The officer said he'd been in a fight." Dorie breathed in shallow puffs of air and patted her chest. "I can feel my blood pressure going through the roof already. I hope he's all right."

"I'm sure he's fine, or the officer would have said otherwise." She hoped. "How can I help?"

"Will you go down to the precinct office for me? I don't think I can handle the paperwork or his attitude right now."

"I'll go." She turned Dorie's wrist between her thumb and fingers and checked the older woman's racing pulse. "You been taking your medication?"

"Yes. And watching my diet. There's not a lick of salt in that spaghetti tonight." Her vehement protest faded on a pant of breath. "It's just stress. And my seventy-year-old heart."

Meghan frowned. She fully intended to help Alex understand the consequences of his actions. "Why don't you lie down? I'll feed the boys, and when I get back with Alex I'll bring you some dinner.''

Dorie shook her head. ''Nonsense. I can feed the little ones. You just bring that teenager home so I know he's safe.''

''I will.''

Reluctant to leave Dorie alone, but understanding that this was the best way she could help, Meghan pressed a kiss to her grandmotherly temple and hurried toward the front door. She slowed her pace as she neared the entryway, thinking something looked odd. She stopped when she realized what was out of place. A large bouquet of yellow roses sat on the hall table. Long-stemmed and studded with statis and greenery. Meghan released a long, low whistle. Someone had spent a fortune.

On one very sick idea of a joke.

Meghan felt a corresponding tension quiver through her muscles, setting her entire body on edge. She looked over her shoulder to Dorie. ''Where did these come from?''

''Oh, those came for you while you were out back. After that phone call, I forgot to tell you.'' Dorie pressed her hand over her heart. ''Imagine. A dozen roses. You must have an ardent admirer.''

Meghan frowned. She didn't like this. She didn't like this at all. ''There are only eleven roses.''

''I didn't notice.'' The older woman shuffled into the foyer beside her. ''Did the florist make a mistake?''

''I don't think so.''

One anonymous rose she could write off as a little weird and donate it to the hospital with the rest of her flowers.

Eleven golden mates showing up on the same day to complete the gift was downright creepy.

''Did you see who delivered them?''

''The doorbell rang during the news.'' She could hear the agitation in Dorie's voice as she picked up on Meghan's tension. "By the time I got to it, the bouquet was on the doorstep and a white van was backing out of the driveway. The sun was reflecting off the windshield and I didn't have my glasses on."

"Was there a name on the side of the van?"

Dorie shrugged an apology. "If I remember, there were some red letters or markings on the driver's door."

Meghan pulled a thorny stem aside to get a closer look at the blank envelope. "And you're sure they're for me? There's no name."

"Honey, my Jim's been dead goin' on ten years now. Who'd be sending an old girl like me flowers?"

Meghan traded worried looks with Dorie. "How did they know where to deliver them? Why didn't they go to my apartment?"

Only John Murdock and the chief knew that this was her second home. And she doubted anyone at Family Services who knew she volunteered here would be sending flowers. She supposed someone could have tried to deliver them at the station house and been redirected here. But John was off duty, too. Who else knew to find her here? Had she been followed?

Dorie tapped her on the shoulder. "Don't stand there gawkin' at 'em. Open the card and see who they're from. Maybe that'll solve the mystery."

An uneasy feeling settled around Meghan's shoulders as she plucked the envelope from its plastic mount. That uneasy feeling knotted into a combination of fear and anger— a sense of violation deep in her gut—as she pulled out the card and read it.

"That's odd." Dorie's confusion echoed her own. "It doesn't say."

Meghan crammed the note into the pocket of her shorts. The discomfiting words were already emblazoned in her memory.

You are truly Kansas City's Bravest.
You know I love you.

Only one man had ever claimed to love her.

And she'd thrown his proposal back in his face and walked out of his life forever.

Chapter Four

The drive into downtown Kansas City gave Meghan plenty of time to plan what to say to Alex, and then dismiss each version of her speech three times over. She wasn't his mother. She wasn't even his legal guardian. She was just a friend. He was a young man who needed someone he could count on. He needed a role model to learn from—someone who could teach him to make smarter choices without compromising his self-respect.

Meghan didn't think she was up to the task. But she had to try. She had to put her own self-doubts on hold, ignore her nagging curiosity about that odd bouquet of roses, and be there for him. Whether he'd admit he wanted someone around who cared or not.

The drive also gave her plenty of time to fuel her paranoia. Every flash of white on the road seemed to catch her eye. Trucks. Cars. Even a white van.

But no red letters on the side. No florist's logo.

Hundreds of nameless, faceless travelers shared the highway with her. Did one of them know her? Had someone followed her from the warehouse fire to the station house? To Dorie's? Was that someone following her right now?

Or was someone from the station playing a tasteless practical joke on her?

If it was a joke, she wasn't laughing. And if she had

picked up a resourceful secret admirer, *flattered* wouldn't be the word she'd use to describe her feeling about the anonymous flowers. She had no interest in gifts from admirers, secret or otherwise. If that admirer thought his boldness or cleverness would be appreciated in return, he was sadly mistaken. She just wanted to know the truth, and then she wanted to put an end to it.

But first things first. Though it was nearly 8:00 p.m., the summer sun was still bright in the sky, giving her the flagging energy of a never-ending day as she pulled up to the white stone building that served as the Fourth Precinct headquarters. By the time she'd secured her visitor's badge at the front desk and pushed the button for the elevator, Meghan had made only two clear decisions. Her first priority would be to make sure Alex hadn't been hurt.

And the eleven roses were going into the trash.

Beyond that? She took a deep, fortifying breath to prepare herself for whatever Alex's story might be. She'd never had much luck with long-term plans, anyway.

The elevator opened up to a maze of desks and partitions, set apart from the hallway by a tall, circular work station. A bank of offices with blinds at each window lined the opposite wall. A handful of men and women, dressed in professional street clothes, sat at their computers or talked on phones. The bulk of the night shift seemed to be made up of uniformed officers, though, wearing their familiar light blue shirts and black slacks.

Meghan clutched at the ID card hanging around her neck and crossed to the sergeant's desk. A tall, female officer with a strawberry-blond braid down her back was arguing with someone on the phone.

"You can't do that." The woman swallowed hard, probably schooling her temper. Unsuccessfully. "Dammit, Danny. You can't keep her this weekend. You know I'm going to Minnesota to see my family. Let me talk to her. Danny?''

She held out the receiver and glared at it for several moments before finally setting it down in the cradle of the phone. The Danny who had her so upset must have just hung up on her. The woman stood and stared at the phone for several moments.

When it seemed as though she might be calming down a bit, Meghan cleared her throat, subtly diverting the woman's attention. ''Are you all right?''

The female officer laughed as she turned around to face her. ''Sure, why not?'' But her red-rimmed eyes looked as if they were fighting back tears. She nodded toward the phone. ''My soon-to-be ex. Need I say more?'' Shutting off the emotional pain she must be feeling, the officer shifted into cop mode. ''Thanks for asking. I'm Sergeant Wheeler. How can I help you?''

''The front desk sent me up here to pick up Alex Pitsaeli.''

Several minutes passed as the sergeant verified Meghan's ID and typed the information into the computer. ''I'll have him brought out. We've had him in one of the interrogation rooms, just to separate him from his buddy.''

Buddy? Not good. Like the other woman, Meghan clenched her teeth and held her emotions in check. She couldn't tell if it was fear or anger or disappointment trying to make itself heard—probably a combination of the three. ''Do you know what they were fighting about?''

Sergeant Wheeler shook her head. ''The preliminary report doesn't say. But from the looks of the kids when they came in, it might be gang related. His buddy's got a Warrior tattoo.''

Definitely not good. One of the conditions of Alex remaining in Dorie's home was that he sever all connections to the Westside Warriors. Though he, too, sported a stylized

W tattoo on the back of his right shoulder, his career as a gang-banger had ended.

Supposedly.

"Is he free to go?"

Sergeant Wheeler nodded. "The papers will give you the date he has to appear in juvie court." She pointed to a row of empty chairs beside the elevator. "Have a seat. He'll be right out."

Meghan chose to pace rather than sit. "Police reports. Court dates." She swiped her loose hair up behind the nape of her neck, then let it filter through her fingers down her back. "How are we going to handle this one?" She supposed most kids had families they could count on. They'd have a parent or sibling who could guide them through their trouble. Right now, all Alex had was her. She cocked her eyebrows into a wry frown. "There's a comforting thought."

About as comforting as the anonymous love note that pressed against her hip inside her pocket. Meghan stopped in her tracks. Why hadn't she pitched the thing? Now it was calling to her. That all-too-suspicious voice inside her head that longed for security was demanding answers. Closure.

She pulled out the wadded card and smoothed it flat between her palms.

You know I love you.

Maybe John had sent the roses, and she was blowing this whole thing out of proportion. They were getting to be pretty close friends. But a dozen roses as a platonic gesture? And wouldn't he have signed the card? Or confessed to leaving her the rose in the fire truck?

She didn't have any family to speak of, at least none alive who'd claim to love her.

Of course, there was always…Meghan caught her breath at the crazy possibility. She'd run into Gideon this afternoon—after almost two years apart from each other. Though he'd touched her so tenderly, his mood had been distant. Cool. As if he was trying to hide something. Surely, he didn't still feel…he couldn't.

Her heart did a crazy flip-flop in her chest. But she quickly squelched the foolish hope with common sense. The reasons she'd had to leave were the same now as they'd been two years ago. Gideon had talked about kids and family and forever.

How long would his love have really lasted when he found out she couldn't guarantee him any of those things? And noble son of a gun that he was, he'd have probably stayed with her anyway—not because she made him happy, but because he thought it was the right thing to do. She refused to sentence him to a life of sacrifice like that.

Maybe the flowers were just a misguided thank-you from a dog lover who'd seen her after the fire. But then, the note didn't make sense.

You know I love you.

She didn't want anyone to love her like this.

She slipped the card back into her pocket, no closer to finding answers than she'd been earlier.

Her therapist had told her that she needed to tell Gideon the truth, that that would be the only way to bring closure to that chapter of her life. She'd come a long way in the past two years, developing the emotional courage she'd lacked for so long. But along with that courage came a sense of responsibility. Gideon deserved to know why she'd turned down his marriage proposal, running out of his apartment and his life with little more than a backward glance. But he didn't deserve any more pain. And she wasn't sure how the truth could do anything but hurt him all over again.

It seemed both a curse and a blessing to have someone else's troubles to worry about for a change.

"Alex." She recognized the sixteen-year-old by his short, stocky dimensions as a young police officer escorted him down the hall to meet her. What the sixteen-year-old lacked in height, he packed on with muscle. He was perfect for the wrestling program at the local high school. He'd even made the varsity team his sophomore year. But that had been last winter. Since school had gotten out for the summer, he'd been moody and mysterious and had missed Dorie's curfew more than once.

Now he'd been detained for disorderly conduct. If he was lucky, the judge would only order community service and not assign him to a probation officer. Meghan shook her head, wishing she knew what had caused his backslide from reformation success to juvenile delinquent.

His thick, black hair curled down to his collar and framed the tiny gold hoops in the lobe of each ear. God, he was a good-looking kid, with the sculpted features and olive skin of his Italian ancestry. But his swollen lip and permanent scowl kept him from being handsome.

The officer handed him off and walked away. Alex stared hard at Meghan's feet, refusing to make eye contact. "I'm sorry."

"I'm sure you are." She had to tread lightly here. But she needed to make a point. She wrapped her arms around his shoulders and hugged him. The kid needed it. So did she. But she kept it brief and quickly pulled away. "Dorie couldn't come because hearing you were down here shot her blood pressure through the roof."

"Is she okay?" At least he had the compassion to care.

"For now. But I have to wonder how much more stress she can handle." Meghan ducked her chin to see his eyes since he wouldn't look at her. "Are *you* okay?"

He spared her half a glance. "Yeah."

"What's this?" She quickly inspected the banged-up

knuckles on his left hand. "You need to clean up and get some ice on that."

"I'm okay."

A typical male protest. She could tell from the downcast tilt of his eyes that he was far from okay. Alex was a pretty bold kid. What his Mediterranean charm couldn't get for him, his fists and attitude often had. Was he embarrassed? Did he feel as guilty as those coal-black eyes looked? "You promised Dorie you wouldn't fight."

"I had to."

"Had to? Why?"

"Yo, baby." A thickly accented voice interrupted from behind her back. "You Alex's other mama? I don't know how a little boy like him finds them so fine."

"Boy?" Alex straightened. His muscles bulged with a bristling tension that put Meghan on guard against his Latin temper. Is that what they'd fought about? An insult to his manhood?

Meghan turned to face the young man who'd accosted her. "Excuse me, but we're having a private conversation."

She guessed from the bruised swelling around his eye that he'd been the one in the fight with Alex. He looked no more than eighteen or twenty. But the kid had money. The gold chains hanging from his neck and the belt loop of his baggy pants, as well as the high-priced lawyer standing beside him in the three-piece suit, were testament to that.

"Ezio." The lawyer looked hot and bored. "I suggest you keep your mouth shut."

But Ezio clearly was used to giving orders, not taking them. The cut-back sleeves of his muscle shirt revealed the W tattoo that marked him as a Westside Warrior. The knife stenciled above the W labeled him their leader. He ignored his attorney's advice.

A whisper of recognition tried to push its way into

Meghan's conscious mind, but the boy's lewd come-on diverted her attention.

"You lookin' phat." He ran his gaze up and down Meghan's body, lingering with bold thoroughness on the loose strands of her hair where it rested at the top of her breasts. A suggestive sweep of his tongue traced his bottom lip. "Pretty hot and tempting."

Alex jerked beside her. "Shut up."

"Alex, don't."

"Excuse me?" Ezio touched his fingers to his chest as if he was the injured party. "Did you say something to me?"

"Enough," muttered the lawyer. The stuffy man inhaled and finally looked her way, as if he found this whole confrontation tedious and beneath him.

The two young men squared off like cocks in a fighting ring, with Meghan stuck between them, trying to calm Alex's protective anger.

"I think Sweet Thing likes me. Alexis is just a boy. She needs a man." With a crude promise of his intentions, Ezio slid his hand toward his crotch. "I'll show you better than a good time, baby."

Alex's curse was swift and graphic.

When he shifted, his chest puffing up to do battle, Meghan planted her feet and shoved him back a step, away from the mocking preen of his baggy-pantsed enemy. "Let it go, Alex."

She'd fended off hotshots before. All by herself.

"He can't talk—"

Alex was strong. Meghan anchored her hands at his shoulders and planted her feet. Oh, God. When had Alex developed such a chivalrous streak? *Other mama?* She understood Ezio's come-on line now. The boy must have hurt or insulted Alex's girlfriend.

Ezio pursed his lips and blew taunting kisses.

Meghan was losing this battle of strength and wills. She angled her face over her shoulder. "Are you his lawyer or not?" Alex's anger radiated through his muscles into her fingers, fueling her own temper. Why wasn't that grown man doing anything to keep these two adolescents out of trouble? "Tell your client to get out of here before I sue for harrassment."

Ezio leaned forward and leered. "Would that be *sexual* harrassment?"

Alex lunged, knocking Meghan off balance. "Stop it!" She yelled too late.

By now the scuffle had begun. Meghan was vaguely aware of a blur of blue from the corner of her eye. A fist flew past her ear and missed its target. Passionate Italian obscenities filled the air. A bell dinged. The elevator door opened to the sound of male laughter. Ezio jostled Meghan from behind. The laughter stopped abruptly. Meghan's shoulder twisted between the hot, sweaty crush of Alex and Ezio charging each other.

"Meg?"

The flurry of motion happened so quickly, she could only process it after the fact. The three men on the elevator were suddenly a part of the fight. Only there was no more fight. At least, she wasn't a part of it anymore.

Strong male arms reached into the middle of the fray and lifted her free. Her feet left the floor and for a moment she was cradled against something hard and warm before being set to the side behind a broad wall of bright royal blue. She recognized the musky scent of the man before the dark hair and fierce eyes registered. "Gideon?"

"What the hell's going on?" he demanded.

Around the protective jut of his shoulder she saw a big blond bruiser come off the elevator next, neatly pinning Ezio in some kind of hold around his arms and shoulders. The third man on the elevator, a barrel-chested brute with an unquestionable air of authority, closed a big hand over Alex's shoulder. "You don't want to do that, son." He scanned the room beyond them, a distinct look of displeasure on his face. "Is everyone off duty here?" His booming voice was a tad less gruff when he nodded at her. "Meghan."

"Hi, Mitch." Gideon's cousin. Captain of the Fourth Precinct. Even Ezio's lawyer was paying attention now.

The female officer ran up behind him. "I'm sorry, sir. I got held up on the phone. I didn't see what was happening right away."

Mitch's brown eyes, so like Gideon's, swept over the woman. He frowned, but his words were far gentler than his scowl. "Danny again?"

"Yes, sir. Sorry, sir."

"Damn." He handed Alex off to Gideon. He fixed his most authoritative glare on the boy. "I'll pretend I didn't see this." He nodded to the officer. "Sarge, get someone to cover your desk. I want to see you in my office." Then his pinpoint gaze sought out Meghan. "Are you okay?"

Meghan nodded. "Thanks, Mitch." *For breaking up the fight and for not pressing charges.* Fortunately for her and Alex, he had a matter of greater concern to attend to right now. She offered an encouraging smile to Sergeant Wheeler. "Don't blame her."

He urged the sergeant away from the scene. "Let's talk."

Ezio squirmed against his captor and yelled at his attorney. "Hey, man, do something! This is police brutality."

"Shut up, Ezio." The lawyer sounded as though he meant business now.

The blue-eyed man with a badge who held the youth had the ability to restrain Ezio and to offer her a lopsided smile all at the same time. "Hey, Meghan. Haven't seen you in a while."

"Josh." Gideon Taylor's youngest brother had an irresistible smile that urged her to smile in return. "I'm glad we ran into each other." Like Mitch, Josh was a cop. She hadn't seen either one in ages, though, and noted that he wasn't wearing the traditional blue and black uniform of the K.C.P.D. He must be working as a detective now. "Really glad."

"Joshua." Josh's gaze snapped to his brother's. "I'm all for getting reacquainted—" Gideon eyeballed the lawyer and the two young men, his expression filled with accusation "—but I still want to know why these two were trading punches." His gaze changed to a different sort of fire when it landed on her. "And I want to know why you were stuck in the middle of it."

The lawyer must have recognized the Taylors as a force to be reckoned with, because *now* he wanted to get involved. "It's just a misunderstanding, Officers. My client and I were leaving."

"By all means." Josh pushed the kid inside the elevator with his lawyer and punched a button to send them on their way.

He blocked the doors until they shut on the lawyer's words to his temperamental client. "You know, my boss won't always send me to bail you out of trouble if you keep allowing personal agendas to get in the way."

When Ezio was gone, Meghan breathed a short-lived sigh of relief. "Thanks, guys."

"No sweat. I'd like to know what that was all about, too." She heard Josh's voice without really seeing the concern on his face.

Her world had shrunk down to Gideon's stony expression. Though he stood between her and Alex, his eyes blazed with questions. He held himself perfectly still.

She was vaguely aware of Josh drifting away from the

elevators, excusing himself. "Well, I promised to show Mitch new pictures of my little girl. Gid? You okay here?"

Josh's concern finally prodded a reaction from Gideon. His expression relaxed into a brief smile. "I'm fine. I'll catch up with you later."

Once Josh had gone, Gideon shoved his left hand into his pocket and stepped away so he could turn to face her. His friendly smile disappeared and he became a harder, darker version of the man she used to know. "Are you sure you're okay?"

Meghan stalled, smoothing the front of Alex's shirt where she'd wrinkled it in her fist trying to keep him out of trouble. This was the world she came from. The wrong side of the tracks. Survival of the toughest. Gideon came from the world of cops and intact families and friends one could count on.

He wouldn't understand her ragtag version of a family.

"I'm fine. It's just been a long day."

She could tell he'd put in an even longer day than hers. He still wore his work clothes. But the rumpled black chinos had molded themselves to the solid trunks of his thighs and the trim cut of his hips, giving him a leaner, more world-weary look. A stubble of coffee-dark hair shaded his jaw, adding to the glower of his expression.

"I'm not used to seeing you at the police station." He inclined his head over his shoulder toward the elevator. "Ezio Moscatelli is a kid I've interviewed before. We thought he was having new recruits set fires as a gang initiation."

"Was he?"

"We couldn't prove it." His mouth thinned into a grim line. "I can't say I'm thrilled to know the two of you are acquainted. The kid's too damn cocky for his own good."

Once, she would have run her fingertips along the masculine friction of his evening beard growth, coaxing a smile from him to ease the stress of a taxing day. Gideon was a man who took on more responsibility than he should. He'd once said her gentle massages were the only thing that gave him the escape he needed when he got entrenched in a problem he cared too much about or couldn't fix. He'd said she gave him the ability to reground himself and move on.

She curled her fingers into her palm to keep from reaching out to comfort and reassure him now.

"I just met that kid a few minutes ago." She settled for calming his concerns verbally. But she didn't want to discuss gangs while Alex was around. "Quite frankly, I'm glad he's gone. I've had enough trouble for one day."

"Who's this?" Gideon shifted to include Alex in their conversation.

"Alex Pitsaeli, this is Gideon Taylor. He's…" *A former lover. The man I betrayed.* Her breath rushed out in a self-conscious sigh. "Someone I used to work with." She hurried to cover the awkward pause and complete the introduction. "Alex is a foster teen at Dorie Mesner's home. You remember Dorie, don't you?"

"Sure. Nice to meet you."

Alex stared at Gideon's outstretched hand as if it held a knife. "What?"

Meghan pressed her lips together, wishing she knew the secret formula to dispel adolescent rudeness.

But Gideon didn't seemed offended by the snub. If anything, he seemed to relax, as if he was right at home dealing with distrustful teenage attitudes. But his hand never moved. "It's the customary way men greet each other when they've been introduced."

She couldn't help but notice the subtle jerk in Alex's shoulders at the word "men," and his inclusion in that category. He covered his startled reaction by rolling his shoulders and shuffling on his feet. But then slowly, as if that imaginary knife might still be able to stab him, he reached out and grasped Gideon's hand. "Mr. Taylor."

Gideon held on a moment longer, silently demanding that Alex raise his chin and make eye contact. Once Alex did, he rewarded the teen with a pleased look. "Gideon'll do fine," he offered.

Meghan felt a grateful smile warm her from the inside out. Gideon was a natural. He talked to Alex with respect, and effortlessly commanded it in return. Alex was already standing a little taller. And the tension that left him too eager to talk with his fists dissipated as the two "men" chatted about school and whether or not the Chiefs could put together any kind of defense this fall.

Thank you, thank you. The words filled her silent heart and spilled over to soothe her misgivings about helping Alex.

Maybe some of that buoyant energy showed itself in her face or posture. Or maybe Gideon was too observant to miss even the subtlest of nuances about people.

His chocolaty gaze swept over to her, catching her unaware. "Meg?"

She'd been staring at him. Smiling and staring and feeling the same pride and longing that had been her constant companions back when she and Gideon were together. But they weren't together anymore. A flush of rueful heat warmed her cheeks and she looked away.

"We'd better be going. It'll be bedtime before we get any dinner into this guy."

Gideon angled his body, placing himself in her path to the elevator panel, stopping her as effectively as he'd protected her only moments ago. "Do you have a minute?"

To talk? Alone?

She had her excuse ready even before she fully understood her instant panic. "I really should get Alex home."

"It's about the fire."

"Oh." The arson investigation. She should be feeling relief instead of disappointment. "Sure. But I need to take Alex back to Dorie's first. She's pretty worried."

Gideon reached behind his back and pushed the elevator button himself. "This can't wait. I'll meet you there."

Chapter Five

"So you can't describe the man you saw in the fire?"

Gideon ignored the pull of moonlight as he walked Meghan down the long driveway to her truck. He had to focus on the facts of his investigation. Not the vibrant, unsettling, surprisingly enjoyable evening he'd just shared at Dorie Mesner's home.

Not the way the reflection of the moonlight gave Meghan's soft skin an almost translucent glow.

Gideon looked up from her gentle profile, breathed in deeply and focused. "You're still not going to tell me why you were in the middle of a fight at the police station, are you?"

The honey and gold waves of her hair danced across her shoulders as she shook her head. "Alex was defending my honor, or something like that. He told me Ezio had been hitting on his girlfriend, Marlena, earlier. I just think tempers were still running hot."

He'd seen the panic in her eyes when the elevator doors had opened onto the fight. He'd seen the wince of pain as she'd gotten shoved between the two man-size youths. He'd felt the clutch of her fingers digging into his arms when he'd pulled her free. And she wanted to dismiss the incident?

"Ezio Moscatelli is a known gang-banger. What does he have to do with Alex in the first place?"

A pause told him she was going to change the subject before she spoke. "I'm more interested in how he got a high-priced lawyer there to represent him. Didn't he say something about his boss getting tired of bailing out Ezio?"

"Makes you wonder who his boss is." Gideon couldn't let it go. He stopped. "You know that design on the basement floor of the old Meyer's warehouse—the markings where kerosene had been poured? I realize it wasn't a random design now. It—"

Meghan halted a few steps ahead of him and turned. "I know. I saw it, too. Tattooed on the back of Ezio's shoulder."

At least she understood why he'd felt the urgency to question her. "The Westside Warrior symbol."

She tucked a stray tendril behind her ear, giving him a clear view of the concern on her unadorned face. "Do you think Ezio or one of his compatriots set that fire?"

"It's a strong possibility." Gideon fingered the remains of a dime-size explosive device in his right hand. He'd found one just like it in the basement of the old Meyer's warehouse and bagged it for the crime lab. "You couldn't make out any distinctive features about the man you saw in the fire today?"

She shook her head and turned back toward her truck. "I wasn't even sure it was a man at the time. All I saw was a blur of black."

"Big blur? Small blur?"

"I don't know. Small, I guess. The heat and smoke and distance distorted my depth perception."

"And you couldn't see if he was carrying anything that looked like a remote or an antenna?"

"I barely saw the blur. It was more like a ghost than a man."

He'd found the same type of electronic trigger at each of the other two arson fires he'd been investigating. Just as an artist's work could be identified by the style of strokes used on a canvas, an arsonist left a pattern when he or she set a fire.

Though the fuel sources had varied in each case, the ignition pattern had been the same. A remote control device triggered from close range lit an accelerant, such as kerosene, which could burn unnoticed for several minutes— even an hour—before its flames spread and ignited an even bigger blaze. It was a simple setup, but the high-tech trigger allowed whoever set the fire ample time to escape and either establish a reasonable alibi or find a place to watch the fire without being noticed.

It didn't matter whether the suspect was a calculating genius or a crazy madman. Gideon had a serial arsonist on his hands.

And Meghan was the closest thing he had to a witness.

He followed the sweet sway of her butt as she walked ahead of him. God, he hated treating her like this. Grilling her with questions. Keeping her at a professional distance.

He should be grateful that he had business to conduct so he wouldn't do anything stupid like…like what? Demand answers to their breakup? Sacrifice his pride and kiss her until she remembered how good it had been between them? Run his fingers through her soft, wild hair?

What did a man with one good hand and three suspicious fires think he was going to do to a healthy, independent woman like Meg?

From the tight set of her mouth throughout the evening, he'd known something was bugging her. But was it just him saying yes to Dorie's invitation to stay for dinner?

Gideon told himself he'd stayed because he needed to ask Meghan about the fire, and the four boys in Dorie's care had been getting too cranky to delay eating any longer.

Besides, the food had smelled good. And he'd missed lunch.

Or was Meghan covering for something that made her even more uneasy?

"Is there anything else you can tell me?"

"I don't think so." Meghan shook her head and apologized for the umpteenth time since he'd started this conversation. "I'm sorry I'm not much help to you."

He wondered if she'd felt as uncomfortable as she'd looked sitting across the table from him, nibbling on her food as if she'd lost her appetite. Dinner had been awkward for him, too. But Dorie, an old friend from when he and Meghan had dated, had managed to keep the conversation going. She'd pointed out how successful Meghan was in her new career, how Meghan had gotten pamphlets from area colleges and was planning to finish up her degree— and that Meghan wasn't seeing anyone at the moment.

Subtle. Not.

"Unless the roses mean something." Dorie had rolled her eyes, feigning a casual interest in fishing for information. "You didn't happen to send her a bouquet of eleven roses today, did you?"

"Dorie." Meghan's warning had gone unheeded.

"The card was unsigned." Dorie had busied herself by twirling a forkful of spaghetti on her plate. "She doesn't know who to thank, and I thought maybe…"

Gideon hadn't known about any flowers being delivered to Meghan. He hadn't known anything beyond the twinge of jealousy he'd had no right to feel. He and Meghan were history. Her anonymous admirer could give her a whole damn garden, if that's what she wanted. Her current love life wasn't any of his business.

Looking across the table, he's seen her lips press together as tightly as a clam refusing to give up its pearl. Was she frustrated by the anonymity of the gift? Hurt that he hadn't sent the bouquet? Embarrassed by Dorie's shameless matchmaking?

He'd never had the chance to find out. Eddie Pike had interrupted, "We're not allowed to wear our hats at the table." Gideon had forgotten he'd had the thing on. Quickly whipping it off, he'd smoothed his hand over his short hair but had no chance to apologize. Eddie had moved on. "If you and Meghan are friends, how come I haven't seen you before?"

He'd lost control of the evening soon after that. But he didn't mind.

Truth be told, he'd loved the noisy give-and-take of conversation among the kids. He'd answered questions on everything from smoke jumpers to football to the number and type of pets he'd had growing up. The hamster who had been eaten by his sister's cat earned both yuck's and cool's.

The only person at the table quieter than Meghan had been Matthew. Gideon couldn't help but wonder at the kid's background. The little boy had eaten one slice of garlic bread and stared at him with the saddest, most wary eyes he'd ever seen on a child. His single effort to draw him into the conversation had resulted in the boy climbing out of his chair and running from the room.

Eddie's explanation that Matthew never talked to anyone did nothing to ease his guilt.

How the hell had a simple interrogation turned into something resembling family drama night on cable TV? And why did spending time with teen angst and toddler antics and a beautiful blond tomboy leave him feeling more alive and connected to the world than he'd felt in months?

But now the boys were in bed, the dishes were washed, and Dorie had gone into the den to watch the late news.

It was back to him and Meghan. Alone. He wanted to demand answers to personal questions. He should be asking professional ones. It scared him to think how easily he'd slipped into this quiet time with her. It felt crazy—normal…wonderful—to simply be at her side again. But his crippled-up pride and once-burned heart refused to let him trust anything beyond the moment with her.

"I'm the one who should be apologizing." Gideon brushed his fingertips against Meghan's arm, silently asking her to stop beside her truck. The night air was muggy, the hazy atmosphere capturing the heat of the day. But he detected goose bumps on her soft, bare skin. Quickly he snatched his hand away, not wanting the answering shiver of awareness in his body to betray the turbulent mix of emotions inside him. "I'm worried that I scared Matthew."

She tilted her face up to his, her honey-colored eyes wide with compassion. "Don't blame yourself. Even the therapists haven't gotten through to him." Her gaze dropped to the K.C.F.D. logo over his heart. "His and Mark's parents were killed in a house fire. Maybe you reminded him of that."

Gideon tucked his hands into his pockets and shook his head, berating himself for causing the child any pain. "Great. And we're supposed to be the good guys."

"Think of it from his perspective. There were probably dozens of firefighters at his house that night. Dressed in bulky coats and wearing masks that obscure their faces, slipping in and out of the flames and smoke."

"You make us sound like monsters."

"To a four-year-old, we might be. I think he's learning to accept me, but it's taken some time. You're tall, big-shouldered. You wear a black hat." She flicked the bill of his K.C.F.D. ball cap and doctored his worry with a teasing grin. "If he could spend time with you, too, he'd see that you're a man, not a monster."

"I'd like to do that."

"Spend time with Matthew?"

"I'd like to spend time with all of them." He'd once

pictured a houseful of dark-haired boys and fair-haired little girls with honey-brown eyes. Children that he and Meghan had created together. "You know I like kids."

"I know." She sifted her fingers through her hair in a nervous gesture that stirred the long waves around her shoulders, releasing the citrusy scent of her shampoo and the subtler musky scent that was Meghan herself. "But you've already done enough for them."

His lonesome body stirred at the thought of making babies with Meghan. He lifted that masking tendril that had fallen across her cheek again and tucked it behind her ear. "I haven't done anything."

She went still the moment he touched her, her gaze fixed at some vague point near the middle of his chest. "I appreciate you talking to Alex—man-to-man like that at the precinct office. He's a typical teen, trying to figure out what kind of adult he's going to be. But he doesn't have a decent role model to work from. I think it meant a lot that you took a personal interest in him."

"Why wouldn't I?"

She shrugged and turned her face away from his touch. She unhooked the fanny pack that hung around her slim waist. "These boys aren't like other kids, Gideon. They don't have big brothers or dads who can teach them right from wrong and keep them safe."

"They have you and Dorie. From what I can see, they're getting plenty of love."

She refused to take the compliment. "I can relate to them, that's all. It's not the same as having a man around."

The bleak acceptance in her voice twisted like a knife in his conscience. No matter what she'd done to him, she'd already paid too high a price for any betrayal, to him or anyone else. "I'll never understand a father abandoning his own child."

"That's because your dad's a good man. He's strong."

She opened the truck door and tossed the fanny pack onto the passenger seat. "My dad was heartbroken when Mom died."

"And you weren't?"

She still made excuses for a man he couldn't forgive. "She was the love of his life. I think he got lost somewhere inside himself when that virus took her so quickly. He never could find his way back to the real world."

Or to his child. "Do you ever hear from him?"

Her shoulders quaked as they rose and fell in a heavy sigh. "Did you get everything you needed about the fire?"

He interpreted her avoidance of the question as a no. He'd never met Martin Wright. But he'd been around a few times when Meghan's father had made contact from some remote part of the planet to announce he was about to strike it rich. Sometimes it was a phone call or a birthday card when it wasn't her birthday. Sometimes it was a trinket sent in the mail.

But he could bet she'd trade a dozen calls and cards for one good hug, a thousand trinkets for a little bit of guidance and protection. He'd seen her somber moods, her silent tears, her bursts of temper after each impersonal attempt to be a father to her. Maybe that was one reason making a family with Meghan had been so important to Gideon. Somewhere in the back of his mind he'd thought she would jump at the chance to create a whole new family—with babies of their own to parent, a loving man in the house to rely on.

But she'd said no.

Why the hell had she said no?

He realized he was staring at her, his eyes wide and dry from their unblinking search for a reason why, when the cell phone inside her fanny pack rang. She climbed into her truck behind the wheel to unzip the bag and pull out the phone. Gideon blinked and turned away. He had as many unanswered questions to the mystery of Meghan Wright as he did to his current investigation.

"Hello? Yes." Gideon hooked his hands into his pockets and waited. Long ago, his parents had instilled the protective notion of waiting for a woman to be safely at home or on her way before a man left her alone late at night. "Thank you, but... Wait a minute—" Chivalry turned to curiosity as the tenor of Meghan's voice changed. Her cool politeness stuttered on a gasp of air. Her next words were clipped with a sharp, defensive edge. "Who is this? How did you get this number?" Gideon stepped closer, bracing one hand on the door and the other on the roof of her truck. The dome light cast a harsh glow on her pale features, emphasizing the tight set of her mouth. What the hell? "Wait. What do you mean—"

She slowly pulled the phone from her ear and stared at it as if it would reveal an answer her caller wouldn't give.

Gideon gently laid his right hand on her thigh, not wanting to startle her. "What's wrong?" She shifted her quizzical focus to him, her eyes wide, frightened. Something territorial lit in his veins. "Meg?"

"He said I was as pretty as a yellow rose."

An uncharacteristic anger simmered beneath the surface of his cool facade, demanding answers, if not action. "*He* who?"

She squeezed her clammy hand around his, subconsciously asking for his strength and support. "He said I should get a good night's sleep. That he was going to put me to work again tomorrow."

Meghan was too spooked for Gideon to keep either a self-preserving or professional distance any longer. He scooped her out of the truck and wrapped her in his arms. She linked her hands behind his waist as she had so many times in the past and nestled her head at the juncture of his neck and shoulder.

Her trembling body sank into his and familiar urges awakened. The tingling of skin at the soft press of her breasts against his harder chest. The lambent heat in his groin as the strong muscles of her thighs butted against his. The tender warmth around his heart as her arms held on as if she never wanted to let go.

He tunneled his fingers beneath the casual tumble of her hair and rubbed comforting circles at the nape of her neck. "I take it you don't know this guy and that it wasn't a wrong number."

She shook her head, rubbing the silky crown of her hair beneath his chin. "He called me by name."

"Any bozo could have gotten your name off the TV news as many times as your interview has played today." But this fan had clearly rattled her cage. And triggered the alarm on his considerable protective instincts. "It's probably just a crank call."

"He said he'd love to see me in action again." A shiver cascaded through her. She dragged her palms around to rest against his shoulders, then went stiff in his arms and pushed away from his comfort. "Gideon. I think your arsonist sent me those flowers. And I think he's going to set another fire."

"CAN'T YOU SPEED things up, Taylor?" Daniel Kelleher twisted the plastic evidence bag with the microchip combustion trigger between the fingers of the black leather driving gloves he wore. The entrepreneur seemed to expect some kind of medal for deigning to meet with Gideon at the old Meyer's Textile building on short notice. "I have investors to report to, and a construction crew that's costing me a fortune every day I hold them on retainer. You're going to put me out of business if I can't get this project under way soon."

Gideon had worn his Class A uniform this morning to

meet with Kelleher. The navy-blue twill was already absorbing the heat of the day, but the shiny silver badge pinned to his chest and gold captain's bars on his collar glinted in the sunshine and called attention to the official nature of his investigation. Not that Kelleher seemed to care. His griping avoidance of even the simplest of questions bordered on irresponsibility. Or cover-up.

Was the guy hiding something?

"I can't allow you to bulldoze a single brick until I determine who set fire to this place," said Gideon, carefully studying the other man's agitation. "I imagine your insurance adjustor will want answers to the same questions I have. Two fires on devalued properties you've recently acquired—am I the only one who thinks that sounds suspicious?"

Kelleher's green eyes narrowed. "Are you accusing me of something?"

Gideon didn't rise to the other man's taunt. "I'm just curious why you're not interested in finding out who's behind these fires."

"Believe me, I want to know." Kelleher paced to the warehouse's knocked-out doorway and traced his gloved fingers along the charred brick frame before leaning against it. "But progress can't always wait for everything to fall neatly into place. I have to move forward. I'm fifty years old, Captain Taylor. I've made and lost a fortune twice already." He squeezed his hand into a fist around the triggering device, giving a dramatic finish to his speech. "I'm a visionary. I see things the way they can be. Then I make them happen. Forgive my impatience, but I don't tolerate people or crises that stand in my way."

Kelleher's most recent crisis had nearly cost Meghan her life. She'd been thrust into a spotlight she hated, and now she had a potentially dangerous fan because of it. Last night Gideon had fallen into a familiar role as her champion and protector. He'd had her in his arms. The weight of her, the scent of her, the feel of her soft skin and silky hair had granted him a few moments of remembered heaven. For those few moments out of time, everything had felt centered in his world again.

But then she'd pushed away, denying Gideon the right to hold her. Maybe their love couldn't be rekindled. Maybe happily-ever-after just wasn't in the cards for them.

But Gideon was more than an old flame. He'd been her friend long before he'd been her lover. She might not need his touch the way he needed hers in the middle of his nightmares, but she still needed his expertise.

And if that phone call was indeed their arsonist, a man who was playing with Meghan's peace of mind as well as with fire, then the need to find the truth had just doubled in importance.

At six-two, Gideon was by no means the tallest of the Taylor brothers. But he was more than big enough to get this job done. He strolled over to the doorway beside Kelleher, using his superior height to a subtly intimidating advantage. The warehouse owner wanted to act all big and bad, throwing around talk about his money—whether it was coming in or going out of his accounts apparently didn't matter. In reality Kelleher wasn't even six feet tall. The *big man* was just a lot of talk.

So he was damn well going to answer Gideon's questions. Now. "Losing those properties could be a huge tax write-off for you."

"Not as big as the money I'm losing each day I have to delay razing this building and transforming it into my dream." The older man laughed as if Gideon's suggestion was ludicrous. "I suppose next you'll hint that I burned the place down myself to save construction costs."

"It would take more than a fire to knock down these old walls." Even with the surrounding grass and foliage turned a dull, lifeless brown from the summer drought, the warehouse sat in a beautiful location.

Dramatic granite bluffs gave way to tree-frosted hills that sloped gently down to the river. Though the river itself was too low to be seen over the levee, the Missouri cut a graceful, meandering path as it turned east to flow across the state. The floodplain on the opposite side of the river had been converted into an industrial complex that now lay abandoned. A soot-caked foundry, an aspirin factory, a trucking center. Decades of industrial progress had taken their toll on the natural beauty and resources of the river.

If Daniel Kelleher truly was a visionary, why couldn't he raze one of those eyesores? Why was he intent on destroying one of the few beautiful architectural masterpieces left on the river?

"What are you planning on building here?"

"A casino. Hotel. All the amenities that go with them."

Gideon reached over Kelleher's shoulder and plucked the evidence bag from his hand. "You're sure you've never seen a device like this before?"

"It reminds me of a blasting cap for dynamite or plastique, only it's more sophisticated. I've seen construction crews use something like them." Kelleher rubbed his hand across the top of his short, gray-blond hair and blew out a frustrated sigh. "You say that's what started the fire?"

Gideon slipped the device back into his pocket. "Actually, this is the one used to ignite the fire at your Arlington Road property two weeks ago. But it's identical to the one I found here last night. I'm seeing a disturbing pattern."

Kelleher's green eyes narrowed. "You think I'm being targeted?"

How the fires had been set had been relatively easy to figure out. *Why* they'd been set was a considerably more challenging puzzle. "Do you have any enemies who'd like to see your building project fail?"

Kelleher jabbed his finger in the air and pointed outside. "Look upstream for your answer, Captain. I have as much right to buy property and build a casino on it as Frank Westin does." He brushed a film of dust from the shoulder of his linen jacket and resumed his pacing, into the heart of the shelled-out building. "Right now he's got a monopoly on the Missouri River gambling business. The last casino that tried to compete against his Oasis was closed down in less than a year for illegal practices." He spun around to face Gideon. "You want to discuss illegal practices, you talk to Westin. Word is, he hired an accountant to infiltrate his competitor, Vegas Alley, and doctor the books."

"Where did you hear this *word?*" Gideon asked.

Kelleher shook his head. He pulled back the front of his jacket and splayed his fingers at his waist, creating a casual posture to mask the hushed, conspiratorial tone of his voice. "There's gossip around—at city zoning meetings, on construction sites. At the state gambling commission. Of course, Westin denies it. If he thought I was spreading rumors, though, slandering his reputation…" He dragged the tip of one gloved finger across his throat in a crude mockery of death. "I might find someone doctoring *my* books. Or worse."

Interesting, Gideon thought wryly. An easy excuse without any proof to back it up. He didn't like men like Kelleher, who saw people and places as business opportunities. Sources of revenue instead of individuals with feelings and history and character. Kelleher's impatient opportunism hadn't done anything to endear him personally, either. "So you're saying Frank Westin isn't above burning down your property to put you out of business?"

"I'm saying the man's got mob connections. Or don't you read the paper? He wouldn't actually dirty his hands with something like this, but he has the money and influence to get someone else to do it for him.''

"That's one hell of an allegation."

Kelleher leaned in, daring Gideon to join his conspiracy theory. "Talk to him. Ask Frank Westin about the fires. Maybe he thought my building was blocking his view." When Gideon didn't play along, Kelleher straightened in a huff and strode to the parking lot outside. "It's nearly 9:00 a.m. I have clients waiting. Contact my secretary when you have answers for me."

"Just one more question." Gideon had yet to figure out whether this guy was just an arrogant ass or one very good actor. Either way, he wouldn't be so easily dismissed. "Where were you last night between ten and eleven?"

Keeping his back to Gideon, Kelleher's entire body rippled with a shrug. Gathering his patience? Controlling his temper? Buying time to make up an alibi? Finally he turned around. "Why?"

Gideon refused to be baited. "You don't know where you were?"

After another lengthy pause, Kelleher relented his defensive posture. "If you must know, I was working late in my office, trying to figure out the best way to fix this mess. If the insurance doesn't come through, I could go broke."

Gideon wondered if he could get Mitch or Josh to put a trace on Meghan's incoming phone calls, just to see if this self-absorbed megalomaniac could account for himself. Kelleher was up to something, he could tell. He just wasn't sure what.

Arson? Stalking? Fraud?

"Were you alone?"

"Yes." His opponent's crafty smile indicated he was on to Gideon's subtle interrogation game. "I don't have time for anything but work, Captain. Ask my ex-wife."

The crunch of gravel outside as another vehicle pulled

up diverted both their attentions. Gideon's senses buzzed into alert mode. But his state of sudden hyperawareness had nothing to do with his investigation and everything to do with the woman parking her truck.

Both men watched as Meghan climbed out. Her golden braid fell in a neat rope down the center of her back. Lighter wisps of sun-streaked hair blew around her face, framing the warm glow of her softly freckled skin.

She walked toward them, her shoulders set in her meet-the-world-head-on posture, a consummate professional. Since she wasn't working a fire or hanging out at the station, she wore her Class A's, as well, complete with silver badge and K.C. and F.D. collar pins. It never ceased to amaze Gideon how a plain white T-shirt and navy uniform—worn by men and women alike in the department—could look so utterly feminine on Meghan's body.

The modest cut of the shirt and dress pants clung to every lean curve, showcasing the trim cords of muscle in her arms as much as the subtle swell of her hips. He didn't suppose there was any one feature of Meghan's fit body that jumped out at him. It was the whole beautiful package...

That Daniel Kelleher seemed to be sizing up, as well.

Biting down on his misplaced territorial instincts that immediately flared to life, Gideon stepped toward her and welcomed her to their meeting. "Meg," he greeted her. "Thanks for stopping by."

"No problem. I'm on my way to a day-care presentation, anyway."

In a controlled sweep of motion, Gideon slid his gaze over to Daniel Kelleher's interested smile, then back to Meghan. If Kelleher's expression was easy to read, hers was an impenetrable mask. God, it frustrated him when she locked down like that. She'd been that way when they'd first met. It had taken weeks to coax that first laugh out of her, longer still for her to risk a bona fide argument with him.

It was as if she had some magic spell she could recite to turn off any outward semblance of emotion. If she was nervous or worried or eager, he'd never know it. But she'd be killing herself inside to keep it all in check. He'd learned that much about her in the year and a half they'd been together.

Something was bugging her.

He hoped it wasn't regret about the comforting embrace they'd shared last night. Or the fact he'd asked her to spend more time with him this morning.

Positioning himself between the two, for no other reason than he could sense something was making Meghan feel particularly vulnerable, he introduced them. "This is Firefighter Meghan Wright. Daniel Kelleher. He owns the property."

"Nice to meet you." Meghan politely shook hands.

But when she would have pulled away, Kelleher's fingers tightened their grip. "You're that girl from TV. The one who saved the dog." His grin turned into a full-blown smile. "I saw your Channel Ten interview on the national news this morning as a human interest piece. Nicely done. You made Kansas City look good."

"Uh…" The mask slipped. Meghan's forehead wrinkled with an embarrassed frown. "Thank you."

"Absolutely." He finally released her, but not after he'd run his sly gaze across her body. "You look taller on television. There's not much to you, is there."

"I meet K.C.F.D.'s height and weight requirements."

Gideon stepped in to defend her. "She's earned her spot in the department. If she couldn't get the job done, she wouldn't be in that uniform."

"I didn't mean to indicate otherwise. I think she fills that uniform just fine." The guy was flirting with her. Definitely not Gideon's intention. "You're just more of a sweet little lady than I realized."

Gideon's purpose for inviting Meghan here had been more than met already. Now he just needed to debrief her on her reaction to Daniel Kelleher. "Kelleher, I thought you had a meeting to get to."

"I do. I just couldn't resist taking a few minutes to meet K.C.'s current celebrity. Thank you for trying to save my building."

Meghan tucked a wisp of hair behind her ear. "It was a team effort."

"Don't be so modest." He bowed his head at a debonair angle and bid her goodbye. Then he snapped back to business mode and addressed Gideon. "Captain Taylor. I'll be looking for your report."

His sleek black Beamer kicked up gravel as he sped off toward the highway.

Once the dust had settled, Meghan released a huge breath and stormed past the yellow crime scene tape into the warehouse as if she could leave everything behind her if she just walked fast enough. "God. It's been like that all day. It started with a call from Mayor Benjamin this morning, congratulating me. If I was a man, yesterday's fire would have stayed yesterday's news."

Gideon followed at a more deliberate pace, wondering at the intensity of her reaction. This was more than annoyance or discomfort. "Is that why you're upset? Because of all the publicity? You did a heroic thing, and should be congratulated."

Meghan whirled around to face him. "I did my job. Period." Even in the charred interior of the warehouse, with its lacework of shadows hiding the expression on her face, he could tell from her stiff posture that she was silently venting her temper. She clutched her hand at her waist and breathed in deeply. "I'm sorry. You needed to see me about the fire scene again?"

"Partly. I wanted to let you know that I pulled up the data files and verified the design burned into the basement floor at the trigger site. It's the Westside Warrior symbol. Though it was a pretty sophisticated setup for a gang to use. Of course, an expert could teach them how to create a remote delayed fire."

"Or it could be a diversionary clue, to lead you to the wrong suspect."

"Possibly." He'd considered that part of the M.O., as well. "But the last two arson fires had no symbol."

"Maybe it was better hidden at those sites. We could look again. Or maybe the Warriors didn't think you were giving them enough credit, so they left a signature." He could see she was thinking like an investigator now. "Is that why you wanted to see me? To bounce ideas off each other?"

"Partly. You do have a creative way of looking at things. Gideon slipped his left hand into his pocket and broached the next subject carefully. "Actually, the reason I called you was that I wanted you to meet Kelleher in person."

"Oh?"

"Did his voice sound familiar to you?"

She shook her head. "I've never met him before."

"That's not what I asked." He strolled toward the ladder that would lead them into the basement, hoping her natural curiosity would put her off guard.

She rose to the unspoken challenge. Meghan fell into step behind him. "What are you after, Gideon? Do you think Daniel Kelleher torched his own place?"

Chapter Six

Gideon had his own suspicions about Daniel Kelleher. He intended to run a thorough background check on the man, including financial statements and proven or alleged contact with any criminal activities. In particular, he was looking for a connection to known arsonists and gang-bangers.

But he didn't need Meghan to do research. He wanted to tap in to her eye for detail and observation—if she'd play along.

"How are you this morning?" he asked.

"Fine, I suppose. The guys at the station won't let a little extra publicity keep me from my regular schedule. I'd never live it down if I showed up late or tried to gold-brick."

"I meant the flowers and the phone call. You were pretty shaken up last night."

He could hear the defensive hackles tightening her voice behind him. "I was tired. It was a long day."

Liar. She'd been scared to death.

But he let her have her excuse. Gideon stopped at the head of the ladder and turned to face her. "The man who called you on the phone and threatened you—did it sound like Kelleher?"

"No." She stopped in her tracks at the emphatic answer. Then retreated half a step. "I don't think so. Kelleher seems like an articulate man—a pretty smooth talker. The person on the phone whispered. It was a croaky, froggy voice.''

"As if he was disguising it?"

"Maybe." Her arms went around her middle, hugging herself as she replayed the conversation in her head. "It made me think of my uncle Pete. He drank so much, it damaged his vocal cords so that he talked in that ruined voice all the time."

Gideon pressed her for details. "But you're sure it was a man?"

"The pitch seemed lower than a—" Suddenly she was shaking her head and backing away. "I thought you wanted to talk about the fire. Not my personal problems."

"Personal problems?" A match struck inside Gideon, heating his temper to a slow simmer. "We've got something slightly more serious than a *problem* to deal with right now. That lunatic threatened to set another fire. Because of you. Because he wants to see *you* fight fires. To me, that not only puts the city at risk, it puts you in danger."

"Then save the city. I'm not your concern anymore. We're finished."

"There's a difference between being finished and walking out without so much as a 'go to hell' or any other kind of explanation."

She was backing away from him now, closing down the lines of communication all over again. "I can't do this right now."

"When would be a good time, Meg?" Gideon rarely gave vent to sarcasm, but he hadn't been at his most rational since their breakup. He paced after her. "Were you secretly married? Did I hurt you? Bore you? Do you hate kids? Want a different career? Did you find someone better?"

"No." Her hands were out, pleading with him now. "None of those things. It's my fault. Completely. You wanted…'' She took a deep breath, gathering control of her thoughts. ''It would never have worked between us. Not for forever. And you're a long-term kind of man.''

He wouldn't argue that. Her honey-brown eyes glistened with tears, but he couldn't seem to let it drop. ''Why? Why wouldn't marriage to me work?''

''Not you. Me. Marriage to *me*. I couldn't let you give up your—'' She sniffed back a sob and spun around. ''I don't want to do this right now. I have to get to work.''

She would have bolted through the door if Gideon hadn't reached out to stop her. He'd never laid a hand on her like this. Never used anything but a gentle touch. But he grabbed her now. He snagged her by the wrist and hauled her back a step. She stumbled into his chest and twisted around to free herself, but he grabbed the other wrist and held on. ''Talk to me. We meant something to each other once. Tell me why we don't anymore. Just explain it once and I'll let it go.''

Gideon froze the instant he saw his two stiff, withered fingers lying against the tanned perfection of her bare forearm.

Instantly regretting his pointless burst of frustration and pent-up hurt, he released her and stuffed his hands into his pockets. ''I'm sorry if I was rough. I know your uncle used to…ah, hell.'' He had to turn away. ''You'd better get out of here. You have your safety presentation to give.''

Maybe Meghan was more stunned by his sudden mood swing than he was. A confused vulnerability widened her eyes and pressed her mouth into words that didn't come easily. ''You didn't hurt me. I know you never would. You have a right to your anger. Gid—''

''Go on.'' He stood rooted to the spot and willed her to leave. ''I just wanted you to identify Kelleher if you could. I do think he's up to something. I'm sorry things got out of hand.''

Damn. He looked away, deep into the burned-out recesses of the building. *Hand.* What a freakin' bad choice of words.

"I know you're trying to help." He could sense her angling to make eye contact, trying to placate him. Her hands patted the air, trying to soothe the beast inside him that only existed in his nightmares. "That's your nature. You deserve…"

His silence finally achieved what his demanding questions could not.

She was much calmer, almost emotionless, when she spoke again.

"I didn't grow up the way you did, Gideon. We come from two different worlds. You have the right to aspire to the kind of long-lived happiness your folks have found together. I turned you down because I didn't think I could give you that. I couldn't help you achieve that rose-colored future you always talked about. A healthy family. A distinguished career. Growing old together. I still can't give you what you want, what you'd need to be happy." She inhaled a cleansing breath. "I didn't want to disappoint you further down the road. I knew you'd stay with me, even after you realized your mistake. But you wouldn't be happy. And it would have killed me to see you suffer like that."

"All I needed was *you.*" His words were little more than a husky whisper in the shadows.

"You needed the woman you thought I was. Not the real me."

With that nebulous explanation she was gone.

The real me?

She wasn't Meghan Preston Wright? An independent firefighter with a defensive chip on her shoulder and a heartful of hurt? A sensuous woman whose inability to back away from a challenge was rivaled only by her unwillingness to commit to a relationship?

The puzzle of their mysterious breakup grew more intricate and twisted by the day. Had he fallen in love with a pretense? Been deliberately deceived? Did he need to get to know her all over again? Dig beyond the secrets they'd shared and find the hidden truths?

She seemed to believe he wouldn't like those truths. That he'd suffer because of them.

He pulled out his left hand and tried to make a fist. He'd found plenty of ways to suffer all on his own. He was no longer in a position to make any kind of demands on her. His future plans had altered the moment she'd walked out the door of his apartment two years ago. They'd changed irrevocably the night he'd lost Luke Redding.

She was right. He'd always pictured himself being connected to one woman, sharing one family. He'd always pictured *her* in a front porch swing beside him, looking out over a yard filled with their grandchildren, knowing the life they'd shared had been fruitful and full of love.

But she couldn't see that same picture.

How could she think loving her was a mistake? Why was she so sure she'd disappoint him? If she thought her childhood spent in foster homes made her somehow inferior to his intact family, she was wrong. Everyone had troubles to deal with, but he'd always believed that, together, they could work through anything.

Like a partner's death.

Painful rehab.

The ignominy of being taken off the front line.

Maybe he had more empathy for her decision now than he'd had two years ago. But he still didn't understand why. *Why* would give him the release he needed to close the chapter on his time with Meghan. *Why* would heal his heart and allow him to move on.

Gideon closed his eyes and breathed in deeply, in

through his nose, out through his mouth, centering himself in the midst of his chaotic thoughts.

Through the deep quiet of his meditation he heard the scream.

"Gideon!"

Galvanized by protective instincts that time and injury and doubt could never erase, he ran outside, his long legs swiftly taking him to Meghan's side. "What? What is it? Are you hurt?"

She stood at rigid attention a few feet in front of the hood of her truck, one hand clasped tightly at the side of her waist, the other pressed to her trembling mouth.

Had she heard him?

Did she even know she'd cried out his name?

"Meg?"

He followed the sightline of her unblinking eyes to the windshield of her truck.

A yellow rose had been hooked beneath the wiper blade.

"Son of a bitch." How? When?

Gideon cupped his hand around her right shoulder and moved behind her, folding his left arm across her chest and hugging his body around hers, shielding her from…from what? Unseen danger hovered in the air around them—a palpable, stalking, invisible threat. The violation of the gift was made all the more menacing by the tranquil, sunny normalcy of the day.

"Did you see anyone?" he asked in a hushed urgency against her ear.

She shook her head. "It was just there. Fifteen minutes ago it wasn't." Her fingers curled around his forearm and squeezed, betraying the tension she felt. "This is getting old fast."

Good. She was getting mad. Down beneath her fear, she was getting mad.

He scanned the perimeter of the deserted parking lot,

looking deep into the tall weeds and grass surrounding the abandoned site, and into the trees beyond. There was no dust on the road to indicate a vehicle driving away. And the site had been so overrun with firefighters and press and curiosity seekers, that it was impossible to tell if the man-made pathways of crushed plants were from a few moments ago or yesterday.

Had Kelleher come back? Was someone else keeping an unwelcome watch over Meghan?

With no visible suspect to pursue, Gideon circled around her, tucking her behind him as he walked to the driver's door.

"Get rid of it." She ground the request between clenched teeth. "Just toss the damn thing away."

He lifted the wiper and pulled the rose free. She latched on to his shoulder and biceps and leaned in beside him for a closer look. A tiny envelope dangled from a ribbon tied to the thorny stem.

Gideon glanced over his shoulder. "Is this like the ones you got yesterday?"

She nodded. "I'm up to lucky thirteen now."

"This isn't just a prank." Or a sick joke that he suspected terrified her more than she let on. "This is evidence. We're going to use it to put a stop to this," he promised, pulling his handkerchief from his pocket.

He wrapped the cloth around his fingers before ripping the card from the ribbon and flinging the rose off into the weeds. He couldn't toss aside Meghan's fears so easily. Her fingers tightened their anxious clutch as she peeked around his shoulder to watch him open the unmarked envelope and read the card inside.

What might have sounded like teasing from a trusted friend sounded instead like a scarcely veiled threat. A taunt. A dare. Another puzzle to be solved.

A warning.

Better get back to work, my love.
Or the numbers won't add up.

"What does that mean?" she whispered. She drifted closer, until the jut of one small breast brushed against his back.

He squeezed his eyes shut to ignore his body's instant, interested flare of heat, and focus on the task at hand. She wanted comfort from him. Calm reassurance. Not claim-staking, territorial lust.

In a clear case of mind over body, of necessity over desire, Gideon wrapped the card and envelope inside the handkerchief and turned around. He took Meghan by the shoulder and pushed her back a step so he could hunch down and look her straight in the eye. "It means you're calling in to get someone else to cover your presentation. You and I are going to pay a visit to the police department's forensic lab."

Maybe she felt some of those same illicit sparks herself. She tried to pull away. "I'll call the police myself. I can't let you help fix my crazy life this time. I don't want to depend on you. I don't want to hurt you again."

"Screw that. This is about the job. Your safety. Not *us*." He released her and slipped the card into his shirt pocket. He straightened to his full height, sensing she needed his strength as well as his expertise right now.

He gentled his voice to argue this as logically as he could. "Look. The wall that's between you and me may never go away. I don't know what secrets you're keeping, but it doesn't change the fact that you're in trouble. And that your trouble has something to do with my investigation." He resisted the urge to brush aside the curling tendril of hair that fell across her face and obscured the seeking scrutiny of her eyes. "Think of it as a professional courtesy, if you have to. I'm not letting you go anywhere by yourself until I figure out what all this means.''

She pulled aside the windblown lock of hair herself, giving him a glimpse of her wavering will. ''You don't have to do that for me, you know. I'll figure something out. I'm not your responsibility.''

That hesitant consideration of help from this independent woman twisted at something male and potent deep inside Gideon.

''Every citizen of Kansas City is my responsibility.'' He was only interested in one particular citizen at the moment, but she didn't want to hear that. ''I'm not real comfortable with you being out in the open like this where anyone can see you. Especially since we can't seem to spot anyone else. If you really want to be nice to me, come with me now so I don't worry.''

Her shoulders finally softened with a resolute sigh. ''All right. You can drive me back to the station house. I'll be surrounded by my crew there. How's that?''

''It'll do for now.'' He touched Meghan's elbow and turned her toward his silver Chevy Suburban. ''We'll grab your stuff and ride in my car. I'll send someone out for your truck.''

Thankfully, she moved quickly once she'd agreed to cooperate. They were buckled in with the engine running when she spoke again. ''How did he find me?'' She was looking out the front window, but her self-blaming thoughts were turned inward. ''I mean, how long has he been following me, waiting for the right moment to make contact? How could he be so close and I didn't even see him?''

Gideon reached across the seat and across miles of emotional distance to squeeze her hand. ''I don't know, sweetheart.''

The endearment slipped out and caught them both unaware. For one interminable moment their gazes locked and all their history—all their fears and concerns, all their un-spoken desires—passed between them.

The good. The bad.

The passion. The tenderness.

The dreams they'd shared. The ones they'd shattered.

Gideon released her abruptly. He started the engine and shifted the Suburban into gear.

"I don't know the answer," he admitted. Then he pushed all doubt from his voice. "Yet."

"ANY IDEA WHAT the 'numbers' clue means?" asked Mac Taylor, Gideon's older brother by two years, and a forensic pathologist with K.C.P.D.

Gideon leaned his hip against the stainless-steel counter at the Fourth Precinct's newly rebuilt crime lab and watched his big brother work. "The odd number of roses, maybe? First one, then eleven. This morning's makes thir-teen. Did you find anything when you dusted for prints?"

Mac adjusted his bronze-framed glasses and shook his head, still poring over the data on the computer screen in front of him. "Whoever wrote it either wore gloves or wiped it clean."

Gideon had dropped Meghan off at Station 16, assured himself that she had plenty of friends around to keep her in sight through the end of her shift, and put in a call to Mac. "Her fan knows enough about what he's doing to cover his tracks. He's baiting her." Even if Mac couldn't give him a new lead, he could confirm what Gideon already suspected. "This isn't just coincidence, is it? It's more than a shy groupie with a crush on her who happens to have a really lousy sense of timing, isn't it?"

"This guy is deliberate, not shy." Mac's right eye nar-rowed as he spotted what he'd been searching for. He'd been blinded in his left eye during an explosion at this same lab over a year ago. He typed in a command and the printer went to work. "He has a plan, and he's inviting Meghan to become a part of it." Then Mac shrugged. "Either that, or he's a neat freak."

Gideon grinned at the supposition. His brother was a scientist, not a profiler. But he trusted Mac's educated guesses more than most men's sure bets. "I appreciate you processing the evidence so quickly."

Mac waved aside the gratitude. "You never ask for anything. Running a few tests is hardly calling in a favor." While the printer scrolled out data, Mac pushed his chair away from the workstation and leaned back to analyze Gideon across the white and steel room. "So tell me, Gid— what's going on here? I thought you and Meghan were history."

"I knew the inquisition would hit sometime." After Josh and Mitch had seen him leave the precinct office with Meghan last night, he figured it was only a matter of time before the rest of the family found out. "I don't suppose the fact that I'm thirty-five years old and can take care of myself means anything?"

Mac lifted his hands into the air in mock surrender. "You know we're just worried about you. I don't have to be a scientist to figure out that you've had plenty to be hurt and angry about the past couple of years. You're not one to share a lot, but we always figured you two would end up married."

"To be honest, Mac, so did I." Gideon pushed away from the counter and crossed to the window to look out into the bright sunlight that reminded him so much of Meghan. "But I guess she doesn't see herself as a traditional married woman."

"What about untraditional?"

He started to laugh at the question, but then he realized Mac wasn't joking. Is that what had stopped Meghan from saying yes? Had he talked so much about babies and fixing up a home in the country that she thought that was what he expected her role to become in their relationship? Was that the role she thought she couldn't play?

Gideon's smile faded. Meghan Wright was just about as far removed from June Cleaver and tradition as a woman could be. But that didn't mean she wouldn't make a great mother. It didn't mean she wasn't—correction, hadn't been—the right woman for him.

He guessed there was still plenty of talking to be done between them. But next time maybe he was the one who owed *her* an explanation.

Gideon turned to face Mac. The intense scrutiny of that one eye had him wondering whether or not his brother was reading more into his feelings about Meghan than he was willing to admit to himself. "Relax. I'll watch my back and be careful. But I'm not going to walk away from her. If there's any chance that her fan and my arsonist are the same guy, then I'm the best man to help her."

His answer seemed to satisfy Mac. For now. The blond pathologist blinked and turned his attention back to the printout. "I dusted her truck for fingerprints like you asked. The only clean sets I got off it were hers and yours. And some kids'. The prints were a smaller size. You want me to run them through the database?"

"No." The boys at Dorie Mesner's foster home had had plenty of opportunity to leave their mark on Meghan's truck. And none of them could be involved in something like this. "What about the handwriting on the card?"

"Standard calligraphy. This guy's more than artistic. He's a perfectionist." Mac stood and handed Gideon the printout of the note, enlarged and laid out side by side with a page from an artist's calligraphy handbook. "There's not a line or swirl out of place."

Gideon studied the pictures. Whoever had written the note had copied each letter precisely, right down to the forty-five-degree angle stroke of the pen. "That same profile fits a high-tech arsonist."

"So you're hypothesizing that your man and Meghan's stalker are one and the same?"

Gideon rubbed his fingers across his chin and jaw, wishing he had something more to go on. "You got *any* facts I can use to back up that theory?"

"I can trace the make of ink on the card, if you want, but I'm guessing it's a felt marker you can get at any office supply store."

"And the card itself can probably be found at a dozen floral shops in the area."

"Try a hundred shops." Mac's gaze circled the lab. "There isn't much to go on here, Gid. Maybe this is just some lonely guy and his fascination with Meghan will pass once the news stories about her die down."

Gideon slipped on his K.C.F.D. cap and straightened the bill. "I hope you're right."

Mac fell into step beside him as he headed for the door. "That sixth sense of yours trying to tell you something?"

"That sixth sense has been unreliable since..." He had to switch the printouts to his crippled hand to get the door. "The accident."

"Then trust the facts you do know. And trust your experience. You've studied fires and the people who set them for a lot of years." Mac clasped a hand around Gideon's shoulder and gave him an empathetic squeeze. "Do you think the person who sent that note could start a fire?"

"Yes."

"Do you think Meghan's in danger?"

That question took longer to answer. Meghan had been scared enough—twice—to turn to him even though she insisted they didn't belong together. "Yes."

Mac slapped him on the back in a brotherly sort of hug.

"Then do your job. And let one of us know if there's anything else we can do to help."

"Ms. WRIGHT? Ms. Wright?"

The late-afternoon sun beat down on the top of Meghan's head, draining her of energy and making it all too easy to ignore the insistent voice that drummed in her ears.

The only advantage to the one-hundred-degree weather she could see was that the hoses dried out more quickly and could be loaded onto the trucks sooner. Her shift was almost over and she was ready to crash after spending the better part of her day fighting this one-story blaze in the North Kansas City business district. The building looked like a total write-off—but no one had gotten hurt beyond some mild cases of heat exhaustion—and they'd prevented the fire from spreading to the adjacent structures on either side.

Though few fires were *standard*, at least this one lacked the dramatics of yesterday's warehouse blaze. It had felt good—therapeutic, even—to simply go back to work and fight side by side with her unit. For those few hours she could concentrate on the job at hand and shut out thoughts of stalkers and an old lover who made her feel safe and unsure of herself all at the same time.

She had to stop turning to Gideon for comfort. But he made it too easy to be drawn to his immeasurable strength and intuitive heart. She had to be stronger. She had to somehow help his investigation in whatever way she could, and still maintain her emotional distance. Or both of them would wind up getting hurt all over again.

She'd almost told him everything this morning. The rational side of her was determined to come clean of all her humiliating secrets so Gideon might finally understand why she'd walked out. But that fragile, wounded part of her that had lacked courage two years ago still reveled in the idea of him being kind to her. Loving her. The idea that, in some modern miracle of a world, it wouldn't be such a crime to still love him.

"Keep dreaming," she chided herself and returned to her work. Eventually she'd wear her body out enough that her brain wouldn't have the energy to think or fear or dream about anything. She wiped the sweat from her forehead with the back of her hand and pushed her sunglasses up onto the bridge of her nose before picking up the next length of flat hose. Hoisting it first onto her hip, and then onto her shoulder, she grunted when it fell into place. She breathed deeply beneath its weight and turned toward the trucks parked in the street.

"Meghan? Meghan!"

This time she let the voice register. She lifted her gaze from the littered pavement and saw the woman in the figure-hugging turquoise suit waving at her from behind the yellow cordoning tape that blocked off the fire scene. Meghan's breath puffed out on a weary sigh. "Oh, boy."

Saundra Ames tucked a strand of her long, auburn hair behind one ear and smiled at having snagged Meghan's attention. "May I ask you a few questions?"

Her cameraman stood to one side, his film already rolling, judging by the camera's bright light. Great. He was getting a nice shot of her sweating for the nightly news. Since she wore dark glasses, maybe she could pretend she hadn't noticed the reporter. But Saundra Ames was too sharp for that.

"It'll take just a few minutes of your time. I promise," she said.

John Murdock walked up beside Meghan, hauling his own load to the engine. He leaned down and whispered, "You want to do that again?"

"Not really."

He towered up in full, big-brother mode. "I can make an excuse for you."

Meghan managed half a grin for his sake. "Thanks, but you better not. I've already been spotted. If I answer a few questions, maybe she'll go away and leave us alone."

"Ms. Wright?"

Meghan fixed a smile on her face and waved to Saundra.

"Are you sure about this?" John took her hose in one of his protective-gloved hands and hooked it over his own empty shoulder. "I bet I could take her."

Meghan laughed, grateful for the chance to lighten her mood. "Better save your strength. She looks like a regular barracuda." She patted his arm to send him on his way. "Thanks, anyway."

As John strode toward the engine with his double load, Meghan pulled off her sunglasses and tucked them into the neckline of her T-shirt. Then she primped her hair, trying to stuff as many of the loose ends back into her braid and off her face as she could.

She strolled down the empty sidewalk to the perimeter of the scene and shook hands with the reporter. Saundra's long, manicured fingers were as perfectly buffed and shaped as the reporter herself. "Ms. Ames."

"Saundra, please. And may I call you Meghan?"

Hadn't she already? "Sure."

Leaving the yellow tape between them for an "interesting camera shot," Saundra smoothed her own hair into place and licked her lips to make them shine. Another minute passed as the cameraman centered them in the shot and Saundra introduced herself and the segment.

"It looks as if the city has adopted you as Kansas City's Sweetheart. What do you think of the honor?"

Meghan fiddled with the glasses at her neck, trying to dispel the self-conscious tension she felt. Uncle Pete would be laughing hysterically at the idea of her being *any*one's sweetheart. She ignored the distant voice inside her head and smiled for the camera. "I think that'll be a hard one to live down at the station house. I prefer to think of myself as just one of the guys."

A small dent formed between Saundra's eyes, as if the answer had displeased her. She pushed for a different response. "But you should be celebrating what sets you apart. You're unique, a woman fighting on the front lines of a dangerous job. That's not all that common, is it?"

"Maybe it's a little unexpected," Meghan agreed. "The job is demanding—for a man or a woman. But there are women who succeed in the profession. One of our stations has a lady captain, and there are several women with administrative duties who've come up through the ranks."

"Is that your goal—to rise through the ranks?"

Back to the flagship-for-successful-women role. Meghan took a deep breath and tried to steer away from that topic. "I'm happy where I am right now. I love the challenge of fighting fires. I wish I wasn't so busy, though. Two big fires in two days isn't all that common."

"Of course." The microphone hovered closer to her face as Saundra shifted gears in her questioning. "What can you tell us about today's fire? Preliminary results indicate that the fire at the old Meyer's Textile warehouse was deliberately set. Is there any indication that this was an arson fire, as well?"

The human interest story took a sudden turn into the hard-hitting-news-story zone.

Feeling closed in, Meghan tilted her chin away from the mike. "The scene commander could give you a more accurate report. But it looks like this was burning for a while, down in the basement, before the people in the office next door smelled smoke and called it in." She glanced over her shoulder at the blackened U-shaped space between the neighboring buildings where the office complex had once stood. "Apparently, the company was doing some repainting of the interior so, fortunately, no one was at work today."

"But was it arson?" The microphone loomed larger. "Are we having a crime wave to go along with our heat wave?"

"Ms. Wright?" A tiny voice in the crowd turned Meghan's attention from the camera. A dark-haired girl, maybe seven or eight years old, stepped forward, holding out a tiny notebook and pen. "Can I have your autograph? I'm going to be a firefighter, too, when I grow up."

Meghan wasn't sure what to do. The youngster seemed sincere, so earnest with her big brown eyes and gap-toothed smile. Meghan smiled at the girl, then looked up at Saundra. She couldn't tell if the woman was pleased or put out with the interruption. "Is this okay?"

"Certainly." Saundra smiled and pointed to the little girl, silently directing the cameraman to include her in the shot. While Meghan signed her name, Saundra sought out the child's mother. "May I?"

With an approving nod, the interview shifted to the child. Though grateful for the reprieve, Meghan didn't envy the kid suddenly being thrust into the spotlight. "What do you think of Meghan Wright?" Saundra asked, kneeling beside the girl.

"She's cool." The girl looked up at Meghan. "Tell the dog hi."

Meghan smiled. "I will."

"Will you sign our shirts?" A group of three preteen girls pushed forward, and suddenly there was a growing, overwhelming rush of attention.

Saundra Ames straightened to her fashion-model height and spoke to the camera. "As you can see, Meghan Wright is once again the hero of the day. One woman on the front line, risking her life day in and day out. As these mysterious fires continue to burn throughout Kansas City, we can take hope in knowing that we are not only protected, but inspired by the very best. Reporting for Channel Ten news, I'm Saundra Ames.''

"'Continue to burn?'" Meghan challenged the choice of words. "That's a little dramatic, isn't it? You'll start a panic. We've controlled each fire."

"Dennis, keep rolling the tape and get shots of the kids." Saundra handed off the microphone and smoothed the hips of her silk suit. "Yes, but they're increasing in frequency and damage estimates. If these were grass fires, I'd attribute them to the long, dry summer. But my instincts tell me there's a story here. Four fires in three weeks? At least one of them proven to be arson?" She reached out to shake Meghan's hand. "The fire investigation office was extremely closemouthed this morning, making me doubly suspicious. But I think you and I are becoming good friends. Call me if you find any answers."

Gideon should be handling this conversation. "You really should—"

Saundra reached out to shake hands, dismissing her. "Thank you so much." Then she spun toward her cameraman. "Dennis, I'm going to the van to call in my voiceover. Bring the tape when you're done and we'll start editing for the six o'clock edition."

"Ms. Wright?" A man, no taller than Meghan herself, stepped up to the yellow tape. Two wispy strips of light brown hair at either side of his head kept him from being completely bald. The large round lenses of his glasses made him look like a bug. "I work next door. I wanted to thank you personally for keeping us safe." He held out a pocket calendar and opened it to today's date. "Would you?"

Apparently her fifteen minutes of fame made her popular with more than just dogs and children. But the gentleman was too shy to be threatening. Meghan took his pen and scribbled "Best wishes" and her name. "Thanks."

"Meghan, sign mine."

"Mine."

"Tell the dog..."

Did every person in the city want her autograph? As the crowd surged forward, a swell of panic rose in her throat. "Wait, I—"

Almost as one, the crowd froze, obeying an unmistakable authority.

A sudden heat spanned the small of her back. A familiar hand. Protecting her.

Gideon.

"That's enough, folks. Ms. Wright has more work to do."

The panic eased out through the simple, supportive contact. Gideon's strength and calm flowed into her via the same warm, intangible connection.

But his hand disappeared as she gratefully turned from the crowd and fell into step beside him as he led her back to the fire scene.

"Thanks for the rescue," she offered with half a laugh.

His lips brushed against her temple as he bent his head and whispered for her ears alone. But despite the unintended caress of his mouth, his tone was less than tender. "We need to talk."

Chapter Seven

"That's your idea of keeping a low profile and hanging out with friends?" Gideon marched to the far side of what had once been one of the building's rear offices. His boots sloshed in the standing water as his long legs carried him through the debris of charred furniture and melted plastic partitions. "Signing autographs and discussing my case with a reporter?"

Meghan planted her hands on her hips and tilted her chin in defiance. How dare he? "Do you think I enjoy being held up for public scrutiny?"

"I don't think you enjoyed it, but it was a foolish risk to take." Gideon peeled off his sunglasses and nailed her with a reprimanding look. "What were you thinking?"

"Saundra Ames asked me for an interview. I thought if I gave her what she wanted, she'd go away and leave me alone." Meghan shrugged and waved her hands in front of her, as baffled by the press's ongoing interest in her as by Gideon's reaction to it. "She thinks there's a story here."

"There *is* a story here." His blunt statement doused her defensive temper and replaced it with curiosity.

"What do you mean?"

He switched the glasses with a brown paper evidence bag he pulled from his pocket. With his right hand in a plastic glove, he opened the bag and reached inside. She noted the stiff, scarred fingers of his left hand holding the bag and remembered how strong and sure both hands had once been.

But before she could either treasure the memory of his confident touch or mourn the loss of his easy dexterity, he pulled out another detonator. He held the fried cube of components in the open palm of his hand. "Our friend left his calling card in the basement."

"Oh, my God." Meghan sank onto the remains of a charred metal desk before her knees buckled from the shock. "Is it just like the others?"

"Identical." He dropped the detonator back into the bag and sealed it. "And anyone in that crowd outside, or any building on this block, is close enough to have started the fire and hung around to watch it burn."

"And they could be home right now, waiting to watch it again on the evening news." She dropped her gaze to the muck of water-soaked debris on the floor. "I suppose you found another Warrior symbol, too?"

He nodded. "On the basement floor. Probably drawn with paint thinner or any of a dozen chemicals on hand in the building for the remodel."

An image of Ezio Moscatelli's arrogant face taunted the corners of her mind. He seemed like the kind of creep who'd get off on watching someone else flounder or suffer. He'd enjoy seeing how much trouble he and his compatriots could cause. Was Alex smart enough to keep his distance from Ezio? Or would he succumb to the dares and teasing? Could he be a part of this destruction?

"Oh, damn." Her words fell on an anxious sigh.

"'Oh, damn' is right." Gideon stalked across the room, closing the gap between them until he knelt in front of her and looked up into her face. But she could see in the whiskey-brown depths of his eyes that it was worry, not anger, driving this confrontation. "What were you thinking?

You're giving this guy all the publicity he could ever want. And you're plastering your face out there, front and center, where he might think he's getting to know you real well.''

Meghan shot to her feet, not bothering to correct his misassumption about her concern. Whether it was Alex or her own sorry hide she needed to protect, she'd bungled the job. "I didn't tell Saundra anything about how the fires were started. I didn't even confirm they were arson when she asked." She curled her hands into fists and pumped the air in frustration. "I was trying to make it my *last* time on camera. So there wouldn't be a next time. I just want this circus to be over.''

"So do I.''

"Then how do we—''

When she turned around, John Murdock stood only a few feet away, filling the skeletal rectangle that had once been the doorway to this office. "Are you okay, Meghan?''

She heard Gideon rise to his feet behind her, a silent leviathan who cast a big shadow over her shoulder and made the skin on her back and scalp tingle with the nearness of his heat. "This is a private conversation.''

John stood his ground. "Not if she doesn't want it to be.''

Oh, Lord. This is not what she needed right now. Ever. Two grown men fighting to see who could best protect her. Especially when, deep down, she knew she needed to take care of herself.

She stepped to one side to distance herself from the pull of Gideon's body and to allow a back-and-forth view of both men. Each man wore an expression that commanded the right to her loyalty. Neither man looked ready to back down from the unspoken challenge between them. Uncle Pete would have a field day with this standoff.

Imagine, half a woman—unworthy of the attentions of even one man—having to deal with two men at once.

The memory of that lecherous pug of a man suddenly intruded, triggering a volatile, strengthening response in her veins. Her therapist had told her time and again that anger was a far healthier response than fear. Fighting off Pete's image fueled the adrenaline in her blood. She broke the awkward silence herself.

"C'mon, guys. I feel like this is the playground at school and I'm the kickball." She started the introductions and urged them to be civil. "John, have you met Gideon Taylor? He's a captain with the fire investigation unit."

"I've heard of him." Nothing warm and fuzzy there.

She turned to Gideon, hoping he'd work with her to defuse the tension. "This is John Murdock. We're a team at Station 16."

He offered a curt nod. "Murdock."

John eyed him as if he was trying to remember something. "You used to ride down at the Twenty-third. Did you know Luke Redding?"

Oh, my God. Meghan swung her gaze up to Gideon and watched him bristle. Not that the signs were obvious. But she recognized the thinning line of his mouth, the subtle swell of his shoulders. John had hit a major nerve. "I knew him."

She recognized the desolation turning his dark eyes into opaque masks and wanted to comfort him. She'd known Luke, too. He'd been Gideon's partner and best friend. The night Luke had died, she'd heard that Gideon had been taken to the hospital—that he'd been hurt badly enough to end his career.

She fought the need to go to him now, just as she had that night. Back then, she'd finally driven to the hospital in the wee hours of the morning. But his family was there—brothers, parents, his sister. He had more love and support than she could ever give him. So instead of the former girlfriend making an unwelcome appearance, she'd snuck out the way she'd come in, locked herself in her apartment with a pillow and a box of tissues and cried for all Gideon had lost.

But she was a stronger person now than she'd been then. She could be there for him now. Even in this small way. She could risk the protective feelings she couldn't then. "Did you need something, John?"

Her partner seemed momentarily taken aback when she faced him, clearly allying herself with Gideon. But his stance quickly relaxed from over-the-top protector to good buddy once more. "We're ready to pull out. But we're off the clock. Most of us are heading down to Mack's Bar for a beer to unwind. You wanna come?"

She laid a hand on John's forearm. "I appreciate the invitation, but I'm beat. And I still want to spend some time with the boys at Dorie's." She gave him a gentle squeeze. "Tell the guys I'll catch 'em next time."

He looked down at her intently. "You're sure? If this isn't comfortable for you..."

She glanced back at Gideon. He said nothing to make her stay, but she read the undoctored pain in his eyes. It wasn't much of a gift, but it was one she could give. She smiled at John. "I'm sure. Gideon's an old friend. I'll see you tomorrow."

John eyeballed Gideon over her shoulder one last time, then nodded to Meghan. "Tomorrow, then."

The tension left the room along with John and she breathed a little easier. But when she turned to Gideon, a different kind of tension hung in the humid air between them. It was a tingling essence of hyperawareness she couldn't quite put a name to.

"Old friend, huh?" His eyes were awash in a turbulent emotion that belied the stillness of his posture and resonated deep inside her, unsettling her.

She tucked a loose strand of hair behind her ear and

wondered at the pulsating rhythm of her body's response to Gideon's dark mood. "Sorry about that. He's a little overprotective."

"So am I." He was back to hiding his left hand in his pocket again. Hiding parts of his body and personality he never had before. She wasn't sure she understood this harder, darker version of the man she once loved. "He cares about you."

"I never had a big brother before. John takes the role very seriously."

His gaze caught hers, and the seriousness in his expression forestalled her effort to smile. "Are you sure his feelings are brotherly?"

"Of course they are." She'd never thought of John in any other light. "Come on. Are you saying you've never gone all macho to protect your sister when you thought she was in trouble?" The few times she'd met Jessica Taylor, she'd struck Meghan as a creative, self-sufficient woman with a competitive edge and a laid-back sense of humor. She reckoned she'd have to be, to put up with six brothers who took their love and protective roles very seriously.

"There's a difference. I'm actually related to Jessie."

"Thanks for pointing out that I wasn't blessed with any siblings." Meghan clutched at her stomach in a habitual defensive gesture. How had she gone so quickly from offering compassion to wanting to throw something? "John knows that and he's filling the role."

"I'm not begrudging you the relationship. I know growing up for you was tough, that you wound up alone more often than not." Gideon moved closer, his expression apologizing for touching on a sensitive topic and being such a downer. "I never kept you from anyone or anything." When he reached out to cup her cheek, she flinched away. His hand curled into a fist and dropped to his side. "I just think you should be careful who you trust right now."

"What are you saying? That John has some freaky idea that he's in love with me?" She circled around him, heading deeper into the soot-coated maze of furniture, not wanting to even think what he was suggesting. "That he sent me the roses and made that call last night?" She spun around to face him. "And then he stood behind me, manning the same hose, while we put *his* fire out?"

Gideon stood utterly still, neither accepting nor denying the implausible scenario. "I wouldn't trust anyone right now, Meg."

"Not even you?"

She caught the quick glance down at his hands before he turned away and started sifting through the wreckage. "Especially not me."

"What does that mean?" Gideon was a quiet man by nature, but his silences always meant something. A profound thought. A splendid surprise. A deep consideration of the best way to share bad news.

But he had no explanation for her this time. Maybe she should have gone with John.

But Gideon had needed her to stay. Or so she thought. Now she wasn't sure. Her heart was all twisted up with care and regret, with fear and need. With love she should have kept a tighter rein on in the first place.

Maybe Uncle Pete was right. She could try to do the right thing a hundred times in a row and maybe get it right only once. This wasn't that one time.

When she couldn't stand the quietness any longer, she bent and picked up a battered picture frame. Water had seeped in through the cracked glass and damaged the photograph inside. But the main image was still visible. A team picture from a few years back. Probably the office coed softball team, judging by the matching T-shirts and ball caps. Smiling faces of men and women, arms hugged around each other, fingers veed-up in victory.

Something about the picture felt familiar. But maybe it was just the wish for what the photo represented that felt familiar.

It was a picture of people who shared a bond. People who could trust each other and work as a team. People who had done the job right. People whose past lives didn't stand in the way of finding future happiness.

She broke the awkward silence herself, needing to hear something besides her own depressing thoughts. "That's too bad. You're the one person I do trust. The one person I know would never intentionally hurt me." She reverently set the picture on a desk and picked up a trophy that must have sat beside it. "The one person I could never blame if you did hurt me."

"It's not about retribution, Meg. I'm not trying to control you or your friends or your life. I just want closure so I can move on and quit wondering how you could claim you love me and yet not want a future with me."

She laughed. One wry little sound that spoke of regret, not humor. "If all I had to do to make you happy was love you, I would have said yes."

She wiped off the engraving at the base of the trophy and scanned the words before setting it next to the photo.

"Now who's being cryptic?" His dark brown eyes met hers across the room, and the bond they'd shared instantly flared between them. Now? Did she tell him now how miserable they'd have been together?

An after-image of this morning's message blipped into her brain. Meghan blinked and looked away. She was so consumed with giving Gideon the peace he wanted that the words almost hadn't registered.

"Gideon." The longing turned to quizzical in his gaze as she carried the trophy across the shell of the room to him. "This place is an accounting—" she corrected herself. "*Was* an accounting firm. Chadwick and Burlington."

"Yeah?" He took the trophy and read the inscription. "C.B. Accounting. Inner-City Softball. First Place.'

He didn't see it yet.

She pointed to the words. "*Numbers*. That note this morning said something about the numbers not adding up. Like at an accounting office." Her lungs nearly constricted with the anticipation of making a connection. Of finally being able to have something from the past twenty-four hours make sense. "He was giving me a clue about where he was going to set this fire."

"That card was too vague to connect the threat to a specific building. That message could apply to dozens of accounting firms and businesses."

His rational response couldn't douse the first glimmer of hope she'd had since that first rose had been placed on her coat. "There must be something specific about *this* office. He had to have it planned before he gave me the rose this morning."

Gideon must have seen something important in the observation, too. He pushed the trophy back into her hands and punched a speed-dial number on his cell phone. She followed him as he headed to the front sidewalk for clearer reception.

"Who are you calling?" she asked.

"My brother Josh. I'm going to have him run the name of this place, see who owns it. Get a list of employees and clients."

Meghan continued her impromptu cleanup while he made the call. "I should feel relieved that he finally left us a clue. Instead, I feel like a very large clock just started ticking down inside my head." She looked to Gideon for agreement. "This is going to get a lot worse before it gets better, isn't it?"

He had no argument for that. Just an intense look that promised he'd stick with her. For now, at least. "Detective

Josh Taylor, please," he spoke into the phone. "His brother Gideon."

Meghan righted a line of chairs that had sat by what was once the front window. "Do you think if we could have figured out his message sooner, we could have prevented the fire?"

Gideon shook his head. "Let's not second-guess ourselves. He doesn't want to give away too much information. He must be on a real power trip, toying with you like this. And since he was successful in setting the fire and getting you here, I'm sure he'll try again."

Providence. Just as Gideon said the words, something crunched beneath Meghan's boot.

She froze in place, then slowly lifted her foot to inspect whatever had been damaged. Her breath whooshed from her lungs and she nearly fell over trying to move away. "Gideon."

Half drowned in a deep puddle of water on the front sidewalk, its stem snapped in two, its vibrant colors dulled by a coating of muck and grime, lay a yellow rose.

Gideon swore, his damning words a forceful contrast to the bleak helplessness that threatened to overwhelm her momentary confidence. "I'll call you back, Josh."

She latched on to his forearm as he moved behind her and wrapped his arm around her chest, pulling her farther away from her stalker's calling card. This time she made no pretense about not wanting Gideon's sheltering touch. "He was here."

While they'd been talking. In those few minutes between escaping the spotlight and the crowd dispersing. Unseen by the press or police or her fellow firefighters.

Had he dropped the rose before he could attach a note? Or was there some sinister symbolism to the trampled ruin of that delicate flower? Her blood thickened like ice in her veins, then raced in a feverish pace that left her feeling light-headed. She swayed into the unmoving wall of Gideon's chest and held on for sanity's sake.

"Enough of this game." Gideon shifted positions so that he had her tucked to his side. His careworn gaze swept the bustle of the city street as it returned to normal. "I'm not letting you out of my sight until this thing is solved."

It was a high-handed announcement that she normally would have railed against. She couldn't handle day-in, day-out contact with Gideon and walk away from this investigation with her heart and conscience intact.

Funny thing was, even as he loaded her into his Suburban, she never uttered a single protest. And when he climbed in behind the wheel, she reached across the seat and clung to the reassuring grasp of his hand.

MEGHAN PAUSED on the back porch to watch the scenery.

It wasn't the sun setting beyond the downtown Kansas City skyline. No, this scene was right here in Dorie Mesner's backyard.

Lined up at varying heights along the garage wall. Four naked backs.

An intoxicating flood of hormones mingled with the happy serenity of honest labor on a muggy summer evening. Dorie's garage needed painting. And while three of the four laborers were actually scraping the old paint and cleaning the surface, the fourth was equally busy with his dry paintbrush—sometimes dusting the side of the garage, sometimes dusting the dog who ran around their feet. Sometimes chasing the dog. Sometimes running between the legs of the grown man and laughing from down deep in his belly when the man scooped him up high into the air.

Gideon. Alex. Eddie. Mark.

Meghan felt a contented grin curve the corners of her

mouth. She shifted the tray she carried to rest on her hip and simply watched, nourishing her lonely soul.

This was the break she'd needed to push aside the cloud of doom that had settled around her since finding the rose at the fire scene that afternoon. But she wouldn't go as far as acknowledging the idea that this felt an awful lot like the blissful future Gideon had once envisioned for them. Home. Children. Security. Love.

"It's just temporary," she reminded herself with a whisper. Happiness had always been a temporary thing for her. She'd learned not to bank on it, but to appreciate it while she could. So, making the most of this brief interlude, she allowed herself to enjoy the view awhile longer.

One back in particular caught her eye. Long and lean, Gideon's tanned, supple skin undulated over waves of muscles that started at his broad shoulders and tapered down to the waistband of faded jeans that softly cupped his tight, perfect butt with the familiarity of loving hands. The sheen of sweat glistening across all that bare skin was icing on the cake.

Meghan felt the high temperature and humidity seep in through her pores, matching the luxuriating warmth pooling inside her. Her lips parted, seeking a breath of cool air for a body that was slowly overheating.

For a man who shunned the spotlight almost as much as she did, Gideon Taylor was one beautiful piece of work, commanding the eye and begging for a touch.

The ice-filled glasses rattled on the tray in her hands as she fought her body's instinctive reaction to the call of Gideon's. Four heads turned at the betraying sound. Her idyll had ended.

"Hi, guys." Her croaky voice betrayed the lingering tension she felt.

Fire bloomed on her cheeks as Gideon's gaze questioned hers. She spied a lambent recognition of the hunger she must be projecting, felt the matching spark of pure, physical desire. But the glimpse of answering hunger that flared in his eyes was quickly lost behind the patter of thirsty boys and a charging puppy.

Fortunately, Gideon was a merciful man. He offered her a dazzling smile and invited her to join them. "If that's cold and wet, bring it on."

She started down the steps. "Lemonade with plenty of ice. Will that do?"

"Sounds perfect."

Tools were thrown to the ground as she sidestepped Crispy and met them halfway. For a few seconds she was inundated by thirsty boys and thank-yous and a hug around her legs.

"My lem-ade!" Mark grabbed the tray and tilted it down to his level.

"Whoa, there." Gideon saw disaster coming the same time she did.

Meghan snatched the sipper cup with its lid and Gideon rescued the last two glasses before the tray clattered onto the patio. She pressed a hand to her chest and grinned in admiration. "Nice save, cowboy." She thanked Gideon. She handed Mark his cup and palmed the top of his head. "Next time wait until I give you your drink. We almost spilled all this on top of you." She shuffled her fingers through his downy hair and bent to press a kiss to his crown. "I just want you to be careful. Okay?"

His startled look changed to a wide-eyed smile. "'kay."

Then he trotted off to join Eddie and Crispy on their romp through the yard. Alex had already downed his lemonade and returned to finish scraping the soffit under the eave of the garage roof.

That left her and Gideon, standing alone in a pocket of quiet where chaos had reigned a moment ago. She picked up the tray and Gideon handed her a glass. "Here. Great timing. We're almost finished with this side and the back. Thanks."

"You're welcome."

He tilted his head back and took a long drink. Meghan watched the long column of his throat with helpless fascination. That most innocent of actions had become a sensual experience for her. A stubble of dark brown beard shadowed his jaw and neck. And the utterly masculine contour of his Adam's apple, riding up and down his neck with each swallow, made her lips tingle with the urge to catch it and kiss it.

She took a drink from her own glass, hoping the icy liquid trickling down her own throat would be enough to cool the untimely awakening of her libido. With his drink half emptied, Gideon pressed the chilled glass to his cheeks and forehead. His quest for relief from the heat flexed the toned ridges of muscle across his chest and shoulders. It stirred the musky scents of man and heat from the crisp, T-shaped mat of hair that spread from nipple to nipple and thinned in a line down to his navel and disappeared behind the top button of his jeans.

Though she clearly remembered where that distinctly masculine trail led, she valiantly tried to continue a normal conversation. "I can't believe how much you've gotten done in one evening."

He took another drink and she had to look away to concentrate on what he was saying. "Alex is doing most of the work. That kid has something eating inside him."

"At times I think he's half afraid he won't live to be a man." She watched as Alex attacked a particularly stubborn spot. He scraped the paint and blew away the dust and rubbed it with his hand until it was perfectly primed. A familiar, protective anger churned in her gut, effectively turning her lusty thoughts into more maternal ones. "He survived a father who beat him unconscious more than once. He joined a gang…''

Meghan sucked in her breath and zeroed in on the stylized blue-black W on the back of Alex's shoulder. After an awkward pause she released the breath she'd been holding. Gideon wasn't an idiot. "I guess you saw his tattoo."

Gideon nodded. "Westside Warrior. Just like the symbol burned into the floor at the last two fires."

"Alex is a good kid. He—"

"I know he's not a gang member anymore. Dorie wouldn't let him through the front door if he was." His resolute statement eased some of her fears. "He didn't set those fires."

"But maybe some of his old friends—enemies now, I guess—did. You don't think he's hiding any secrets about it—do you?"

Gideon watched Alex continue to work without a break. The sun-carved lines beside his eyes deepened with a frown. "I'm not sure he'd admit it, but he's too anxious to keep what he has here. You and Dorie. I think he likes the responsibility of being a big brother. If he thought his enemies had put any of you in danger, I think he'd come forward." He glanced down at Meghan. "He said something to me about another guy hittin' on his girl. Flirting, not physically. Maybe that's all that's bugging him right now. He *is* sixteen."

"He told you about his girlfriend?" It had taken her the entire car ride home from the precinct office last night to pull those details out of him.

"Yeah. We've been talking. Well, mostly I've been listening." His frown transformed into a mischievous smile that made him look almost as young as Alex. "By the way, if Dorie is missing some Tupperware, you might check Eddie's room. He said he needed a container for the snails he found to live in.''

Meghan didn't bother with an "O-oh, gross." She looked beyond Eddie's confession to the bigger picture.

"I knew you'd be wonderful with children." Meghan hesitated, but then she gave in to what she wanted—no, what she needed—to do. Bracing her hand against one bare shoulder, she rose up on tiptoe and kissed the dimple beside Gideon's mouth, blinking back the unexpected sting of tears as she dropped back onto her heels. "Thank you for being so good with my boys. And not holding what I did to you against them."

She could feel the thunderous beating of his heart beneath her palm. But she couldn't tell if it was their potential audience or his considerable self-control that kept him from responding with nothing less subtle, nothing more precious than the light stroke of his fingertips across her cheek. "I told you I'm not into retribution. I'm not sure what I feel lately. But I would never hurt you. Or them."

She centered her gaze in the middle of that broad, inviting chest. "I suppose I know that intellectually, but..." She pressed her lips together and inhaled deeply, flaring her nostrils and working up the courage to force herself to look him in the eye again. "I have a voice inside my head that tells me you get what you give. And I hurt you, so there's going to be payback for me somewhere along the line."

His eyes narrowed and studied her for so long without comment that she had to speak again to keep from running into the house.

"I'm not crazy," she tried to explain. "It isn't that kind of voice."

But he understood that she was talking about a memory. "Who told you that? Your father? That's a pretty morbid philosophy." Gideon ground the low-pitched words like an accusation between his teeth.

She'd heard that eye-for-an-eye adage the first time she'd

refused to let Pete Preston treat her like a girlfriend instead of his niece. She'd been Alex's age. Sweet sixteen. She'd told Pete no and slapped his face.

Seemed as though he'd been paying her back ever since.

"Meg?" His hand was on her face again, a stronger touch this time. His fingers slid into the hair at her temple as he cupped her cheek. "Do you honestly think I'm going to walk away from you when you need me? At the very least we're colleagues, and it's part of the unwritten code that I back you up. But seeing you these past two days tells me there's still more than that between us. I think we owe it to ourselves to figure out exactly where we stand."

"But what if I hurt you again? What if you're kind and gentle like before and I still…" Guilt choked the words in her throat.

Courage, Meg, she coached herself. She had to move past the shame. *Tell him.*

"I lived with my aunt and uncle for a year or so when I was a teenager." It was a shaky beginning, but she leaned into the warmth of Gideon's hand and discovered the strength to go on. "Uncle Pete's nickname for me was…" She swallowed hard. *"Freak."*

She felt the tremor in Gideon's hand as he held his reaction in check. But he never took his patient gaze from hers. "Good thing I never met Uncle Pete."

"Yeah, well—"

Alex's scraper tore the air with an abrasive screech, then clunked into metal. "Ow! Son of a bitch!" She and Gideon turned in unison and saw the teen throw down the tool then shake his fingers as if he were flinging something off the tips.

"Hey, watch your mouth," warned Gideon, his tone firm, not angry.

"Are you okay?" asked Meghan.

Alex turned around and mumbled an apology. "Yeah. It

just stings. Gid, could you give me a hand? I think I need someone taller.''

Gideon's hand had slid down to her shoulder where the calloused pads of his fingers singed the exposed skin beside the strap of her tank top. She could see he was torn between the needs of the teen and her pathetic story. She twisted and tried to scoot free, absolving him of guilt and removing the tempting contact. ''It's okay. Go.''

''I'll be there in a sec.'' Gideon looked at Alex, but didn't release her. ''Don't hurt yourself.''

''I already did that.''

While the boy fussed and fumed and picked up the scraper, Gideon released her. But she'd retreated less than half a step before he caught her again, beneath the chin this time. The unexpected contact was an incendiary spark to dozens of nerve endings. Her lips parted on a startled breath of anticipation.

Whatever damage had been done to his left hand, there was no mistaking the strength in his right. Like steel sheathed in velvet, his fingers and thumb spanned her jaw and pulled her close. He pressed his lips to hers in a kiss that was swift and thorough and over before she could either respond or protest. She felt cherished and hot and full of questions.

His eyes probed her face and hugged her with reassurance. ''You'll tell me later?''

He made it sound more like an expectation than a request.

Meghan nodded. If she found the courage once, she could find it again. ''Go on. I want to get the kitchen cleaned up before we leave. You finish up out here.''

He released her as quickly as he'd taken her in hand, gave her his empty glass and strode over to Alex. ''Hey, let me help with that.''

They discussed ladders and architecture while Meghan

practiced breathing evenly again. She collected glasses and
made sure Eddie and Matthew were playing safely on the
swing set before retreating into the house as quietly as
she'd appeared.

She found Dorie dozing on the couch in the den. Meghan
shook her head and smiled. The older woman took on too
much. As much as she loved the boys, she needed to be
paying more attention to her own health needs. Offering
her some rest, at least, Meghan tiptoed in to turn off the
TV and retrieve Dorie's half-empty lemonade glass.

Back in the kitchen, Meghan inserted the glass into the
last empty spot on the top dishwasher rack and wondered
if she should make room for the glass she'd carried up to
Matthew's room. Though Gideon had issued the invitation
to help with the garage to all four boys, Matthew had opted
to go upstairs to play. At least he hadn't run from Gideon
the way he had the night before.

Meghan added soap and started the dishwasher. If Matthew needed some time and space to get used to a big man
like Gideon, or just that there was a stranger in the house,
she'd give it to him. She'd checked on him when she took
him his drink. Matthew had been looking at his books, not
crying or sulking.

Another look out the back window over the kitchen sink
and she had all her precious charges accounted for. She
marveled at Gideon's patience as he held the ladder for
Alex and carried on a conversation with Eddie. She went
still for a moment, standing with suds up to her elbows,
acquainting herself with the inexplicable peace she felt inside.

She lightly licked the rim of her lips, remembering the
brief possession of Gideon's mouth. *He* was doing this to
her, she suspected. Surrounding her in the normalcy of how
others lived. Listening to her. Showing kindness to her boys
and former foster mom. Wrapping her up in his gentle pa-

tience and fierce protection. Gideon was making her care again. Reminding her that she had never stopped caring.

It was a beautiful world he was creating for her.

But it was a world *she* could destroy.

With that sobering reminder to burst her contented bubble, Meghan closed the curtains and pretended that scrubbing pans was the most important job in the world.

She'd managed to replace the shield that guarded her heart by the time Gideon and the boys burst in through the back door.

"Mission accomplished!" Gideon beamed as he deposited Mark on the countertop and tugged the boy's shirt on over his head before slipping into his own. "One more day and we'll have everything ready to paint."

"I'm hittin' the shower." Alex grabbed a handful of cookies and headed toward his room downstairs.

"Do we have any salad? What do snails eat?" asked Eddie, already standing in front of the open refrigerator.

"Shh," she cautioned them all with a finger to her mouth, "Dorie's napping." She closed her mouth to contain her own laughter as all four made just as much noise apologizing. "Stop it. You guys are terrible." She slipped into Mom mode and closed the fridge door. "Boys first, snails later. I want all these dirty clothes in the laundry and everyone in a bath or shower. Now."

As the boys quietly marched off to do her bidding, Gideon grinned. "Me, too?"

An instant image of his tall, naked body soaping down in her shower interrupted the authoritative flow of her thoughts. Her lips suddenly burned with the memory of his kiss. She pressed them tightly together to conquer the urge to put her hand there to reveal to Gideon just what she was thinking.

Feeling her emotional detachment rapidly eroding, she crooked a finger and asked him to follow her out through the dining room. "There's a bathroom at the top of the stairs. You can wash up at the sink in there."

"I remember." He'd mounted four stairs in two strides when he stopped.

Meghan's nose wrinkled up at the same moment. A faint hint of sulphur hung in the air. "Do you smell that?"

Gideon wasn't grinning anymore. "It's up here."

"Smoke."

Chapter Eight

A familiar bolt of adrenaline shot through Gideon, heightening his senses and turning on a rusty radar that had died that night with Luke Redding.

Fire.

Meghan dashed up the stairs ahead of him. "Matthew!"

Reawakening the firefighter role that beat in his blood, he hurried behind her to the landing. An anticipatory energy thrummed through his nerve endings, making each movement quick and precise. "There."

A whispery carpet of light gray smoke seeped from beneath the closed door at the top of the stairs. Meghan's decisions were quick and instinctive and right on the money. She spread the flat of her hand against the closed door and checked for heat on the other side.

Assured that it was safe to go in, she opened the door. "Matthew, honey, are you in here?"

Smoke rolled out into the hallway behind her. There was finally enough of it rising in the air to trigger the smoke detector. The piercing alarm cut right through Gideon's brain, adding to the charged urgency in the air. He kept the tension in his body under tight control, forcing rational thought to the forefront. Where was the kid? Gideon added a louder voice to the search. "Matthew?"

Gideon hovered in the doorway as Meghan swept aside

the smoke and entered the room. "Talk to me, sweetie,"
she begged.

A quick assessment of the bedroom indicated the fire was
contained. Smoke had risen to the ceiling and was settling,
but hadn't filled the room yet. The only identifiable flames
shot up from the tall, metal trash can near the window.
"The curtains."

Meghan saw the fuel source ignite the same time he did.
She reached for the trash can. "Ow."

He could hear the others moving about downstairs, responding to the alarm. "Meghan?" Dorie's voice was high-
pitched with panic. She'd had a rude awakening to danger.
"Gideon? Boys? What's wrong?"

Gideon debated his next move for about half a second.
He yelled down the stairs. "Dorie, get out of the house!"

She was a smart enough lady not to ask questions.
"Boys!"

The metal can with the Chiefs logo must be hotter than
an oven. "You all right?" he asked Meghan. He rushed in
and ripped down the curtain panel, stomping out the flames
beneath his boot before they could take hold. He reached
for her hand. "Let me see."

"No. I'm fine." She crossed over the closet and slung
open the door. "Matthew?"

If the lack of an answer alarmed him, Meg must be worried sick. "We'll find him."

"I know." She coughed once and knelt down, checking
the hidden recesses of the closet. "Matthew?" When she
turned he could see the redness in her eyes. Smoke irritation
or tears? "He isn't here."

She needed a comrade-at-arms right now, not comfort.
"Where's the fire extinguisher?"

"Under the kitchen sink."

He was already out the door. "I'll get it. You keep looking."

Gideon bounded down the stairs and ran to the kitchen, passing Dorie with Mark in her arms. "It'll be okay." He paused only long enough to tweak the little one's nose and to visually reassure the older woman. "I want everyone outside just as a precaution, to make sure we're all accounted for."

Dorie's breath came in shallow pants. "Is Matthew still up there?"

"We'll get him." Gideon opened the doors beneath the sink and snatched up the extinguisher.

Dorie was right behind him. "But Matthew won't call out if he needs help."

Gideon spun around and reached out to comfort her with his right hand. But his left hand didn't respond to the quick transfer and the extinguisher slipped and crashed to the floor. "Damn." He crushed what muscles and nerves were cooperating into a useless fist and scooped the red canister up with his right hand. "I have to go."

Alex ran up from the basement. "What's going on?"

"There's a fire," warned Dorie. "We can't find Matthew."

A contained fire for right now if he could get back upstairs to help. But Gideon didn't have time to explain. He looked straight at Alex. "Get Dorie and Mark out of here."

The young man put his hands on Dorie's shoulders and started backing out toward the patio door. "What about Eddie?"

Dorie glanced over her shoulder to answer. "I sent him outside already to put the leash on Crispy."

Gideon was hurrying toward the opposite exit. "Alex, you make sure he's there and then all of you stay put until I come for you."

"Yes, sir."

He didn't wait to see them leave. He believed Alex would get the job done.

The smoke was filtering down the stairs now as Gideon climbed them three at a time. "Meghan?"

She was an efficient piece of work to behold as she darted from the second bedroom into Dorie's master suite, keeping her head and doing a methodical search for the missing boy. "He's not in the first two rooms or the john."

"Good girl."

His praise fell on her retreating back. As it should be. He went to work himself.

Not trusting his hand to fail again, he tucked the extinguisher into the crook of his left elbow, pulled out the pin and squeezed the handle. In under a minute he had the trash can and the surrounding floor covered in white, suppressive foam.

He blinked against the stinging cloud of smoke and coughed out a cleansing breath. "It's out."

The intense heat had melted the rug beneath the can, and the flames had left scorch marks on the wall. Other than the lingering smoke getting into anything that could absorb the odor, the damage was minimal. But it could have been worse. A lot worse.

He didn't give himself time to savor the tiny victory over a fire he could defeat. The piercing cry of the smoke detector was an unnecessary reminder of just how dangerous this fire could have become. And how deadly it might have been for a little boy who didn't heed its call.

He opened the bedroom windows to bring in fresh air and vent the smoke, then went in search of Meghan and Matthew. "Meg?" He opened the smoke detector casing and ripped out the battery to stop the ear-splitting noise. The shock of sudden silence hurt his ears almost as much as the alarm had. "Meg, did you find him?"

"In here."

He jogged down the hallway into Dorie's bedroom.

Meghan was stooped in front of the sliding-closet door. "Is he okay?"

She gathered the silent little bundle of boy into her arms and stood. "Mostly scared, I think." She brushed Matthew's curly hair out of his eyes and wiped the tears from his cheeks. A matching tear trickled down her cheek. "Oh, sweetie, we were so worried about you."

When she hugged him tight and buried her nose in his hair, it punched Gideon right in the gut. Meghan had so much life experience to share, so much patience and empathy with children. She had so much love in her heart she needed to give away. And the unfiltered love of a child might well be the only thing that could heal her wary heart.

Overwhelmed by the image of mother and child—bound by the heart, if not by blood—and the unexpected magnitude of relief at finding them both safe, Gideon closed the distance between them and wrapped his arms around them both. He nuzzled his nose in the smoky scent of Meghan's golden hair, just as she had nuzzled Matthew. The size of his hug was just right to hold them both. "I'm glad you're both safe."

Though he made no sound beyond a few soft sniffles, Matthew's body trembled inside the double embrace. Remembering the way Matthew had run from him at dinner last night, Gideon wisely pulled away so he wouldn't add to the boy's anxiety.

Gideon brushed a hair that had stuck on the dampness of Matthew's cheek. "You gave us quite a scare there, buddy. You need to run outside to a safe place when there's a fire."

Matthew pulled away from even that gentle touch and buried his nose in Meghan's shoulder. The rejection hurt, but he didn't want to compound the four-year-old's fear. Gideon backed off yet another step. With Meghan's hands literally full at the moment, he could best help by simply doing his job. Every fire had a source, and it was his nature to try to identify it. "Did he say anything about the fire?"

Meghan shook her head. "Is everyone else okay?"

At least he could reassure Matthew in that way. "Your brother and Dorie, Alex, Eddie and Crispy are all in the backyard. They're fine." He summoned that calm demeanor that allowed him to stand back and observe what others could not. Even on a scale as small as this one, a fire could talk. He touched Meghan's arm and ushered her back into the hallway. "Why don't you go out and see them while I do some cleaning up and nosing around up here."

"Sure." She stopped a moment and backed up, pushing her elbow into his hand. The intentional contact warmed him like an intimate caress. When she looked up at him and smiled, he knew his professional detachment had just been shot to hell. "I'm glad you were here. For a lot of reasons."

He looked down at his hand. He'd almost failed her. But she didn't need to know how close they'd come to losing control of the fire. "Me, too."

He let her precede him down the hall and waited at the top of the stairs until Meghan and Matthew disappeared from sight. Gideon sighed. It was a heavy, weary breath that sat like a weight upon his heart. He'd tried so hard not to care about Meg, to harden himself to her independent spirit that desperately needed someone to care. He'd tried to focus on the woman who worked overtime to pretend she didn't need anyone at all, not the world-weary soul underneath who loved these four boys more than she'd probably ever admit to herself.

He wouldn't deny the physical attraction that sparked like kinetic energy between them. But she wasn't the woman he'd loved two years ago. This Meghan was tougher, stronger—and yet more vulnerable and more aware of other's feelings than the woman who'd walked out on him. He was her friend. Her protector.

And he was dangerously close to becoming the man who loved her. Again.

But until he believed she understood what commitment meant, until he believed she wouldn't break his heart all over again, he'd need to watch himself. He needed to remember that she wasn't his woman. These weren't his children.

This wasn't his life.

He was an arson investigator. Not a husband. Not a father.

After checking out the landing window and counting heads to make sure everyone was together and safe, Gideon went back into the bedroom Matthew and Mark shared. He just wanted to make sure there was nothing dangerous for the boys to get into before the room was cleaned up.

But Gideon's curiosity made the informal investigation a little more thorough. He knelt in front of the trash can and used the tip of his pen to dig around to see what he could find. "I wondered."

He sat back on his haunches and said a little prayer—guidance for himself and peace for a frightened, lonely soul.

At the bottom of the trash can he'd made an unfortunate discovery. A cigarette lighter that had probably belonged to Dorie's deceased husband.

And the charred, brittle remains of three small cardboard children's books.

"You think Matthew set the fire?" Meghan couldn't quite fathom the possibility. She studied Gideon's profile as he negotiated the twists and turns of Blue Ridge Boulevard en route to her apartment. He was serious. She was incredulous. "Would a four-year-old who lost his parents in a fire really be playing with a lighter?"

"I don't like it, either. But my gut tells me Matthew knows what happened." The streetlights from the old, working-class neighborhood threw enough light into Gideon's Suburban that she could read his grim expression. "It wasn't spontaneous combustion, and he was the only one upstairs. He stayed close enough to watch, but then, when it got out of his control, he tried to put it out and cover up his mistake. He shut the door and hid."

Meghan reluctantly concurred to the possibility. "I saw something that looked like a towel wadded up in the trash can—as if he'd tried to smother the flames."

His big shoulders expanded in a shrug. "I'm stumped as to the *why,* just like you."

"You don't think…?" She couldn't even say the words. A phantom pain sank its talons into her gut and twisted her up with fear and anger. Surely her stalker hadn't found his way past three adults to sneak into the house and endanger her boys.

Gideon's intuitive spirit understood. He reached for her hand and closed it in his reassuring grip. "No way. Our friend with the roses uses a very high-tech means to start a fire. Arsonists have a definitive style to their work. This one was too simple to be the same guy."

She turned sideways in her seat to face him, finding comfort in his gentle strength and expertise. She stretched her arm across her lap and hung on to his hand with both of hers. "I don't know what I'd do if something happened to Matthew. Or any of those boys."

He spared her a look that warmed her through and through like a cup of rich, dark coffee. "They'll be fine. We'll keep a close watch over them."

We? She liked the sound of that. The idea of her and Gideon on the same side again drizzled through her and offered her a fleeting sense of hope. She nestled into her seat, taking comfort in just watching him and in holding his hand.

They turned north onto Sterling Avenue and drove several miles in companionable silence before they reached Sugar Creek, the tiny suburb near the river where she lived. The low hum of the engine vibrated through her muscles and left her drowsy and relaxed. Her long day was finally coming to an end and her body was ready to drift off to sleep.

But her brain wouldn't stop its wondering. As much as she hated Gideon's theory, she suspected he was right. She'd seen the end of a towel burning inside that trash can, as if someone had stuffed it on top of the flames to try to smother them.

"Do you think that was Matthew's way of trying to communicate something? Dorie said she'd call his therapist in the morning. Oh, God." She sank back into her seat and hugged her arms around her waist. She wished her next thought had never popped into her head. "You don't think it's just a fascination with fire, do you? That he's set other fires before?"

Gideon's weighty sigh matched her own. "Maybe he thinks the firemen will come and bring his parents back. I don't know."

The Suburban's air-conditioning chilled the bare skin on her arms and legs. But that cold was nothing like the arctic blast of dread gathering inside her. "Matthew couldn't have set the fire that destroyed his home. That would mean he accidentally killed his own parents."

Gideon's right hand tightened in a white-knuckled grip around the wheel. Control. No matter what emotions buffeted around inside him, he managed to keep them under control. Except with her. She had the dubious honor of being the one person who could make him lose it.

"Even if he just *thinks* he killed them—" with his reaction firmly in check, Gideon finally spoke "—that's a
terrible burden for anyone—especially a child his age—to
bear." Meghan wondered at the burden Gideon carried over
Luke Redding's death. Maybe he had much more in common with the boy who was afraid of him than even he
realized. "I plan to spend some time at the computer tomorrow. I want to read the investigator's report about the
Grimes fire. Hopefully, it will show some other cause besides playing with matches. And then we can explain that
to Matthew."

There he went with the *we* stuff again. The chill around
her heart began to thaw. She mentally put herself on guard
against the deluge of emotion that was sure to follow. "You
should be a father, Gideon. You know just when to get
tough and when to listen."

That earned her half a smile. "I had a great role model."

"Your father, Sid, is a wonderful man. He and Martha
raised you guys right." She'd always been envious of Gideon's upbringing. And a little intimidated by his large, loving family who seemed to be able to weather good times
and bad with support and unity and patience. A visit to his
parents' condo for a boisterous Sunday dinner with all of
Gideon's brothers and their wives and his sister had seemed
like an alien world to her.

He slowed and turned onto her street, heading toward the
apartment complex at the end of the block. "I've always
wanted that. Kids of my own." He glanced her way, and
there was no mistaking the wistful regret in his voice. "I
used to dream about having kids with you."

"I know." Meghan felt her heart sink into that empty,
disfigured pool of secrets inside her. She looked out her
window into the night, unable to see the houses pass by
through the veil of tears she didn't want him to notice. She
couldn't afford to get caught up in his dreams again. No

matter how beautiful and perfect they might be, she knew they were unattainable.

But Gideon refused to hold anything against her. "I guess I'll have to settle for spoiling my niece and nephew right now."

Meghan didn't say another word until he pulled into a parking space near her apartment door. Her throat ached from the effort to conquer her tears. She had to cough first, to speak. But by the time he killed the engine and lights, she could actually look at him with a friendly smile. "Thanks for the ride. And thanks again for helping at Dorie's."

She wasn't surprised when he climbed out of the Suburban to walk her up the stairs to the door of her second-floor apartment. His gallantry was one of the first things that had attracted her to Gideon. Every woman, no matter her age or appearance—or "independent personality" as he'd so kindly described her first antagonistic encounters with him—deserved his protection and respect.

She slid her key into the dead bolt and unlocked it. When she inserted her key into the doorknob lock, however, it turned without any resistance. Hmm. But she shook her head and dismissed any concern. She hadn't gotten much sleep, and her day had been so long she'd probably just forgotten to turn the lock inside before leaving. The dead bolt had been secured, anyway. She was still safe.

Tucking a loose strand of hair behind her ear, she turned and smiled up at Gideon. "Good night. And thanks again. I'm glad you're going to help Matthew."

But to her surprise, Gideon reached around her to turn the knob and push open the door. "Get inside in case someone's watching."

Right. He was smart enough to still be thinking safety. But instead of shutting the door and waiting for her to lock herself in, he pushed his way in behind her and locked the door himself. Inviting himself in. Making himself at home. She stepped farther into her living room and turned on him. "What are you doing?"

"I said I wasn't letting you out of my sight." He faced her with a lazy smile that made the walls of her small apartment feel as though they were closing in. Gideon seemed bigger than ever, by comparison.

"I didn't think you meant twenty-four hours a day." There was too much need, too much hurt, too much history between them. The air in her apartment was rapidly filling with the charged ions of energy that pulled them together time and again. A floodgate of foolish hopes had been opened the moment she'd dropped her guard and kissed him. Now, unless she got some time to herself to regroup, she couldn't be sure she'd have the strength to close it again. "I'll let you drive me to work in the morning. How's that?"

"Not good enough for my peace of mind." Two long strides carried him into the center of her living room. He looked around as if reacquainting himself with once-familiar things. "Don't worry. I'll keep this as impersonal as you need it to be. I can sack out on your couch."

"My couch isn't big enough for you."

"Then I'll hit the floor." He looked straight at her then, the casual repartee in his voice doused by the intense darkness in his eyes that brooked no argument. "You're not getting rid of me tonight."

Meghan moved, needing to break away from the spell of such a promise vibrating through her and sinking into her very bones. She tossed her keys and fanny pack onto the kitchen table. "All right." She chose to surrender this argument, not wanting to charge any more of those ions. "I'll just get you a blanket and a pillow. I have a sleeping bag around here, too."

"Not just yet." He cut off her path into the hallway and

back rooms. He formed an intimidating wall that left her nowhere to go but to retreat. And yet she didn't have to. His voice was amazingly gentle, and the tender stroke of his fingertips across her cheek even sweeter. "You were telling me something important about your past, at Dorie's, before we got interrupted. I want to hear the rest of it."

"Right now?" She dropped her gaze from his and turned her cheek away from his touch. She needed time to prepare for this.

With the persistent gentleness of a trainer soothing an injured animal, he tunneled his fingers into the hair behind her ear. He stroked his thumb along her jaw to the point of her chin, then tipped her face up to his. "I know you're tired, but we're alone for once. We won't get interrupted. I want to listen to anything you have to say." His voice was a husky whisper. "It's been two years since we simply sat and talked. I miss that."

Meghan was done for. She lost herself in those dark, loving eyes and knew she couldn't turn him away. Not tonight.

"Me, too."

She mimicked his touch on her, running her fingers along the sandpapery stubble of his beard before sliding her palm across the short silk of his hair and cupping the back of his neck. The slight parting of his sensual lips fascinated her. Her own mouth felt suddenly parched and she touched the tip of her tongue to the rim.

"Meg."

Those mesmerizing lips breathed her name in a dark voice. She watched intently through hooded eyes as that mouth drifted closer. Or maybe she was the one moving.

She reached up and traced her fingertip along the hypnotic edge of that bottom lip. So fine. So full. So handsome. Her breath seeped out in a helpless gasp. She stretched up on tiptoe as the mouth descended. "Gideon."

Their lips met in a kiss of pent-up passion and long-denied need. Her feet left the floor as he skimmed his hand down her back, squeezed her bottom and lifted. Meghan wrapped her arms around his neck, squishing her breasts against the hard plane of his chest and rubbing her palms against the silky softness of his hair. Using his left arm simply as a pinning brace against her back, he was strong enough to hold her, suspend her, carry her to a place of passion and shelter she thought she'd forced her body to forget.

His mouth opened hotly over hers and his tongue plunged inside, claiming what was his, demanding no less from her. Her shorts rode up and she felt the hot possession of his hand on the skin at the back of her thigh. And still they kissed.

A thousand memories exploded inside her head. Memories of the raspy stroke of his tongue against hers, memories of the salty tang of his skin as she tasted his chin and jaw and mouth, memories of the tingling rush of ecstasy that built pressure at the pebbling tips of her breasts and the achy juncture of her thighs. Memories of how her heart hammered in her chest and her breath came in short, stuttered gasps. Memories of cherishing and being cherished, of loving and being loved by Gideon.

He'd taught her to kiss like this. Taught her to ask for what she wanted, such as planting little samples of kisses against his mouth while she squiggled free of his grasp and dropped her hands to his waist. She tugged his shirt free from his jeans and slipped her hands beneath to scorch her palms against the smooth skin of his back.

He backed her against the wall and helped himself to the same kind of liberty, pulling her shirt from the waistband of her shorts and tugging it up to her armpits, exposing the functional cover of her bra to his greedy hand.

Hand.

One hand.

Meghan arched her body into his, shamelessly inviting him to explore whatever he could touch. But though his desire was evident in the warm, wet forays of his mouth and the bulge in his jeans, his left hand rested against her hip, refusing to join the embrace. "Gid...Gideon. What...?" She began to pull away, punctuating each request with an apologetic kiss. "What's wrong?"

"Nothing." He drove her back against the wall with the force of his mouth and the thick pressure of his thigh between hers. "For the first time since forever, this finally feels right."

Her body was weak with passion, yet primed for more. Still, Gideon was holding something back. With a huge quest for self-control that would rival the master himself, Meghan brought her hands to his stomach and pushed him back a step.

"No. We have to stop," she protested on a ragged whisper. He kissed her one more time before she could work her hands up to frame his face and hold him where she could look up into his eyes. "Gideon, what's going on?"

"That's two years of frustration, sweetheart, trying to catch up in one kiss." He rested his forehead against hers, accepting the end of their embrace, clumsily righting their clothes as they each struggled for even breaths and saner thoughts. "But you're right. I said we'd talk."

That wasn't what she'd meant. Was he the one keeping secrets now? Was he self-conscious about the scars on his hand? Afraid she'd be repulsed by its touch? She supposed she understood that kind of self-preservation better than anyone. And though hiding his pain or any self-perceived shortcoming gave her a glimmer of understanding about the frustrated compassion and feeling of being shut out he must have felt with her, she backed off and let the subject drop.

Like her, maybe not all of Gideon's scars were visible.

She stroked her fingers along his jaw one last time before he backed away and broke contact completely. She couldn't help but notice he held up only one hand in a wry gesture of surrender.

She pushed away from the wall and offered them both some time to reestablish their composure. "Give me a minute to freshen up. We can sit on the couch."

"Cuddle or coffee?" It was a question from old times. Nights or mornings after making love, they'd used the contented afterglow as a quiet time to discuss the world and each other, and become even closer. Sometimes their talks had been energizing, illuminating. Sometimes they'd been more intimate.

She thought of how hard this was going to be and how much strength he could give her. She balanced that consideration with the knowledge that he'd probably want nothing to do with her when she was done. The need to tap into her own self-sufficiency won out. She still smiled with her answer. "Coffee."

"Fine. You do whatever you need to do, and I'll go start the coffee-maker."

"Do you remember where everything is?"

He walked around the corner and disappeared into the kitchen. "If nothing's changed."

Alone in the hallway, Meghan took a deep, steadying breath. She pressed her lips together, still tasting him there. She cradled her palm against her belly and tried to ignore the unintended portent of his words. "Nothing's changed."

Grateful for the reprieve, Meghan went into the bathroom and shut the door. The reflection in the mirror showed a tired woman—her shorts and shirt rumpled by a trying day and a needy man, her eyes wide and dark with the remnants of passion, her mouth pink and swollen.

She remembered the night she'd looked in the mirror and seen the cut across her lip, the bruise darkening her cheek, the wild look of fear and self-loathing in her eyes. As she unzipped her shorts and prepared to do her business, the network of fine, pale scars across her abdomen caught her eye. The spiderweb of lines, bisected by one long mark, served as a visual reminder of all she had lost. Of all she could never have.

But a stronger spirit, one kindled by the need to survive and boosted by the patient teaching of one good man, banished the tortuous images from her mind. "Go to hell, Uncle Pete."

She could do this. It might be harder than fighting any fire, but she could tell Gideon the truth.

Meghan tucked in her shirt and pulled her hair back into a ponytail. She ran cool water in the sink and splashed her face until a healthy color returned beneath the freckles. She dusted a hint of blush on her cheeks and moistened her mouth with lip balm.

When she reached for her toothbrush, she hesitated. The bristles felt damp. Odd. Usually they were dry and ready to be used again by the end of the day. Meghan set aside her misgivings, refusing to be deterred from her intention to tell Gideon why she left him two years ago, and why neither one of them should put too much hope in a future relationship working out, either.

Opening the door, she inhaled the stimulating aroma of brewing coffee and stepped across the hall to open the linen closet. She moved a stack of washcloths back to the shelf with the towels and reached behind to pull out her spare blanket.

When she had the blanket tucked under her arm she froze. She'd moved them *back* to where they belonged? An erratic pulse of unsettled energy danced along her nerves. She was pretty much a creature of habit. She always kept her towels and washcloths together. When had she moved them? Had she?

She pushed the closet door shut on an uneasy breath and slowly turned to face her bedroom door. She'd need to get an extra pillow for Gideon off her bed. But suddenly the prospect of entering her own personal, private sanctuary didn't even seem like such a sure, safe thing.

Meghan moved closer, determined not to be afraid in her own home. She was just spooked by that trampled rose and on edge with her resurrected feelings for Gideon today. She knew how to handle herself in tough situations. She wasn't such a wimp that she couldn't open the door to her own bedroom.

With that enervating determination to see her through, she reached for the doorknob and turned it.

And screamed.

Chapter Nine

Meghan's scream ripped through Gideon's heart and tore him free of the pointless debate that had consumed him.

He ran from the kitchen to the back of her apartment. Past the spot where he'd nearly made love to her, beyond the self-conscious doubts about his hand that even she had been able to recognize.

He burst through her bedroom door and halted midstride, swearing one vivid, pithy word at the scene inside.

Meghan stood next to her bed, clutching a plaid blanket in her arms so tightly, she was shaking. She stared with unblinking focus at the note pinned to her pillow.

Some son of a bitch was going to pay for this.

He shut his protective fury off in a dormant corner of his mind and concentrated on absorbing every pertinent detail of the violated room—including the ashen pallor of her face.

"Meg?" Slowly, he moved into the room, not wanting to startle her.

"He was here. Where I sleep. He used my toothbrush." Her voice sounded cold and distant.

He carefully sidestepped the trail of yellow rose petals strewn across the floor and walked toward her. The air in the closed-off room was pungent with the oily perfume smell of hundreds of petals littered across her bed and pillow.

"Sweetheart." He quietly alerted her to his presence behind her. He pried the blanket from her grasp and turned her unresisting body into his arms, slowly backing toward the open doorway. With his eyes glued to the sick message lying in a dent where someone had rested his head on the pillow next to hers, Gideon murmured soothing little nothings into her ear, holding her close against his heart.

Once they were free of the smell and the words, he closed the door. He pressed a kiss to her temple and released her just long enough to pull out his cell phone and punch in a number. Then he grabbed her keys and fanny pack, tucked her beneath his arm and led her outside onto the front porch balcony.

"How?" she asked on a voice that was half dazed, half disgusted. "Why?"

"I don't know, sweetheart. But we're gonna find out."

The blank look in her honey-colored eyes worried him. It might still be eighty degrees out, but she was in danger of going into shock. He unfolded the blanket and wrapped it around her shoulders.

"Taylor here." His call to the Fourth Precinct had picked up.

"Josh, give me a second." Gideon didn't bother to identify himself. His little brother, the detective, would be able to figure it out.

He tucked the blanket beneath Meghan's chin, but couldn't manage the blanket and the phone both. She blinked and looked up at him with cognizance and a spark of emotion in her eyes. She was back with him. "I'm okay," she reassured him, taking over blanket duty for him. "Make your call."

Gideon didn't mind a bit when she snuggled up close to his chest. He draped his left arm around her shoulders as he turned his focus to the grisly business at hand. He could hear her breathing deeply, feel her heart pound back to life in her chest, its adrenaline-charged rhythm beating in quick time with his own.

"I'm back." He spoke into the phone.

He could hear the hesitation in Josh's voice. "Is this an official call or are you backing out of baby-sitting tomorrow night?"

Oh, damn. He'd completely forgotten he'd promised to watch his niece. He squeezed his eyes shut and prayed for calm.

"Both," Gideon had to answer.

Sometimes he forgot that Josh wasn't his baby brother anymore. He was twenty-eight, not that spindly-legged kid who used to tag along with his older brothers. He was married, with a child. And he was a damn good detective. His voice was deadly serious now. "Talk to me, big brother."

"I know I'm not going through proper channels on this, Josh. But I figured you'd understand the situation." Josh had saved his new wife's life when she'd been victimized by a madman who'd threatened to take away her baby as soon as she'd given birth. "I want to report a breaking and entering at Meghan's apartment. And…"

Gideon once thought he could figure out any mystery. Piece the clues together and come up with the answer for himself. But his crime scenes had never involved twisted messages that toyed with him and triggered such distracting, possessive anger.

They'd never involved Meg.

"I need help identifying a stalker."

Josh asked a few more questions, needlessly reminded them not to disturb the crime scene, and promised to be there ASAP with his partner, A. J. Rodriguez, to officially handle the report from a family member.

"And Gideon?"

"Yeah?"

"We'll find him. You just take care of Meghan."

After Josh hung up, Gideon shoved the phone back into his pocket.

"Is Detective Taylor going to help us?" Meghan asked, putting the emphasis on Josh's new, official title. She was breathing at a normal rate now, though she still huddled close to his side.

"Yeah. We just need to stay put for a few minutes, if that's okay?"

She nodded. "Will you stay with me?"

He dipped a finger beneath her chin and tilted her face up to his. "I said I wouldn't let you out of my sight."

"Don't let me out of your arms, either." She loosened her grip on the blanket and wound her arms around his waist. "That sounds corny, but I don't care. I feel safer when I'm with you."

Gideon breathed in deeply, drinking in the faint, smoky scent of her hair from the fire at Dorie's place, and feeling humbled by the request she'd made of him. Half an hour ago he'd warned her to go inside to stay safe. He'd been disastrously wrong with that piece of advice. Now he honestly didn't know what to tell her. He didn't know what promise he could make and keep.

So he said nothing.

Using his sixth sense of perception as the only weapon he possessed, he peered into the shadows between the street lamps, searching for their elusive friend who could wield such terror and destruction with a beautiful flower and a remote-controlled computer chip.

Assured—for the moment at least—that in a city of hundreds of thousands of people, they were unwatched and alone, Gideon propped his hips against the wooden balcony railing and pulled Meghan into the vee of his legs. With her arms anchored around his middle, he nestled his chin at the crown of her hair and held her close, giving her his heat and strength. Using her quiet vulnerability and shaky trust to calm the vengeful thoughts roiling inside him.

The message written in nice, neat, generic calligraphy played over and over in his mind. He wondered how the bastard had gotten in, who he was. He wondered what the threat about tomorrow meant.

He wondered at the uncharacteristic impulse to do violent damage to the person who wanted to claim the woman he loved.

I touched you today. I tasted you. Did you feel the same electric spark between us that I did?
You're so beautiful in action. As beautiful as a yellow rose. Tomorrow we'll meet again, love, and I'll shower you in more rose petals.
One for every day you'll be mine.
Sleep well.

DETECTIVE A. J. RODRIGUEZ had been about as low-key as they came, thought Meghan as she rode with Gideon up the elevator to his apartment near the city's market district.

Rodriguez's "I see" response to the scene in her bedroom was an unassuming contrast to Josh Taylor's brasher, more graphic reaction to the deviant altar of affection.

Josh had called in the crime lab, then left to wake and interview her neighbors about any unusual activity in or around the apartment complex. Gideon had hovered close by while A.J. asked her question after question, not just about tonight, but about each of the times her *loving* fan had made contact with her. The detective pointed out that her locks had been picked by someone who knew how to use some pretty delicate tools. They'd found other items in

her apartment, slightly out of place, touched or even used
by the sick man who imagined they were lovers.

Except for the possibility of a DNA trace on her toothbrush, nothing in the apartment had discernible fingerprints
besides her own and Gideon's. A.J. had warned her that
they might not get a break on this case unless she recognized someone, or they could put a tail on her to catch the
guy when he next tried to contact her. Of course, K.C.P.D.
lacked the manpower to post a guard on her 24/7, but Josh
had promised to call a few friends and family members to
make sure someone always watched her back.

With Josh himself taking the first watch outside Gideon's
building, Meghan felt compelled to apologize. Again. "I'm
sorry that I got your family involved with this. I never
meant to put anyone else in danger. And now I've jeopar-
dized almost everyone I know. Dorie. The boys. Your
brothers. You." Her sigh echoed inside the elevator. "This
is one twisted mess."

"You didn't do this. *He* did."

Yeah, right. What other freak of nature could attract this
kind of unwanted attention? She looked away and watched
the buttons on the elevator panel light up. Uncle Pete had
once told her she'd never get a man to love her unless she
styled her hair, got a boob job and spread her legs.

A sarcastic, humorless laugh bubbled up in her throat.
Look at what she'd managed to accomplish without doing
any of those things.

"What is it?" Gideon asked, hearing the tiny hiccupping
sound.

She couldn't look at him and not feel ashamed. "I was
thinking about my uncle Pete."

"Don't." He nudged a finger beneath her chin and
forced her to meet his eerily probing gaze. "Whatever that
bastard said or did to you, forget about it. It makes you go

pale and afraid. And neither of those describes the woman I know.''

''A.J. asked me to go to the precinct office tomorrow to look at some mug shots of known arsonists.'' She gently pulled away from his touch, unnerved by the hypnotic perception of his gaze that saw far more than she wanted him to. ''See if I recognize anyone I may have had contact with yesterday.''

''I'll take you.''

Thankfully he didn't push to learn any more about her trip down nightmare lane with Uncle Pete. ''I also want to report for my shift in the morning. This guy is not going to rule my life and have me jumping through hoops or changing my routine.''

Although spending the night at Gideon's would definitely be a change. The last time she was here was when... Her thoughts took a sharp turn into the past.

''I could have gone to a hotel, you know.'' The elevator door opened and, after checking to see that the hallway was empty, he ushered her out ahead of him. ''Will my being here remind you of when you proposed? I don't want to hurt you again.''

He stopped in front of apartment 312 and inserted his key before favoring her with a weary smile. ''I'm a big boy. I'll be okay.'' He brushed a wisp of hair off her forehead. She treasured the kindness more than she should. ''Before we were so rudely interrupted at your apartment, you said you wanted coffee.''

Ah. So he still wanted to talk. Meghan breathed deeply, then let the resulting yawn come. It was after eleven. The late hour was as good an excuse as any. ''Will you let me take a rain check until morning?''

''You owe me the truth, Meg.''

''I know.'' She believed that with all her heart, but...''Can I be selfish and just enjoy your comfort for one night—the way things are between us now? Before I say something that will screw up your willingness to help me?''

''I won't change my mind about that.'' He opened the door and touched the small of her back, guiding her inside. When the door was locked behind them, he turned and gave her a look so deep and raw and intense, she felt it stripping away the protective walls that guarded those empty places inside her, leaving her feeling naked and exposed to the power of his all-seeing eyes. She hugged her arms around her waist to hide her trembling response. But she couldn't look away. His words were both a balm and a gentle warning. ''I'll give you whatever you want or need, as long as you promise not to run out on me again without any explanation.''

A hard bargain. But fair enough. Better than she deserved.

''I promise.'' He watched her for several seconds longer without a word. She shrugged, nervous that her word wasn't good enough. ''Do we shake on it?''

''No.'' He smiled at last and took her in his arms. ''We sleep on it.''

''Gid—''

''Relax. Unlike you, I have two bedrooms, remember?'' He planted a quick, reassuring kiss on her lips. ''Now, do you want to shower first, or should I?''

Too late. Too late.

Gideon thrashed about in his sleep, trapped in the fiery hell that haunted his dreams. He was burning up. Melting. Going mad with the impending grief that would never let him escape. But the images played over and over again.

The impact of raw, compressed air exploding into a ball of flame lifted him off his feet and dumped him on his backside.

''Meghan!''

She was trapped, and he was her only hope.

Gideon shook his head and moaned out loud. The nightmare that had plagued him for three nights in a row had altered with a sickening twist.

He sucked in a deep breath of oxygen from his tank and plunged into the smoke. "Meg, sweetheart," he whispered into his mike, "I'm coming for you. Stay with me, babe."

He paused in the heart of the black, billowing darkness and shut down all his senses except for that finely tuned radar that would lead him to her.

There.

He stumbled into the collapsing boiler room and found her. On the floor. Pinned beneath a ton of burning, warping metal.

"Meghan!"

"Gideon?" He heard her voice like a weak, desperate plea in the distance. "Gideon."

A shadowy figure materialized out of the smoke, charging at him, knocking him to his knees.

He struggled to stand, but his gear was too heavy. His lungs were bursting in his chest, starved for oxygen. "Meg?"

The unknown shadow knelt over her and laid a long yellow rose across her chest like some damned kind of funeral. Then he bent to kiss her.

"Get away from her!"

Gideon lurched to his feet and tackled the shadow. They fought until his energy waned, until his oxygen gauge clicked on zero.

"Gideon?" Unseen hands pulled at him, and still he fought.

He collapsed beside Meghan and the shadow vanished. But the fire blazed up into the skeletal beams of the dying building, searching for him, circling ever closer. Its fiery talons leaped at his throat and attacked. The evil essence of the fire and the shadow were the same. One enemy.

"Meghan." He had to help. He had to save her. With a superhuman effort he rose to his knees and looked into her colorless, unseeing eyes. She couldn't breathe. She was trapped. Dying.

Too late.

He scooped his hands beneath her supine form and lifted. Shoulder to gut. Hand behind knees. But he couldn't. His left hand refused to hang on. He couldn't pull her free. He couldn't hold her. He couldn't save her.

"Meghan!" He screamed her name on a hoarse plea for mercy.

He'd lost Luke. He'd lost them both.

He was too late.

"Gideon." He heard the voice from the fringes of his grief. Strong hands were on his face, on his shoulders, shaking him. He felt a soft tap on his cheek, then a harder one. "Gideon."

Meghan's face swam in front of his eyes, her smooth skin lined with concern, her golden hair falling down around him. "I'm sorry," he whispered, hearing his voice crack with unshed tears from the pit of a distant dream. "I'm so sorry I lost you."

"Wake up, Gideon. Please." She was kneeling beside him now, leaning over him—a sunny savior calling him from his darkest nightmare. Her soft fingers brushed his fevered brow. "I'm right here. Come back to me."

Gideon's breath burst from his lungs as he slammed into wakefulness. He sat bolt upright in bed, tumbling her onto his lap. Welterweight though she might be, she was real and solid. And before she could crawl away, he crushed her in his arms, trapping her supple strength and life-affirming warmth against his body. He buried his nose in the citrusy dampness of her freshly washed hair and breathed in the clean, sunny scent of her.

"You're safe," he whispered against her neck, teasing his lips against her soft, dewy skin. "Oh, God, baby, I thought I'd lost you."

"Gideon." Strong, capable hands brushed the curve of his scalp. "It was a nightmare. Whatever happened wasn't real." She traced the rims of his ears and stroked the taut cords of muscle down his neck and shoulders. Her hands continued their tender massage, slowly pulling him back from the tormenting shadows of memory and imagination. "It's gone and I'm here. It must have been horrible. I heard you cry out in your sleep from the other room. I'm here now. Do you see me? Can you feel me?" She looped her arms around his shoulders and pressed her lips to his feverish temple. "I'm real."

Deep, tortured breaths shook his body and were absorbed into her sweet, feminine strength. He splayed his fingers at the flat of her back and held her impossibly close, soaking in the scent and softness and sensation of her. "Oh, God, Meg. I've needed you."

He admitted the aching emptiness before rational thought censored his heart.

And he thrust his fingers into her hair and captured her mouth with his, pulling her down beside him onto the bed, seeking the life-affirming welcome of her body before the darkness from his past could claim him again.

Chapter Ten

Making love with Gideon had always been a gentle, lei-surely thing. A slow seduction of mind and body. As pa-tiently as he'd taught her about fighting fires, he'd taught her about enjoying and loving sex.

But this was a fiery conflagration that burned out of con-trol, a desperate need for one body to connect with another in that elemental way that celebrated life and trust and hu-manity.

And Meghan was just as eager to lose herself in the moment. To be everything that Gideon needed. To place herself in that ultimate haven of trust and security. To be-long. Truly and completely. To—for this night at least—find her home. Her family. Her love.

"Gideon," she whispered on a catch of breath between kisses. "Are you sure?" His hand skimmed down her back and squeezed her bottom. She wound her leg around his hip, feeling the strength of him already rising to meet her welcoming heat. "Be sure."

"I should be asking you that." He murmured the apol-ogy beneath the point of her chin. "But I don't want you to say no." He pushed up her chin, exposing her throat to his lips and the dance of heat that moved lower beneath the neckline of the old T-shirt she'd borrowed from him for pajamas. "Say yes, sweetheart. Please." He pulled back just as his lips grazed the swell of her breast. His face was a contorted mask of control, his chest heaving in deep breaths that butted against her own. "I'll understand if you don't—"

"Yes, Gideon. Yes."

She framed his smoothly shaven jaw between her hands and guided his mouth to hers for a kiss.

Spontaneous combustion flared in the meeting of lips and tongues and fevered breaths. His hard hand slid up beneath her shirt to stroke the bare skin of her back. His calloused palm traced circles that pulled her ever closer and closer, creating a torrid friction that spread through her body like molten lava.

Gideon's body radiated heat that fed into her own imminent meltdown. His naked torso was slick and musky with the furious struggle from his nightmare and the white-hot strength of his passion. Meghan buried her nose in the raw, masculine scent and ran her tongue along the salt of his skin, catching the tip of a flat, bronze nipple and taking it into her mouth.

"Meg." His body jerked in a helpless response.

Feeling a sultry feminine power, she repeated the action, licking her way toward the other male nipple and laving him until his hips ground into hers through their underwear and one very annoying sheet.

"Witch." He swept her shirt up over her head and pushed her onto her back. As the shirt tangled in her arms, he seized the advantage, closing the moist heat of his mouth over her exposed breast, sucking hard and taunting the nipple with the raspy stroke of his tongue.

Meghan twisted and bucked beneath him. It was too much, too fast. A flashover of flame shot through her to the ends of her fingers and toes, and fanned the heavy, throbbing embers between her legs.

"Gideon. Please." The night was hot. The room was

hotter. The oxygen was being rapidly consumed by two bodies that had been alone for too long, two hearts that had always longed to be one.

"I know, babe. I know."

Answering the urgency of their need, she tossed off the shirt. In seconds the sheet, her panties, his briefs had all disappeared and there was nothing between them. Nothing but hot skin singeing hot skin.

He scooped his hand beneath her bottom and lifted her up to his driving shaft. He plunged into her once. She was slick and hot and primed for release.

He drove into her a second time. The heat bubbled up and threatened to explode. "Gid—"

He stopped up her mouth with a kiss, pushing his tongue inside and claiming her there just as he was claiming her entire body. He was on top of her, in her. Plunging, driving. Taking. Giving. "Now. Meg." His breath whooshed out against her neck. "I. Need."

The moan in his throat foretold the brink of his release. Holding tight to his shoulders to finish this ride with him, Meghan hooked her feet around his hips and opened herself wide. Gideon thrust long and hard, pouring himself into her as her body detonated around him.

When he collapsed on top of her, their bodies spent and sated from their frantic joining, Meghan wondered if she would ever breathe properly again. She hadn't held anything back. She'd given him the solace he'd asked for and found the acceptance she'd needed for herself.

Gideon switched positions before he crushed her, rolling onto his back and pulling her on top of him. He hugged her close while his fingertip traced a tantalizing, languid line along her spine and the curve of her buttock.

She was draped over him like a sheltering blanket, her ear nestled against the hammering beat of his heart. She rode the rise and fall of his chest until their hearts beat at a more soothing rhythm.

"Well." He made a sound that was half a laugh, half a sigh. "So much for separate bedrooms."

Now came the cuddle part. The quiet talking. The regrouping. Meghan snuggled closer, winding one hand behind his neck and holding him as best she could in this position.

He'd been so tense when she'd run in from the spare bedroom to see if the moans and cries of her name had been real or part of her own unsettling dreams. The nightmare that gripped Gideon had twisted his muscles into straining knots. His face had been wreathed with pain, his skin bathed in sweat as he faced the horrors that consumed his slumber.

She'd been frightened for a moment. As frightened of the demon who could make this strong man tremble as she'd been of her stalker tonight.

But then he'd reached for her. Groggy with the stupor of sleep, he'd called to her for help. For once in her life she'd been able to give him something her past and her secret couldn't take away. She couldn't give him everything he wanted, but she'd been able to give him this.

Meghan dipped her finger into the dimple beside his mouth and smiled with a smug, womanly satisfaction.

Everything about him now was relaxed.

Well, not quite everything.

"Are you all right?" he asked, his voice drowsy with contentment against her hair.

She nodded. "Are you? I was scared when I heard you cry out."

He didn't immediately answer, but she could feel the tension building in him again. "I was dreaming about the night Luke died."

"That must have been horrible." She knew the kind of

shock and grief she'd gone through when a fellow firefighter had fallen. The sense of one of her own being taken
clutched at her heart even now. She stroked a soothing hand
across Gideon's face. "I can't imagine what it would be
like to lose your partner that way."

She felt a barely perceptible tightening of his arms
around her. "I was too late to help him. My radar chose
that night to go on the blink. The one night it counted most
in my career. I couldn't get to him in time." She waited
through a long, long silence for him to continue. "What if
I lose it again? When it's really important. What if *you're*
in danger? What good is my creepy talent if it doesn't work
when I need it most?"

Meghan was confused. She moved her contented body
at last, shifting off Gideon and propping herself up on her
elbows beside him. "'Fires are unpredictable things,' a
wise mentor once told me. You stay alert, you stay fit, you
stay smart." She held his gaze when it slid over to hers.
He remembered the skills he'd taught her. "You let the fire
talk to you. You listen and react."

He looked away, finishing the adage for her. "But the
lady can still lie."

Meghan sat up, unmindful of her nudity or the warmth
of the night that made a cover necessary only for modesty's
sake. "I know you did everything you could to save Luke.
He knows that, too. Everyone knows it but you."

The surface of his chest shuddered in an uneven breath.
"I lost more than a friend that night."

Meghan dropped her chin to her chest and looked for the
sheet, feeling the first stirrings of self-conscious awareness.
"So you're human like the rest of us now. Maybe you lost
your confidence in one fire." She set aside her own misgivings and tried to make him see reason. "You're still the
smartest, most thorough investigator in the department. You

can act under pressure, make snap decisions. You took care of the fire at Dorie's house today.''

He shook his head. ''It was a little self-contained fire. And I almost didn't get that job done, either.'' He lifted up his left hand and studied it. ''Because of this damn thing I almost failed.''

''But you didn't.''

''The stakes are higher now. And a lot more dangerous than any trash can fire.'' He rolled over onto his right side, propped himself up on his elbow and faced her. The soft glow of the lamp burnished his cheekbones and jaw, but cast shadows across his eyes. ''I promised to keep you safe.'' The bleakness in his tone was unmistakable. ''Luke couldn't afford to have me fail. Neither can you.''

GIDEON WASN'T SURE how to respond when Meghan reached for his left hand. She sat there beside him, a naked nature-girl temptress, stirring a slow, seeping heat in his blood. He wanted her all over again. But she needed to talk. Or maybe her nurturing instincts sensed that *he* needed to talk.

But not about this.

''Don't, sweetheart.'' He'd just made love with the most incredible woman in the world. He'd escaped into the sunlight of Meghan's generous heart and welcoming body. For those few glorious minutes he'd forgotten all about the past.

He wasn't ready to spoil it by bringing up the doubtful success of their future.

''Let me look. Please.'' She cradled it now between both of her hands. Her soft voice and even softer touch had always been hard for him to resist. He wasn't sure he wanted the useless appendage held up to the light for her inspection, but maybe it was the best way to illustrate his doubts to her. What if her stalker showed up on her doorstep again? At her station house? Her truck? What if he threatened her physically? Trapped her in one of his fires?

Could he do anything? Could he get to her in time? Would he lose her the same way he'd lost Luke?

Yeah, he was a good investigator. After the fact. Someone else, younger, stronger—whole—would have already done the dangerous part. Putting out the fire. Rescuing the victims inside.

Would his only benefit to Meghan be after the fact?

I'll shower you in rose petals. One for every day you'll be mine.

Gideon couldn't let that happen. Meghan might not see a future with him, but he would die before he let that psycho make good on his claim to possess her.

Trouble was, he didn't know how to prevent the guy from contacting her again. He'd already assigned himself her personal protector. But with his track record for saving lives... Even with the best of intentions...

"Can you feel this?" Her curious question brought him back from his exploration of every worst-case scenario.

She was stroking her thumbs across the back of his hand, tracing the intricate web of scars from the original injury and resulting skin grafts. "A little." It seemed inherently wrong to see the ugly thing being cherished by two such beautiful hands. "I feel the pressure, not the actual touch on the surface of the skin."

"What about here?" She dragged her hand along the length of his two stiff fingers. "Can you feel this?"

He shook his head. What was she expecting, a miracle? That he could suddenly clap his hands and it would heal? Luke would come back? He'd have his old job and she'd be his wife?

"There's too much nerve damage. If I look at them and concentrate..." He did just that, staring hard at his hand where it rested between hers. He curled his thumb and first two fingers into a fist. And then—his physical therapist had said to visualize—the last two fingers jerked, more like a spasm than planned movement. He wiggled them again.

"Gideon!" Meghan's delighted cry startled him. She leaned over and kissed him, then kissed the hand itself. It had taken him six months to master that little trick. But her sparkling enthusiasm almost made him believe he had done something miraculous.

For a moment he saw himself through her eyes. Her ready acceptance of his handicap, her guileless hope that any improvement was an improvement to celebrate. Her lighted smile reminded him of all the reasons why he'd wanted to marry her in the first place.

"Does the scarring affect the rest of your hand?" she went on, blithely unaware of how he drank in every nuance of her sunny expression. "I mean…" Her cheeks spotted with color, no doubt remembering the incendiary passion they'd just shared. "I couldn't tell anything before, but—"

"Without the nerves to stimulate them, some of the muscle is atrophying. I do physical therapy to rebuild the muscles that are working and to develop control."

"Then you should use it more, not tuck it in your pocket."

She'd noticed that? Of course, she would. She'd been a stellar pupil, with powers of observation almost as scary as his own. He sat up across from her and pulled a pillow into his lap, letting his hand fall to the side, out of sight. "It's an ugly reminder of losing Luke and the job I can't do anymore."

"It's part of you." She climbed up onto her knees and pulled at his arm, reaching for his hand again. He wouldn't fight her if she insisted on holding it. But he didn't quite comprehend the fire in her tone. "I'm sorry that you were so hurt. I'm sorry that you suffered. But it's a badge of honor, not a mark of shame. You earned it doing something brave and noble. And it certainly doesn't make you any less of a man. That comes from character. And you, Mr. Taylor, have that in spades.''

She took a deep breath and suddenly her mood changed from indignant anger to one of sultry mystery. What was she up to? Her lips pressed together in a tight line, then pouted out. Her honey-brown eyes took on a golden sparkle. She tilted her chin at an angle, her long waves of champagne hair falling back around her neck and shoulders, brushing across taut muscles and strong bones, ending at the soft swells of her breasts.

A helpless man in the face of such utter femininity, he watched it all.

''Meg?''

''Don't sell yourself short, Gideon.'' She pressed his scarred hand flat between hers and teased her fingernails across his palm. ''You can feel that, can't you?''

Gideon nodded, his skin tingling to life beneath her touch.

''Can you feel this?'' She tugged at his hand and guided it up to cover her naked breast with his palm.

''Meg, no—'' He tried to pull away, but she trapped his hand and pushed herself into him. His entire body leaped to life as he concentrated on the uniquely feminine contrast of soft flesh and rigid nipple beneath his touch. He watched with humble fascination his tanned hand on her palest skin. Her eyes drifted shut and she pleasured herself with his weak hand, which, in turn, pleasured him.

With this erotic style of healing, his body certainly wasn't feeling any less manly. ''Yeah, sweetheart.'' His voice was hoarse with emotion. ''I'm definitely feeling this.''

''Use it,'' she commanded, making herself an alluring, demanding physical therapist. ''I have never seen you as anything but a whole man. Heroic. Smart. Handsome.

Stron—'' Her praise halted on a stolen breath as he caught her rigid nipple between his hand and thumb.

"Enough talking," he whispered, leaning in to kiss her throat and make a few demands of his own. He stole her breath when he closed his mouth over hers. "I get the message." He kissed her again. "And I love you for it."

She never once seemed to mind an awkward grab or clumsy caress as, giving both hands equal responsibility in this seduction, he pulled her into his arms and made slow, restorative love to her.

When he was ready to burst and she was begging for completion, he rolled away from her and opened the drawer of his bedside table. He ripped open the foil packet and sheathed himself. Moments later he was sheathed inside her. They held each other close, savoring the healing warmth, the perfect shelter, the love he knew they shared. He kissed her mouth when she cried out her pleasure and Gideon plunged over just after.

But as he led her into the shower to cleanse and cool their well-loved bodies, Gideon made a realization that nearly stole the pleasure of the night from him.

He hadn't worn a condom the first time.

He'd already failed to keep her safe.

BY SUNUP, Meghan's make-believe night of a relationship with Gideon had ended.

"What do you mean, you take full responsibility for last night?" She could tell he was trying to be noble about something.

Had she given him the impression that she didn't feel well and thoroughly loved? That he'd hurt her somehow? Was it his hand again? Yes, she mourned the loss of its full use. She knew how much he had loved his work. But she also celebrated his strength and determination to never surrender to self-pity or to thinking of himself as an invalid.

Did he think she wasn't proud of how hard he'd worked to return to K.C.F.D—to return to life—after such a serious injury?

He drank his last swallow of coffee and carried his dishes across the unadorned kitchen while she sat at the table and finished her cereal. He was a handsome figure in his uniform this morning, navy slacks, blue shirt, comfortable authority.

She'd have to change at the station. But for now his white K.C.F.D. T-shirt and her own shorts suited her fine. But she didn't think this was about forgetting to pack any clothes when they'd left her apartment, either. "In spite of our history and everything that's going on right now, I was a willing participant last night," she reassured him. "I'm fine."

He set his dishes in the sink before turning around. He propped his hip against the counter and crossed his arms loosely in front of him. Uh-oh. He wasn't smiling. The lines beside his eyes deepened as his gaze narrowed, giving him a worried frown. She set down her spoon. Now she was worried, too.

"I mean that I'll be responsible if anything happens to you. I've always worn a condom when we made love. That first time last night I was just out of my mind with need and—" His broad shoulders lifted with an apology. "I don't know exactly what kind of relationship we have right now. But, if you get pregnant, I want you to know you won't be going through it alone."

An abstract thought left Meghan wondering if all the color had drained from her face. She certainly felt lightheaded enough with all the blood inside her rushing down to her toes. She swallowed hard and tried to cover her reaction by looking away and brushing a nonexistent lock of hair off her face.

D-day had arrived. The one her therapist had warned her

she'd eventually have to deal with if she ever wanted to move forward with her life. The day after which she knew Gideon would never look at her the same way again.

She ate another bite of cereal and felt it sink like a rock to her stomach. So much for that delaying tactic. Fate and her own conscience were forcing her to confront the truth. She dropped the spoon and scooted her chair back from the table. "I'm not pregnant."

"Meg, I know the chances of conceiving are slim having unprotected sex just once. But sometimes one time is all it takes."

She stood, steeling herself before seeking direct contact with those concerned brown eyes. "Do you have any diseases I should know about?"

"No."

She carried her dishes to the sink. "Then there's nothing to worry about."

Let it drop, she begged him silently. He didn't. "Are you on the pill?"

Yes, it would be so easy to say. One word. One easy out and she could salvage her pride and skip seeing his disappointment in her. She felt him looking down at the crown of her head, patiently waiting for her answer.

But two years of learning to put Pete Preston's abuse behind her, and her love and respect for Gideon himself, wouldn't let her lie.

"I can't have children, Gideon."

There. She'd said it. Badly. Abruptly. But she'd done it.

But Gideon was a man who hated unanswered questions. "What do you mean? You can't conceive? You can't carry a child?"

"None of it." She moved away from him, needing distance to keep the emotion out of her voice. "I had a radical hysterectomy when I was sixteen. The doctors took my uterus, ovaries, everything. I have to rely on hormones and calcium to keep the rest of me working right.'' She hugged herself, letting her hand slide down past her waist in that self-consciously protective gesture. ''I'm just a shell of a woman inside.''

Just a freak. She blinked and shook her head against the intrusive thought.

''The scars on your abdomen.'' He sounded incredulous. Confused. ''I thought they were from that car accident you told me about. Your aunt was driving. She died.''

''Yep.'' Meghan tried to keep her explanation clinical because she'd lose it if she gave in to the enormity of it all. ''I had severe trauma to my abdominal cavity. Lost a lot of blood. There was no way to save those organs and my life.''

''Sweetheart, I'm sorry.'' One long stride brought him to her side. His arms wound around her, but she pushed him away.

Fiery tears burned her eyes, but she refused to shed them. ''That's why I couldn't marry you.''

The dreadful silence in the room finally caused her to look up into the midnight heat of his eyes. But was that anger—pain?—accusation?—she saw there?

''Because you have scars?'' His voice was too quiet for her to gauge his reaction. He held up his hand between them. ''Like I'd be one to judge.''

She squeezed her eyes shut, wishing understanding didn't mean she had to hurt him. She took a deep breath and looked him straight in the eye. ''Think about it, Gideon. I can't have babies. Ever. Not with artificial insemination or surrogate mothers or divine intervention. Not yours. Not anyone's. Not ever.''

He braced his hands on his hips and inhaled deeply, pushing his shoulders out to proportions that had made her feel sheltered and loved last night. In the morning light she withered beside his indomitable strength. "Why didn't you tell me this two years ago?"

"Two years ago I still believed what my uncle had taught me. That I was no good. That I would never be woman enough for any man. That I should have died in that crash instead of my aunt." She wondered now if Uncle Pete had been right. "I knew how much you wanted children of your own. To plant your seed and create a family like the one you grew up in. It was a beautiful dream. But it's not one I could give you. I knew eventually you'd resent that. You'd resent me. You'd always been so good to me, and I knew I'd end up hurting you."

"You can read the future?" His voice was spooky calm, like the echo of a building that had been gutted by fire.

"Listen to me, Gideon." She didn't need to read the future to know what a life without a family to call your own would be like. "Can you see yourself twenty, thirty, forty years down the road with just me? With no precious babies or annoying teenagers or well-adjusted young adults to carry on the Taylor name? Can you see yourself alone like that, with an empty nest your entire life?"

He hesitated, but he had the courage to be honest. "No."

"Well, that'd be your future with me."

Point made. Heart broken. Dream shattered.

She'd always imagined she'd be weeping when this discussion was over, but her eyes felt strangely dry. Everything about her felt as hollow and pointless as the inside of her belly. While Gideon stood there, silently sorting out his feelings, Meghan moved on. Right now that was all she could do. "I can call a cab to get to work."

"I'll drive you."

She thanked him for his perfunctory offer, but hoped to make a cleaner break of things this time than she had two years ago. "Maybe it's better if I get someone else to baby-sit me until—"

Her cell phone rang and her heart jumped in her chest. Between last night's passion and this morning's confession, she'd managed to forget the outside world still existed. Pressing a calming hand to her chest, she unhooked her fanny pack from the back of the chair and unzipped it.

The clearer tone of the phone once she pulled it out finally seemed to cut through Gideon's fog. He reached for the cell himself. "Maybe you shouldn't answer that."

Meghan waved him aside. "It might be Dorie with news about Matthew." She punched the talk button and put the phone to her ear. "Hello?"

"Meghan, where are you?"

The outside world was back with a vengeance.

Her arm automatically went around her waist in a defensive hug. "What do you want?"

The hoarse, croaky whisper grated across her eardrum, sending shards of fear and anger and doubt plunging deep inside her. "Why did you call the cops? My gift was just for you. You're spoiling our beautiful relationship." He caught his breath in a way that almost sounded like crying. "And now you're on television, telling everyone about us."

"Television?"

"You'd better go to work today," he warned. "I need to see you. I'll keep burning things until you show up."

"No," she begged him. "Don't set another—"

Gideon snatched the phone from her hand. "Who is this?"

His sharp, dark voice echoed in the kitchen. The caller must have hung up immediately. Gideon pulled the phone from his ear and tried to check the number. But the log came up empty. Out of range.

He punched in another number right away, but Meghan didn't wait to hear who he was calling. She backed away and hurried into the living room. She grabbed the remote and turned on the TV, flipping through channels until she found an image that stopped her cold.

"Oh, my God."

In the top right-hand corner of the screen was a still picture of herself, cradling Crispy in her arms, the burned-out remains of the old Meyer's warehouse silhouetted behind her.

Saundra Ames sat behind the news desk, reading from the TelePrompTer. "Police reports indicate that local hero Meghan Wright's apartment was broken into yesterday, and that a message was left for her by the man who may be responsible for the string of arson fires that have been burning down our city, building by building, this summer."

The image switched to a full-screen tape of fans crowding around her, asking for autographs. Saundra's voice-over continued, giving the security-robbing trauma of the last few days a dramatic, even ominous spin. "Could it be that Kansas City's Sweetheart herself is the target of these fires? We'll be following the story as it unfolds throughout the day, and have an update to report to you this evening on the six o'clock edition. This is Saundra Ames, Channel Ten news, reporting—"

Gideon turned off the TV, filling his apartment with an eerie, tension-wrought silence.

"I called Josh. He'll meet us at the precinct office. See if we can get a tracer on your phone." Meghan stared at the blank screen, trying to imagine the face of the man who could ruin so many lives in the name of love. "We'll see about getting Channel Ten off your case, too."

Gideon's reflection loomed up behind her own on the screen. The size and shape of him surrounded her. But he never touched her. Though the Taylor code of honor would keep him from ever abandoning her to that maniac, she didn't suppose there'd be any more tender reassurances.

But then, she wasn't the only one in danger anymore.

She turned to face the man, not the reflection. "I don't know how to warn everyone."

"About what?" The cold-eyed clarity of the arson investigator had completely replaced the somnolent warmth of last night's lover. "What did he say?"

"He's disappointed in the way our *relationship* is progressing. He said he wants to see me today."

She didn't have to spell it out for Gideon. He understood the caller's intent. "He's going to set another fire."

Chapter Eleven

Gideon watched Josh slam down the phone and spin his chair away from his desk. The word he used was less than flattering.

"I take it that didn't go well?" Gideon asked.

Josh tipped his face toward the ceiling and blew out a long breath of frustration. "Saundra Ames is citing First Amendment rights. She says she'll challenge us all the way to the supreme court if K.C.P.D. and the fire department don't let her report the news as she sees fit."

Gideon rose from his perch on the corner of Josh's desk. "Even if the fact she's generating national publicity is putting people's lives in danger?" He plopped down in the seat at the adjoining desk vacated by Josh's partner. "How did she find out about the break-in at Meg's, anyway?"

"She probably got it off the wire. Most of the press— TV, print, radio—have someone assigned to the police beat. They read through our reports. If there's something that sounds like news, they pass it on." Josh adjusted the holster that hung from his shoulder and leaned forward to prop his elbows on top of the desk. "I heard Saundra used to be the weather girl at the university station in Columbia. Now she's reporting our local crime spree for the national news. I guess you can really go places if you look as fine as she does and don't mind stepping on a few toes."

Normally, Gideon would have shot Josh a teasing reprimand for talking about a "fine" woman. Once the family's resident flirt, Josh had given up his appreciative eye for devotion to his gorgeous college professor wife and baby girl. But this morning, not even his little brother's good-natured philosophizing about the feminine gender could coax a smile out of him.

Instead of responding to Josh's efforts to get a rise out of him, Gideon turned toward the row of interrogation rooms. He looked through the open blinds of the first room and watched Meghan flip through another page of pictures in the thick books of mug shots. Pictures of known arsonists and sexual predators. Not the kind of company he wanted her to keep. He couldn't shake the protective fury that tightened his gut into knots each time he thought about that crazy lowlife contacting her over and over again, calling her "love," watching her, leaving gifts. But he'd been able to distance himself from other emotions that had tried to overwhelm him since this morning.

At a time when she needed him to be strong, she'd been the one to get *him* through the night. Comforting. Healing. Talking sense. Her ready acceptance of his handicap and her understanding of his darkest fears had reminded him that he still loved her. And the thing that made this all hurt so damn much was knowing that he would always love her.

I can't have children, Gideon.

She could have smacked him in the gut with a tire iron and he wouldn't have been any more stunned. He'd never known a woman with a bigger heart. She'd grown up without a mother, without much of a father, had known only snippets of love and trust and home in her life. She'd hinted at abuse that made him sick inside, leaving him wondering how much she was sharing and how much of her secret life she was still trying to protect him from.

And still that woman understood love, and that it was more important for her to give it away than to receive it.

She deserved a brood of kids to shower that love upon. But, somehow, he'd always thought they'd be *his* kids.

He watched Meghan blow those curls of hair off her face with a heavy sigh. Then she palmed her neck beneath her gold-and-amber braid to rub at the tension there. She looked pale, tired—about as exhausted as he felt. And he suspected their fatigue had more to do with the stress-filled ride they'd been on the past few days than missing a few hours of sleep to pursue other activities in the bedroom.

He'd felt so damn guilty about using her to find solace from his never-ending nightmares. He hadn't been able to sleep, worrying about repaying her generosity with an unplanned pregnancy.

"Gid?" Through the fog of self-recriminations, he finally heard Josh's voice. "You okay, man?"

Gideon had to blink and look away when he realized he'd been staring at Meghan so long, he'd caught her attention, too.

When those honey-gold eyes narrowed to question him, he pushed his chair back a little too quickly, answered a little too loudly. "You got any coffee around this place?"

Josh raised his eyebrows but said nothing. He just pointed to the snack area behind Gideon.

No children. Not with you. Not ever.

When Meghan dropped that bombshell he'd been so damn mad that she'd never felt it was safe to tell him something like that, he hadn't trusted himself to speak. It was an insult to the kindness he'd always shown her, clear evidence of how little faith she had in him. In them.

Then he'd wanted to make it right for her. Shield her from the hurt and disappointment she must surely feel at being denied what some women took for granted.

And finally he thought he understood her. He *was* proud

of his family. He *had* talked a dozen times in the quiet after making love about having his own family one day. She knew what family meant to him. She knew his dreams and fears and wants and desires better than anyone.

I can't give you that.

And so she'd walked away.

Two years ago, and again this morning, she'd walked away.

And Gideon had let her go.

If that damn call hadn't come in, if Saundra Ames's news report hadn't taunted Meg's stalker into promising to strike again, he'd have let her walk out the door. Without saying a word.

What was he supposed to say?

Could he picture himself forty years down the road without ever having had children of his own? Could he see his children with any mother besides Meghan?

Gideon sipped the fresh cup of coffee, nearly scalding his tongue in the process. But it was enough of a wake-up call to shake him out of his stupor. He'd have to sort out his feelings and rethink his future plans later. Right now he had a job to do. No matter how this turned out between them, he'd made a promise to Meghan. And he was nothing if not a man of his word.

"Hey, Gid." Josh waved him over to his desk. "I think we've got something." A. J. Rodriguez was already sitting at his computer, typing in search data. Josh had surrendered his chair to Meghan and was looking over her shoulder at the open book of pictures sitting in front of her on his desk.

Gideon dumped his coffee and rejoined them. "Did you see someone you recognized?" he asked, trying to keep both eagerness and sadness out of his voice.

She seemed small and alone sitting there. But then Josh was such a big man, standing right behind her. Maybe it was just a trick of optical illusion and had nothing to do with the tight press of her mouth or a downcast gaze that didn't quite meet his. "He was in the crowd after the fire yesterday. He asked me for an autograph."

Josh had no problem being direct. "Does the name Jack Quinton mean anything to you?"

Gideon turned inward and sped through an internal catalog of information until the name popped and a story came to mind. "Yeah. He was arrested for a string of arson fires—some kind of insurance scam—back in the midnineties. My unit worked a couple of them. Isn't he in prison?"

A.J. shook his head, reading information off the computer screen. "He was released from Jefferson City earlier this year. Good behavior. I'll have Sarge pull his file. Check with his parole officer. We'll get a complete history on him."

Gideon looked at the image on the computer screen, recognizing the bug-eyed man with the glasses from yesterday. "If I remember, Quinton had a degree in electrical engineering. He'd know how to put together the remote triggers I've been finding."

Meghan leaned forward in her chair. She might be weary of it, but she was still in the fight. "Then how do you explain the gang signs? The man I saw was never any kind of warrior. Westside or otherwise."

"It could just be a diversionary tactic to throw us off track," Josh suggested. "We have been running alibis for Ezio Moscatelli and his known associates."

Gideon shook his head. "Why leave the triggers behind if he wants to misdirect the police? A remote-controlled computer chip is a pretty distinct signature for an arsonist."

"The man I saw looked like he was in his fifties, maybe sixty," said Meghan. "Maybe he's not working alone. Maybe he's passing along his craft to someone else. Someone younger. Maybe he's hired himself out to the Warriors."

"That's a lot of maybes." A.J. turned his chair toward Meghan. Though Rodriguez projected an image of laid-back nonchalance, the probity of his questions last night and his patience this morning told Gideon the man was thorough. He'd partnered with Gideon's brother Cole until he left the force. Now Josh was his partner. Gideon was relieved to sense that Meghan's case was in good hands with the Hispanic detective. "We don't even know if this is your guy yet," he cautioned. "I'll run down an address for him. Josh and I can pay him a visit. Maybe we'll luck out and find he works in a florist's shop, too."

"If he is our man, you won't find him." Gideon was beginning to understand the way this guy operated. "He'll be out today, looking for Meghan, preparing his next surprise for her."

He couldn't help but be concerned by the sudden pallor of her skin or her noiseless sigh. But it was Josh who closed his hands around her shoulders, offering support and massaging the tension there. Gideon recognized the possessive impulse to warn Josh to keep his hands to his own woman. But he quickly squelched the urge to circle the desks and pull her up into *his* arms for his comfort. His emotions were still too raw to predict what kind of comfort he'd actually be.

But he could still control his instinct and intellect.

Gideon directed his comment to the two detectives. "Your official interest and national press coverage are making this guy nervous. In his mind, he's got a private relationship with Meg that he wants to get back to."

"What if I just don't go to work?" Meghan suggested. "If he knows I'm not there to fight it, maybe he won't set another fire. I can call in sick. The chief would understand."

Gideon shook his head. "I don't think he works that way. He likes seeing you in action. That's where the two of you connect—at the beginning and end of a fire. He'll keep burning things down until you show up."

"Then how do we stop him?" Josh's frustration spoke for them all. "Do we have to set a trap?"

A beat of deadly silence closed in on the group. All eyes turned to Meghan.

No! Gideon wanted to shout. He could see what she was thinking. What Josh and A.J. were both thinking.

"Well." She stood, throwing back her shoulders and lifting her beautiful chin with all the pride and fatalism of an innocent woman being led to her execution. "We all know I'm the only bait he's interested in."

No one liked it, but no one could argue the sense of her words.

A.J. was the first to move beyond the grim mood and put the half-formed plan into action. "I'll write up a warrant request, get Captain Taylor to green-light it. I still want to check out Quinton's place. Gideon, can you go with us to identify whether or not he's got the materials on hand to create these fires?"

Gideon couldn't look away from the bleak acceptance in her honey-brown eyes. "I have to stay with Meghan."

"No, you don't." The serene calm of her voice dismissing him from his promise should have soothed his concern, not put his warning radar on full alert. "You can drop me off at the station. There are good men on my crew. I'll make sure one of them's always with me. And John Murdock watches my back closer than anybody when we're on a call. When my shift's done, I'll call Dorie to see if I can spend the night there. I won't be alone." She picked up her fanny pack and strapped it around her waist, as if volunteering to let Jack Quinton come after her was a done deal. "Quinton hurts property, not people. If I'm never alone, he can't get to me. But you guys will be around to catch him trying, though.'' Her inquiry included Josh and A.J. "Right?"

A.J. nodded. "We'll bug your phone and post a watch at your apartment. If it's not me personally, I guarantee there will be someone you can trust watching you at all times." His golden eyes narrowed to slits, and Meghan seemed to take courage in the dark-haired detective's words. "We'll get this guy if he contacts you again."

"And the fire?" she asked, turning to Gideon for that assurance, at least.

"I'll call your batallion chief and issue an alert. As soon as I'm done with A.J. and my research on the Grimes fire, I'll be there with you, too." She had to understand that he wasn't abandoning her or her boys. Not while they still needed him, at any rate.

"Thank you for remembering Matthew. I'd be forever grateful if you can help him." In the charged silence that followed, his world shrank to just Meghan and the regrets that hung between them. "I'm not holding you to any promises, Gideon. Do what you have to do."

Did he hear an unspoken message in her words? Acceptance of wherever he decided to take their relationship from here? A goodbye?

"I'm all right," she reassured him, trying to absolve him of guilt and take on his pain the way she had last night. Her body seemed to take on a newfound energy when she turned to A.J. and Josh. "I need to freshen up. Then I'll be ready to leave whenever you are."

A.J. excused himself to process the request for a search warrant and wire-tapping device, leaving Gideon staring hungrily after the subtle womanly sway of Meghan's retreating backside.

Josh's big hand, clamping around his shoulder, was the only thing that could tear him away from what felt like goodbye. "So what's with you, Gid? You look like that day in the hospital when the doctor told you you couldn't fight fires anymore. Are you and Meghan on again or off again or what?''

Gideon shook his head, then stepped away to face his brother. He felt old. Tired. Defeated. ''I don't know. I always thought she was the one. But now I'm not sure it will ever work out between us.''

''Why not? If you love her, you can find a way to get through anything.''

''Sometimes love isn't enough.''

''You know, as far as words of wisdom go, those really suck.''

He had no idea. ''You talk too much. Why don't you go catch some bad guys or pick on your sister or something, instead of trying to give me advice.''

Smart aleck that he was, Josh ticked off the answers on his fingers. ''I'm working on it, Jessie's in Chicago, and you're avoiding the question. Do you love Meghan?''

Gideon picked up his K.C.F.D. ball cap, smoothed back his hair and adjusted the cap on his head before answering. ''Yeah. I fell hard a long time ago. But she's not the person I thought she was. And I'm not the man I used to be.''

Josh considered the cryptic response before speaking. ''I don't know what went down, but don't write her off, Gid. Not until all this blows over. I guarantee you, neither one of you needs to be making any major decisions right now.''

When had the baby of the family gotten to be so wise? ''You always wanted to be the big brother, didn't you?''

But Josh's goofy grin was firmly back in place. ''Nah. You're the sage old man of the family. I'm happy being the spoiled-rotten cute one.''

For the first time that morning Gideon found it in himself to smile.

''I GAVE YOU a statement.''

Meghan sat on the edge of the pool table in the station's rec room and crossed her arms defensively in front of her.

Saundra Ames wore a stunning suit of mauve silk today. But her flawless features were marred by an impatient frown. "I need you on camera. Your face is the one the public wants to see."

"I'm sure they're tired of looking at it."

It was amazing, really, to see how quickly the men in her unit had rallied around her request for some friendly protection. The chief himself had given Saundra a tour of the station while others had found a way to detain her cameraman outside. Even now she wasn't alone with the reporter. The men shooting pool and reading a book listened closely enough to make their presence known without interfering with any of Ms. Ames's first amendment rights.

But she hadn't gotten to be a local reporter about to break out in the national market without being relentless. Her rose-tinted lips smiled. "Don't you see? That self-effacing modesty is one of the things they love about you."

"No."

"Then what about a voice-over with a still picture like the one we ran this morning? We used those with great success when I was doing that series of stories about the new prison in Jefferson City. We won regional and national awards with that series."

"Congratulations." Meghan smiled. "No."

Didn't this lady get it? Meghan wanted normalcy to return to her life. Hell. She was just now beginning to appreciate that the good-natured ribbing from the men she worked with was a form of acceptance, not exclusion. And the boys and Dorie offered her some responsibilities, people who would accept her caring.

She might never have the dream life of a family of her own, with Gideon Taylor at her side and in her heart, but she could create some sort of facsimile. She'd known things would change between them once she told him the truth. She'd hurt him deeply, letting him love her, letting him think they had a chance at a future together. If she hadn't selfishly needed his strength and wisdom to feel safe—if she hadn't needed his love to feel whole—she might have taken Uncle Pete's final advice and gone off to live her life alone. Where she couldn't screw anything up. Where she couldn't hurt anyone else.

But she'd learned that she was human, that her feelings counted for something. If a noble man like Gideon hadn't taught her that, she wouldn't be here now. Defending her privacy, her freedom, her life. Protecting her community. Standing tall inside the uniform she was proud to wear.

Meghan clung to the idea that she could be part of a symbolic family, which was a hell of a lot closer to normalcy and happiness than she'd had growing up. She wouldn't have love, but she'd have friendship. And that would have to be enough.

If one sick man and this determined woman would ever leave her alone.

"Don't you feel you have a responsibility to the community, Miss Wright? If the arsonist is leaving you clues that could save lives and property, don't you want to share that?"

Meghan bristled as if the woman had shoved the microphone in her face. "He doesn't tell me where he's going to set his fires."

"So he has contacted you?"

"I didn't say that."

"Has he threatened you in any way?"

Meghan threw up her hands. "I'm not going to answer your questions."

"Don't sell yourself short, Miss Wright." Saundra leaned in as if she was an old girlfriend sharing a secret.

"People will want to know if Kansas City's Sweetheart is in danger."

"Stop calling me that."

"Miss Wright—"

"I think she's answered enough questions." A big shoulder—one very big shoulder—inserted itself between Meghan and Saundra Ames.

John. Thank God. Partially hidden behind his back, Meghan allowed the stress to surface and breathed a sigh of relief. Big brother to the rescue again.

But she wasn't the only one glad to see him. Stepping back to afford herself an assessing view, Saundra Ames slowly took in the novel tucked beneath the swelled biceps, and tilted her head to meet John's downturned gaze. Meghan almost smiled at the reporter's temporarily speechless state. Her rosy lips parted on a sigh. She was interested, but not necessarily on a professional level. If Meghan had been having a better day, she would have laughed out loud. So the high-class Ms. Ames liked her men big and brawny.

"*Ulysses* is an awfully big book." Big? Smooth line.

"I'm a big boy."

"I can see that." Was John buying the reporter's syrupy tone? "Are you a big friend of Miss Wright's?"

"Yes," came John's pointed answer. "Are you?"

His tough-guy banter seemed to please Saundra. She must be thriving on the prospect of being challenged as both a woman and a reporter. "Does a man of your size and apparent enlightenment find it disruptive to work beside a woman of Meghan's stature?"

Did she mean Meghan's diminutive build? Or current media popularity? And was John really going to get sucked into this woman's interrogation?

"She's an equal member of the team, like everyone else."

"Maybe it would be an interesting sidebar to get some

feedback from her fellow firefighters.'' Saundra linked her arm through John's and turned him toward the door. Meghan was relieved to feel forgotten. "Would you mind if I asked you a few questions, Mr....?"

"John Murdock.'' He turned and tossed *Ulysses* on top of the pool table. With his back to Saundra he winked and mouthed the words, *Another one you owe me.* Then he laid his hand over Saundra's where it rested on his forearm. "It all depends on what you have to ask, Saundra. I can call you that, can't I? Why don't we talk outside?"

As the door closed behind them, the two rookies who'd been playing pool stopped their game. "What are we doing wrong, Joe?" Dean Murphy leaned on his cue stick and shook his head. "She's practically drooling over the big guy."

"How many times can you work the word 'big' into a conversation?" Joe Cutler raked his fingers through his blond hair.

Murphy shouted after them, "Don't call him Big John. He hates that."

"Do you think I should get lifts in my shoes?" asked Joe.

Dean shook his head. "You're tall enough."

"Maybe we should be working out more."

The two lovelorn rookies looked at Meghan for answers. She had none. But she was learning how this Station 16 family worked. She pulled a five-dollar bill from her pocket and tossed it onto the table. "Five bucks says she calls him Big John and the honeymoon's over."

Joe reached into his pocket. "I'll take a piece of that. I say they go out to dinner, if not all the way."

Dean laughed outright, throwing in his five dollars. "Murdock might get ticked, but I bet he gets some. She's hot."

Reassured by their unassuming companionship, Meghan

joined their laughter. She returned John's book to his re-
cliner while the pool game resumed behind her. She could
almost imagine life was returning to normal and that the
bottom hadn't dropped out of her world this morning in
Gideon's kitchen. Almost.

"Hey, Meghan, you want to play a set?" asked Joe.

"Sure, I—"

The station alarm rang, stopping all conversation. A familiar boost of adrenaline cleansed her thoughts and sharp-
ened her senses. Tilting her ear toward the intercom, she
followed Joe and Dean into the garage, listening to the
location and assessment of the call being announced by the
dispatcher.

Meghan hurried to her open locker and quickly stepped
into her waiting pants and boots. She slipped the suspenders
up over her shoulders and reached for her turnout coat.
What might look like chaos to an uninformed outsider was
actually a precise, well-rehearsed routine. Within minutes
of the call, her unit, with two trucks and a paramedic van,
was en route to a strip mall located near the river.

She was vaguely aware of the Channel Ten news van
following them. Vaguely aware of the blare of the sirens
and the pitch and roll of the truck. Vaguely aware of the
directions and responses being traded over the radio.

Meghan's focus was on the memory of a sea of yellow
rose petals and a twisted declaration of love. Gideon had
made the fear go away. He'd given her something to hope
for and to care about and believe in. Until she'd destroyed
it.

Gideon wasn't here now. He might never be with her
again.

Meghan dug deep, searching for some reserve of will that
would get her through this. The froggy voice on the phone
had said he wanted to see her.

That meant he'd be setting a fire just for her.

Meghan's heart sank into her boots. Would this be the one?

"THE SUPPORT STRUCTURE looks good, but we've got patches of roof left on this thing." Meghan tested the concrete block wall herself while John controlled the hose behind her. "I think it'll hold. If we hug the outside, what's left of the roof shouldn't be a problem."

The south end of the DK Mall was a wash. The last two stores had been nearly gutted, their glass display windows blown out by uneven air pressures or broken on purpose to prevent potential injury from flying debris. But they were well on their way to saving the rest of the building.

She tried not to be creeped out by the fact the store on the end had been a florist shop.

Static buzzed in her ear while the chief made his decision.

"I need eyes inside to see if that connecting wall is hot." A strip mall such as this one would have been built with periodic fire walls to contain a blaze in one section and avoid catastrophic destruction of the entire facility. But the roof could have dropped fire on the opposite side of the wall, igniting a secondary blaze. Connecting ductwork could carry smoke and airborne embers that, while more than likely would burn themselves out, could still ignite dust or fibers within the ductwork itself. Both possibilities were unlikely, but worth checking out.

"Meghan. Murdock. You're up. Let's try to save this one, folks."

"Got it, Chief."

After handing off their hose to a backup team, Meghan and John ran a quick check of their gear, ensuring the seal on their masks, their gauges and level of oxygen in their tanks. They gave each other a thumbs-up, and John reported in. "We're good to go."

"Report your twenty," the chief ordered. "And stay safe."

With their helmet lights switched on and clean air running through their masks, they went inside. Pockets of flame still burned along the floorboards of the east wall, filling the building with smoke and rising gases. John radioed in their locations while Meghan turned on her handheld flashlight and peered into the cloud of smoke and steam. The gray-black cloud hovered in areas where the roof was intact and drifted upward toward the blue sky above them in areas where the roof had collapsed.

Carefully climbing over the mini mountain of roof and merchandise debris, Meghan left the relative security of the outer wall and headed toward the fire wall. She shone her light above her. "We've got damage to the A.C. conduits. I'm moving west to see if it carried over into the next store."

"Roger that."

John moved toward the back of the building, following his own inspection route. "I'll meet you on the outside in five," he challenged her.

Meghan scanned the braids of bent pipes and metal grating that still clung to the roof yet hung like broken fingers toward the floor. "I'll be there before you," she promised.

The smoke thickened around her as she shimmied down the opposite side of the collapsed section, leading her to wonder if they still had a hot spot buried beneath the rubble. While she could still follow a visual path, she pushed her way past a hanging pipe and oriented herself in position to her destination.

"Visibility's getting down to nothing over here." She bounced on the balls of her feet. "The floor feels solid. I can't tell where all the smoke's coming from. There's got to be a secondary burner in here somewhere." Meghan turned off her flashlight. Similar to the high beams of a car on a foggy night, the light simply reflected back into her face, obstructing her vision even more.

Like ghosts flitting through the air, the hanging debris appeared and disappeared as the thickness and color of the smoke changed. Relying on her innate sense of direction as much as the man-made path of burned racks and display cases, she made her way through the aisles of what had once been a sporting goods store.

A hanging piece of charred ductwork butted against her shoulder and Meghan jumped. She must have gasped out loud because John was on the line immediately. "What's up?"

She shook her head, feeling foolish. "It's nothing. I just got startled."

"I'm heading down to the basement. See if I can find your smoke source there."

"Got it."

Meghan checked her oxygen gauge one last time before the encroaching curtain of darkness swallowed her up. Plenty of air.

Translucent smoke gave way to a viscous curtain of gray and black. Meghan closed her eyes and tried to find that quiet place inside her in which she could detect the faint tinges of sulphur in the air that might lead her to the hidden fire.

There. With a new sense of direction, she opened her eyes. A flash of movement diverted her focus. A shadow darting past. Darker than the black smoke. She froze midstep.

"John? You up here?"

"I'm downstairs," he repeated.

"Are we sure this building's clear?" She turned her head from side to side, knowing there wasn't a damn thing to see out there. "I swear someone just ran past me."

"Mall security said the stores had been evacuated."

A creaking sound became a roaring groan as a ribbon of ceiling material careened out of the mist and swung past her face, missing her by mere inches. "Damn." She jumped to the side as it crashed to the floor.

Her breath rushed out on a stunted gasp. She shook her head and cursed. She was jumpy. That damn stalker with his crazy messages had made her so paranoid she wasn't getting the job done.

"Meghan?" She could hear the worry in John's voice.

"My bad," she said, silently counting to four as she tried to even out her breathing and heart rate. "A piece of the roof just fell in. I spooked myself. I'm checking the fire wall and then I'm out of here."

"Last one out buys the beer at Mack's."

"I hate beer."

"You're buying, not drinking. What do you care?" It was enough of a dare to leave Meghan grinning and determined and able to function again.

She inhaled a deep breath to clear her head and plunged forward. As thick and viscous as pea soup, the smoke forced her to navigate by instinct alone. But hers were good instincts. By the time her hand hit the reinforced fire wall, most of her confidence had returned. "It doesn't feel like anything's been breached," she reported in. "I've got no updrafts or circulation. The fumes are hanging pretty heavy here. Besides our hot spots, I think we've got it."

"That's what I like to hear," answered the chief. "Now get out of there."

"Yes, sir." Only too happy to leave the darkness behind her, Meghan turned, oriented herself against the wall, then headed out toward light and people and fresh air. "I've got your butt beat, John."

"I don't think so."

There was no sound, no shadow to warn her until the instant before something hard smacked her in the head and knocked her to the floor. Her helmet flew off into the black pit of nothingness around her. "What the hell?"

"Meghan—"

Roof collapse? There'd been no forewarning sounds. She was vulnerable now. Her helmet had probably saved her life from the first blow. A second could knock her unconscious or worse. She needed to protect her head. She needed to escape.

She'd pushed up onto her hands and knees when she saw the feet in the layer of clear air at the floor. Black. They moved too fast for shape or details to register. And then they disappeared. "John?"

An unseen figure grabbed her around the throat, jerking her up to her knees. Someone strong. Determined.

Meghan screamed.

She snatched at the hands. They lifted her higher, onto her feet. But they weren't helping her. She felt the jerk beneath her chin, the pinch of hair being plucked from her scalp as her attacker tried to remove her mask.

"No!" She swung out. She clipped an arm with her fist and loosened the grip. She spun around in time to catch a glimpse of shadow. To see a grotesque face, distorted beyond recognition through the smoke and shadows. "Leave me alone!"

But the shadow was stronger.

In a furious battle of kicking legs and twisting bodies, Meghan was thrown to the floor. A flashfire of pain exploded inside her head as she hit or was hit. Groggy and disoriented, she snatched at the hands as they attacked again, but she was no match for him.

He ripped off her mask, exposing her eyes and nose and mouth to the toxic fumes in the air. He ripped off her microphone, leaving her helpless and alone and unable to call for help. He flipped her onto her stomach with a vicious twist, and the distinctive hiss beside her ear warned her he'd just severed the hose to her oxygen tank.

"Why?" She grabbed his arm and held on with all her might. But he shook her off. Meghan skidded across the floor and crashed into a pile of debris that tumbled down around her.

She covered her head with her arms and lost sight of the shadow as it disappeared into the smoke.

After the last of the rubble hit the floor and rolled away into the darkness, Meghan came up for air. But as she breathed in, she coughed, choking on the carbon monoxide.

"Help," she cried between coughs. Her eyes burned and watered with the sting of sulphur fumes. Had John been close enough to know her location? Or was he outside waiting for her? Had they heard her distress? Would they send in a team? How far from the wall had she come? Was she near the front or the back of the store?

Her head pounded inside her skull. She tasted something warm and coppery inside her mouth. She couldn't see. She couldn't breathe.

You freaking screw-up! Uncle Pete's voice was the last thing she needed to hear right now. *Why are you alive when my Rose is gone?*

"Shut up." Meghan whispered the words on half a breath. She deserved to live. She deserved...what? Her brain went fuzzy and she couldn't think.

She leaned back into the rubble. She could just rest for a moment. But the coughing seized her again, tearing deep through her chest, smacking against the pain in her head. She pressed her fist to her mouth to try to muffle the next bout.

That was when she saw the glove clutched in her hand. Looking through a fog of aching head and oxygen-starved delirium, she lifted both hands in front of her face. She was wearing her own gloves.

She'd pulled this black beauty off her attacker. It was *his*.

A renewed sense of adrenaline, that innate instinct for survival that had brought her back time and again from loss and abuse and heartbreak, pounded through her veins.

"Meg?"

Gideon called her Meg. Was she imagining his voice in her head? Imagining his concern as a subconscious comfort to herself?

I'll be with you. He'd promised. Gideon Taylor kept his promises.

"Gideon?" She hadn't the strength to talk now. Only the will to survive. Only the promise to hold him to.

Meghan shrugged out of her tank and gear. Twenty pounds lighter, she staggered onto her hands and knees, staying low and lurching forward, dragging her off-kilter body in whatever direction it would go. It was like being lost in a black hole, a blind cave. No one would ever find her in this.

Not in time.

Chapter Twelve

"Meg!"

Gideon had long since ducked beneath the yellow tape that blocked off the fire scene from the gathering crowd of fans and press and evacuated employees. His official uniform and not-to-be-messed-with air of authority easily cleared his way through the chaos of equipment and firefighters. His search was quick and thorough. And fruitless.

She wasn't here.

The news he wanted to share with her had to wait. Clutching fingers of impending doom tightened around his heart. Where was she?

A tiny, forgotten signal beeped to life in the corner of his mind, turning his attention toward the building itself. He knew the truth, knew it in his bones. "She's still inside."

His instinct to run and find her warred with his fear of failing. He could almost hear her inside his head, talking to her boys on gasping breaths, promising them the things she'd never had. He could see her crawling through the wreckage, her lips pressed into a thin line of determination. She was there. *There.*

He drifted a step closer to the blown-out windows of the building. The black smoke was changing to charcoal gray and silver. The fire was dead. She should be out. He moved in another step, barely hearing the world around him through the pounding pulse in his ears. Sweat popped out on his brow and the small of his back. She needed him. "Meg!"

His next step was thwarted by an unyielding grip on his arm. "Stay clear, Taylor. We're on it."

John Murdock's soot-streaked expression challenged Gideon to defy him. Of all the dumb, territorial, testosterone-filled... Gideon snatched his arm away. He didn't intimidate easily. "Meghan's in there."

"We know. We lost contact with her three minutes ago."

"You son of a bitch. I told you to keep an eye on her."

A twinge of remorse flashed across Murdock's face. "I know. I dropped the ball. That's why I'm going back for a fresh tank of O-2. I don't want to wait until the smoke clears. But we'll find her. You're not the only one who cares about her, Taylor." He tugged on one glove and reached into his pocket for the other. Murdock was already jogging away. "Now let me work."

Gideon. The name flashed in his mind on a softly husky voice. He turned to look, as if he'd heard the plea with his ears, not his heart.

He turned toward the building, tuned in to that awful talent. She was right there. In front of him. Should he trust it? Could love or luck or that fallible radar of his pull her to him? The noise around him faded into silence, the people moving past becoming a blurry after-image in his vision as he focused everything he was on that cry for help inside his head.

Frightening images from his nightmare tried to pop into his mind. But he pushed them aside. He would not lose her. There were some things a man could only stand once in his life. He couldn't stand losing her twice.

Gideon. Help me.

He was already climbing through the front window before he realized his decision had been made. "Help's coming, sweetheart." He closed off his ears and his eyes to the distractions around him, bent low at the waist to buy himself air to breathe closer to the floor, and plunged into the barrier of smoke.

Without the proper gear he couldn't go far, but if his radar was working, he wouldn't need to. *There.* He turned. "Meg," he whispered, conserving his breath.

"Gideon?"

A real voice. Husky and raw.

"Meg?"

He saw her, crawling on her belly, inching forward. Her hair caked with soot and matted to her head. Her hair?

Gideon fell to his knees beside her, rolled her over and scooped her up into his arms. "Where's your gear?"

She pressed her cheek into his chest and grabbed a handful of his shirt in a weak fist. "He was here. Attacked me."

He felt her weight sink against him as her strength ebbed. Gideon swore as her head lolled to the side and he glimpsed the red goo in her hair, sticking along her cheek and jaw. Blood.

"I'm getting you out of here." Without thinking whether or not he could do it, he held her tight in his arms and pushed to his feet. "Stay with me, Meg. Keep breathing."

Who knew what other injuries she'd sustained? Smoke inhalation and the blow to the head were the obvious ones. The oppressive heat would have sapped the moisture from her body, leaving her weak and woozy. But it would also slow the flow of blood from her wound.

Gideon followed his gut and retraced his steps as quickly as he dared, fearing the turbulent emotions inside him—anger, guilt, fear, love, pride and a fierce sense of possession that felt irrevocably violated—would all break free and flood his senses, throwing his sixth sense off-kilter the way it had with Luke. Meghan didn't have the time or strength for him to get emotional or distracted or lost.

Even in her turnout coat and pants, she weighed next to nothing in his arms. There was hardly enough of her to fight an attacker. Yet she fought fires. She fought for her boys. She fought off an abusive uncle.

The only thing she hadn't fought for was him. Them.

Gideon stumbled a step as the observation hit him. But he righted himself and pushed the thought aside. Later. The future could wait. The future was irrelevant if he couldn't save her now.

"I see light ahead." He whispered the reassurance and pressed a kiss to her hairline. Her soft skin was sticky with sweat, her silky hair stringy with greasy soot. God, she was beautiful. From the inside out. "The smoke's clearing."

She felt her head nod against him. "You came."

"Shh, babe." What it must be costing her to speak. When he hit clean air, he stood straight and shouted an order. "Medic!"

"Jus' like you promised."

Her words were lost in the sudden onslaught of noise and help and the outside world. He carried her straight toward the ambulance, heedlessly noting the path cleared for them by John Murdock and others.

"How badly is she hurt?" A woman's voice and a bright light blindsided him. "Dennis, are you getting a shot of this?" Gideon kept moving until Saundra Ames jabbed a microphone in his face. "Can you tell us what happened? Was Miss Wright contacted by the arsonist before the fire?"

"Get that damn thing out of here!" He had no qualms about shouldering the woman aside. Two other firefighters moved in to block the camera, and Gideon left them behind. "Medic!"

With more than enough hands to help, he laid Meghan

on the waiting guerney where she was quickly stripped of her coat. An oxygen mask was placed over her nose and mouth. The EMT pushed him aside to check her head wound and vital signs.

"How is she?" Gideon hovered at the fringes, refusing to let Meghan out of his sight.

"She's conscious and responsive. You need to let us work." They hooked up an IV and rolled her toward the ambulance.

"Gideon?" The second she called his name, he was there beside her, taking up her hand in both of his.

"I'm here."

She was trying to talk beneath the mask. On a frustrated cough she tugged it down to her chin and whispered, "The glove. I got his glove."

She didn't need to explain whose. She'd stolen a clue from her attacker. "I'll find it," he promised.

"Now, sir."

Gideon stepped back as they loaded her onto the ambulance. A lack of space and an order from the batallion chief kept him from climbing in beside her. If he had his way, Meghan Wright would never be alone again.

But he had work to do before that could happen. Before he could even pray it would happen.

"I'll be okay." She lifted her head and gave him a small smile. "My boys need me."

The EMT replaced her mask and closed the back doors.

Gideon stood rooted to the spot and watched the ambulance drive away. "So do I, sweetheart. So do I."

MEGHAN HATED hospitals.

She'd lost her mother, her aunt and a chance at a normal life inside one hospital or another.

She couldn't bear to think what this visit might cost her. But it had seemed imperative to the doctor that she be kept overnight for observation. Two stitches in her temple, another IV bag and fluids to drink, a fair night's sleep and half a dozen different tests on her lungs later, she was chomping at the bit to get out.

She'd have snuck out in the middle of the night if there hadn't been a Taylor brother of one shape and size or another stationed outside her door since her arrival. Whether chatty or tight-lipped, polite or distant, they'd formed an intimidating presence between her and anyone who tried to come see her who hadn't been cleared by the doctor. But they'd also prevented her escape, forcing her to settle for phone calls to Dorie and the boys, and to John and her chief, to reassure them of her condition.

Even floral deliveries had been turned away to other patients in the hospital once the cards had been removed. Fortunately, there'd been no yellow roses in the lot.

There'd been no Gideon all night, either.

She'd tried to lessen her bitter disappointment by telling herself he'd just been doing the job he'd promised to do when he'd rescued her yesterday. He was an honorable man, with a special gift for finding his way when no one else could. And she shouldn't read anything like forgiveness or hope in the tender crush of his arms or the soft comfort of his words or the heated concern in his eyes.

Meghan climbed out of bed and paced the room again, doubting that Gideon's oldest brother, Brett, would be any easier to get around just because he wasn't a cop. He'd been big enough to fill the whole doorway when he checked in with her, and the petite detective who was his wife didn't look like anybody she should mess with, either.

She was trapped in this sterile hellhole. Trapped and alone and slowly going mad with worry.

Who had attacked her? Why? Had the glove she'd pulled off his hand provided any kind of clue that could help? Was Gideon coming to see her? When?

"Oo-oh." She clenched her fists and shook her head with frustration, immediately regretting the impulse as a throb of pain beat a retaliation against her temple.

Gideon's soothing patience and steady presence had calmed her fears at the fire scene. But she shouldn't keep expecting that from him. He needed to move on with his life, to find the mother of his children. One of these days she'd have to figure out how to move on with her own life. Alone.

Back to trapped and going mad while she waited for the doctor to release her, Meghan turned on the television. She flipped through the channels, stopping on a national morning news show when an all-too-familiar image caught her eye. "Oh, my God."

A panoramic view of a low, flat building billowing smoke segued into a shaky, hand-held, close-up shot. Even cloaked in a blue uniform, she recognized the cut and dimension of Gideon's broad back. The glimpses of the woman he carried in his arms looked like a bedraggled rat. Her.

While her latest nightmare played out on national television, Meghan upped the volume to listen to the evenly modulated voice of Saundra Ames.

"—the third property owned by Daniel Kelleher to be targeted by the arsonist. A fourth property, C.B. Accounting, was once owned by Kelleher's former fiancée, Cynthia Burlington. After Ms. Burlington's death in a car accident ten years ago—"

Ten years ago? Meghan's hand automatically went to her waist and sank lower, cradling the stab of phantom pain in her abdomen. Ten years ago she'd been the sole survivor of the crash that had taken her aunt Rose and the driver of the other vehicle. A woman. Meghan squeezed her eyes shut, trying to come up with a name. She should call A. J. Rodriguez and have him check. Did she have a connection to Daniel Kelleher beyond putting out fires in his buildings? Or was his loss simply a very sad coincidence?

"Kansas City police are looking for this man, Jack Quinton, a recent parolee from the state penitentiary." Saundra's voice cut through Meghan's speculation and turned her attention back to the TV. A mug shot of the bug-eyed little man who'd asked for her autograph stared back at her. He looked so timid. Defenseless. Had that old man really waited for her in the dark of his fire and clobbered her upside the head? "Having served time for arson, Mr. Quinton is wanted for questioning in the fires."

"Isn't living through it once enough?"

Meghan's heart skidded into her throat at the dark-pitched voice from the doorway. She wiped away the moisture that had gathered at the corners of her eyes and feasted on the tall, dark-haired man who had finally come to see her. "Gideon."

Despite the fear and uncertainty that still toyed with her conscience, the omniscient light in his dark brown eyes was a balm to her battered soul. Freshly shaven and dressed in jeans and a black T-shirt and his K.C.F.D. ball cap, he was a handsome, sexy, world-weary man. It was the last observation that tugged at her heart, that made her want to go to him to stroke away the frown that lined his forehead. But she didn't. She couldn't be sure her touch would be welcome.

Tearing away her hungry gaze, she looked up in time to see Saundra Ames conversing on a split screen with the national news anchor. Meghan shook her head. "Jack Quinton might be the one person who hates all this publicity more than I do."

She turned off the TV and crossed to the far side of the room, pressing her lips firmly together and hugging herself tight. "I wondered if you'd be coming. You probably have some questions, I suppose."

"The questions can wait."

She glanced over her shoulder to meet his gaze. "Thank you for saving my life yesterday. I don't know if I had the strength to make it out on my own."

He tossed the overnight bag he carried onto the bed. "You would have made it. It isn't in you to give up."

Though his compliment hinted at double entendre, Meghan brushed it off with a laugh that grated through her tender throat. This polite mutual admiration society was testing the endurance of her lonesome heart. She needed to break the tension before she screamed. "Please say you brought me something decent to wear in that bag."

"Well, I could point out the advantages of a backless hospital gown from my perspective."

Meghan clutched at the back of her gown and spun around, feeling an embarrassed heat flood both sets of cheeks. That almost sounded normal. Flirty. When she saw the gentle curve of a smile on his face, she knew something had happened.

"What's going on?" It wasn't like Gideon to be secretive.

But he neither acknowledged nor denied that that line had been an invitation to welcome old feelings. He reached into the bag and pulled out a folded-up piece of white cardboard. "I've had some very interesting conversations in the past twelve hours or so, but I'll fill you in later. Let's get you checked out of this joint and home first." He held up the cardboard between his fingers. "I stopped to check on Dorie and the boys last night. They made you a card."

Meghan gasped with joy at the precious gift. Of the card and his caring. "Thank you."

"I didn't want them to worry. We finished scraping the garage and started priming it."

"You have been busy." His steady influence would have minimized the disruption in the boys' routine, given them the same sense of security he'd always given her. "I'm sure having you there helped."

He strode across the room, eating up the distance between them. When he was close enough, he handed her the card. But to her surprise he kept moving closer. He folded his arms around her and dragged her up to his chest.

"I missed you." His ragged sigh stirred the hair at her crown. "I thought I'd lost you all over again."

Meghan snuggled beneath his chin and wrapped her arms around his waist, forgetting for the moment that distance provided a buffer of emotional self-preservation. She buried her nose in the clean scent of his chest and felt his strength all around her, sheltering her, becoming part of her. "I wish I could make a miracle happen, Gideon. I wish I was woman enough to make your dreams come true."

"Shh." He palmed the back of her head and massaged gentle circles there. "We'll work on miracles later. Right now let's just take it one day, one minute, at a time. Okay?"

Meghan nodded. More curious than hopeful at the cryptic promise of his words, she reluctantly let him go. "Okay."

"I'll get the paperwork started while you change," he said.

She opened up the card and laughed out loud, then clutched at her throat as pain and pride and pleasure made her want to cry. Illustrated and signed by Dorie and the boys—from Mark's scratches to Alex's painstaking drawing of a heart—the bent-up concoction was a work of art. And the dearest message she'd ever received. But one corner of the cover was punctured and smushed. She displayed the damage for Gideon to see. "What happened to it?"

A hint of a bemused smile eased the fatigue from his expression. "They gave it to Crispy to chew on. Apparently, Eddie thought she'd want to wish you well, too. I don't think the paw on the ink pad worked the way he expected.''

"Oh, no. Did they make a big mess?"

"As if Dorie really minded." That was a yes.

Like doting parents, they shared a laugh that reminded Meghan of all they could be together. And all they never would be.

With that sobering thought, the laughter ended.

"Get dressed," Gideon ordered. This was the investigator at work again. The superior officer whom she respected and admired. The gentle man she loved had gone with the laughter. "We have a couple of stops to make before we get to Dorie's house."

MEGHAN'S NEED TO PROTECT her sanity from more sick mind games and physical trauma just wasn't quite letting her grasp what Gideon was trying to say. "So now *two* men want me dead?"

"Jack Quinton doesn't want you dead. He wants you to complete the relationship he starts when he sets those fires." Gideon steered his Suburban off I-70 toward the heart of downtown Kansas City. His post mortem of the DK Mall fire had revealed the "starter" items she'd come to expect: the remains of a remote triggering device and a crudely drawn Westside Warrior emblem burned into the floor. "He likes seeing you in action, remember? Not dead."

"So who else would try to knock me unconscious and leave me to suffocate?" She shivered at the cruel notion. "And why?"

"Your notoriety could be drawing too much attention to someone's plan."

She touched the bandage at her temple and shook her head. "It can't be the Warriors, then. They *want* the pub-

licity—to show what big, destructive excuses for men they
are so that the competition runs in fear of them."

He smiled at her assessment of Ezio Moscatelli and his
gang-bangers. "I don't think it's about making a statement,
either."

"You figured something out, didn't you?" She studied
the intent line of his profile, which gave nothing away.
"You said that you went to Jack Quinton's apartment with
Josh and A.J. Do you plan to share what you found?"

He stopped at a red light and finally looked her way.
"No sign of Quinton. But definitely the tools of his trade.
Disassembled electronics, a pay stub from—get this—his
sister's floral shop. Apparently she gave him a job making
deliveries when he got out of prison."

"Floral deliveries?" Meghan's breath whooshed out of
her lungs.

"Easy." Gideon reached out and brushed a lock of hair
away from her bandage. "There's more."

She concentrated on the gentle touch. She pressed a hand
to her chest and forced herself to breathe in and out again,
instead of thinking how easy it had been for Jack Quinton
to conceive and carry out the torment of the last few days.
"Let me guess, he drives a white delivery van."

"With red letters. Just like Dorie described." He tunneled his fingers into her hair and cupped the side of her
neck in a protective, comforting gesture. "But we also
found a shoebox full of cash."

"How much?"

"A little over ten thousand dollars."

Meghan's long, low whistle conveyed her surprise. "So
someone paid him to set those fires?"

Gideon pulled away and turned his attention back to
driving as the light changed. "Or paid him to teach them
how. A.J.'s issued a warrant for his arrest. Once they track

him down, he'll be arraigned for arson. Conspiracy to commit. Accessory.''

"But not assault." She heaved a sigh that was part impatience, part grim acceptance. "This is where the second man comes in, right?"

"Jack Quinton is a little guy," explained Gideon, his voice gravely impersonal as he led her through his reasoning a second time. "According to A.J.'s report, he's not any taller than you. Even the size of his fingerprints are tiny for a man. The glove you pulled off your attacker came from someone with bigger hands."

Meghan collapsed back into her seat. She'd expected finding out who was behind the fires would fill her with relief, if not elation. But the damn torment wouldn't end. All she felt was the impending sense of dread that lingered in the pit of her stomach.

"So who hit me?" She turned her face to the window and looked up at the gloomy portent of the overcast sky. She hadn't seen clouds for so long, she'd almost forgotten what they looked like. She wouldn't even begin to hope that they'd get the rain the city so desperately needed.

She'd given up on hope the minute she'd given up on a future with Gideon. She'd accept his promise of caring and protection now because *now* was all he could give her. And a few cherished days with Gideon Taylor in her life was more than she had ever deserved. She'd store up this memory of a good, caring man in her life to reflect back on the next time her ugly past reared its head.

She tried to keep herself in the moment and to not start mourning her empty future until she got there. Gideon slowed the vehicle and pulled into the posh business district just east of the Plaza. "Where are we going, anyway?" she finally asked.

"To see a man with big hands."

"YOU STILL THINK Frank Westin's out to get you?"

Meghan was impressed. Gideon barely batted an eye as

he took Daniel Kelleher's tirade about big business and organized crime and missing golf games in stride. But she suspected there was something more than showing off his cool-under-pressure facade involved when he invited her to accompany him on his interview with Kelleher.

Meghan continued her polite inspection of the entrepreneur's posh high-rise office, and tried not to flinch at Mr. Kelleher's sharp-toned response. "Yes, I think he's out to get me. This is the fourth property of mine that's been destroyed by fire. Frank Westin wants to put me out of business. There aren't many of us left in this town who can compete with him in the realty investment market." The fifty-something man sat in his chair for all of two seconds before jumping up and pacing another circle around his desk. "And why the hell are you holding up those insurance reports, Taylor? Isn't it clear I'm the victim here?"

She felt Gideon's gaze slide over to hers at the mention of the word "victim." She turned away from the painting she was admiring and smiled back at him. Daniel Kelleher was a blustery blowhard who was testy because his golf date with the mayor had been put on hold until after this meeting. Along with the buttery-smooth leather golf glove he wore on his left hand, his tan slacks and green, short-sleeved polo shirt bespoke wealth. But the muscles on his burly forearms indicated he'd worked hard to earn that money. Maybe he had a right to his attitude. She didn't take it personally.

With a slight nod, Gideon returned his attention to Kelleher. "Yes, these are clear cases of arson. But until I have a man in jail, I'm not signing off on anything." Gideon stood and pulled a photograph from his wallet. "Do you know this man?"

Kelleher glanced at the picture and snorted with contempt. "Sure. His picture was splattered all over the news this morning. Jack Quinton.'' He handed back the picture and positioned his arms across his chest in a defensive front. ''The police think he's the one who burned down my buildings.''

''Would he have any reason to hold a grudge against you?''

''I've never met the man. But I'd like to talk to him. I'm sure Westin hired him.''

As Gideon ran through a list of potential connections between Kelleher and Quinton, Meghan crossed over to the glass-fronted display case that housed myriad plaques and trophies and photographs. Starting with the picture of his high school baseball team, the self-made millionaire had mementoes from a variety of sporting events that spanned more than thirty years.

Gideon's probing questions and Kelleher's heated answers faded into background noise as Meghan zeroed in on one photograph in particular. She'd seen it before. Those same people. That same logo on their shirts. Meghan closed her eyes and sorted through the past few days. A softball team. She slowly opened her eyes and matched the photograph to her memory. She'd seen that same photograph in the wreckage of a fire.

''C.B. Accounting,'' she whispered out loud.

Meghan turned, in a bit of a daze, not realizing she'd spoken out loud until Gideon asked, ''What's that?''

She turned back to the display case and pointed to the picture. It had seemed familiar to her when it had been water-damaged and scratched by broken glass. Looking at the clear copy, she now knew why.

She pointed to the woman on the back row of the photo. Linked arm-in-arm with a younger, darker-haired Daniel Kelleher, she smiled confidently. ''Who is this woman?''

Meghan's somber, fearful mood had even affected Kelleher's temper. Suddenly quiet, he crossed to the glass and studied the picture with her. There was nothing hard or accusatory in his tone when he answered. "Cynthia Burlington. She used to work for me." He pressed his fingertips to the glass as if he were giving it a loving touch. "I divorced my first wife to marry her. I never did, though."

Meghan squeezed her eyes shut, seeing Cynthia Burlington's face as clearly as her own reflection in the mirror. "Why didn't you?"

Kelleher sniffed and turned away. "She died. During our engagement. A car accident out on old Crackerneck Road in Independence."

She could barely breathe, much less speak. "Crackerneck Road?"

Meghan sank into the nearest chair and let the memories come.

"Yeah. It was late. It was raining. There are too many turns and big trees on that road. When she rounded the corner and the other car was there, she had no place to go."

"I'm sorry."

Meghan was pulled into the swirling vortex of her past.

THEY ZIPPED around the curve. She clung to the armrest and stared at the ball mitt in her lap, too afraid to look over at the woman behind the wheel. She apologized again, wishing it would make a difference in the speed of the car or the temperament of the driver. "I'm sorry practice ran late, Aunt Rose."

"Sorry, nothing. I told Pete I'd have dinner on the table when he came home. He'll be pissed at both of us now." Though Meghan had her permit, Rose had insisted on driving. She knew the roads better. She could drive faster.

"I'm sorry." What else could she say? Rose's foot pushed on the accelerator. Even with her seat belt on,

Meghan slammed into the car door as they whipped around the turn. And saw the bright, huge beams of two headlights. "Rose!"

The squeal of brakes, the blare of horns, and then—no more.

"MEG!"

She snapped back to the present and found herself staring deep into Gideon's eyes. The dark brown orbs blazed with that almost-psychic light of his, searching deep into her own for understanding. He was kneeling in front of her. He absorbed the trembling of her shoulders within the grasp of his hands. "What is it, sweetheart? Where did you go?"

"Is she okay?" That was Daniel Kelleher, standing off to the side.

Gideon's hands were moving now, skimming across her hair and face, checking her for signs of renewed trauma. "She sustained a head injury yesterday," was his brief explanation. "Are you with me?"

She nodded, then lifted eyes that felt raw toward Kelleher. *I killed your fiancée,* she wanted to confess. She remembered the pictures from the papers, if not the crash itself. *I was there the night she died.* Her hands went down to cover her belly. "I'm sorry about the accident."

"Thanks. But you weren't driving that car."

"No, but…" Could a man still hold a grudge for ten years after losing the woman he loved? Guilt and grief hardened into something a little tougher. She swept her gaze along Kelleher's arms. Looking. Remembering. Large hands. Black gloves. A struggle for her own life. Did he recognize her? Did he blame her for that night? Uncle Pete had.

"We'll talk later, Kelleher. I need to get Meghan home." Gideon pushed to his feet and pulled Meghan up beside him. With his arm anchored at the back of her waist, he guided her toward the door.

"Wait." One small word, one clutch of her hand, and Gideon stopped. The dimple beside his mouth had creased into one long line, betraying his concern. Despite the baffled worry in his eyes, he let her turn around to face Daniel Kelleher. "One last thing, Mr. Kelleher. May I see your hand?"

His sentimental mood had been replaced by the cutthroat businessman once more. "I don't think so."

"The glove," Gideon demanded, backing her up both literally and figuratively.

Kelleher shrugged off his defensive posture. "Whatever." He unsnapped the wrist of his golf glove and slipped it off, holding both hands up for her to inspect. "Satisfied?"

"Yes." She rallied her strength and looked up into his piercing green eyes. "Thank you."

"Sure." He followed them out the door and called down the hallway after them. "Get me the answers I need, Taylor. Or I'll find them myself."

Meghan didn't relax until she was buckled up in the front seat of Gideon's Suburban.

He turned on the engine, started the air-conditioning and turned to face her. "It's your turn to share."

"I was in the car crash that killed his fiancée."

He reached across the seat and stroked her cheek. "I thought it might be something like that."

As much as she loved his comforting touch, she discovered she didn't have to doubt her own judgment or strength each time one of the terrible memories from her past tried to tear her apart.

"There are no bruises on his hands and arms."

Gideon pulled away and leaned back against his door. "Okay, that one you can explain to me."

She exhaled a cleansing breath. "I got in at least one good shot at the man who attacked me in the fire yesterday. That's how I freed myself and got the glove."

"So we're not just looking for someone with big hands but—"

"—someone with big hands that have been in a fight."

Gideon sat forward and shifted the engine into gear. "Damn. I wanted it to be Kelleher. The man's an arrogant SOB."

"And I wanted it to be Jack Quinton." Despite Gideon's assertion that he couldn't be her attacker, she wanted to take a look at the man's arms and hands, anyway. She pressed her lips together in a frown. "One man claims he loves me, but doesn't want to share me with the world. Another might think I'm responsible for his fiancée's death. It's a little disconcerting to wonder if anyone else out there might have a motive for wanting me dead."

"Try not to think about it right now. I'm taking you home."

With her stalker still at large, and more unanswered questions than ever, Meghan felt that unsettling cloud of danger around her growing, slowly eating up the good things that were left in her world.

Home. Without Gideon at her side and children of her own, she wondered if she could ever truly find her way there.

Chapter Thirteen

"You got a minute?" Gideon set the last of the dishes on the drain board beside the sink and leaned one hip against the counter. Meghan, bent over at the waist, loading dishes onto the bottom rack of the dishwasher, afforded him a tantalizing view of her shapely rump.

"Sure. What's up?" she asked, picking up another stack of plates and bending over.

He couldn't pinpoint what it was—the lean curves of her body, her graceful athleticism, just the fact it was her—that transformed every move she made into a joy to watch. Even something as humdrum as cleaning up the kitchen became an erotic stimulus if Meghan was a part of it. When she put away the bread in the pantry and butted the door shut with a swish of her hip, Gideon had to close his eyes to temper his body's lusty response to the innocently seductive movement.

He had to tread very carefully through the next few hours of his life or he could destroy everything that had ever truly mattered to him. As far as Meghan was concerned, their love affair had ended because a tragic twist of fate had set them on two very different paths. Maybe they didn't have a future together. But he wouldn't strip her of her self-worth the way her uncle had, simply because life hadn't worked out the way he'd planned it. He'd already done her a terrible wrong and he had to make amends.

As she pushed her hair off her face, the exposed bandage at her temple reminded him of the scars on her belly and the ones hidden inside her that made her think she wasn't enough for him. Her father's abandonment and Pete Preston's abuse had done their damage. But instead of understanding her sacrifice, instead of helping her heal, he'd mistakenly verified what she already believed about herself. *He* was the one who made her think she wasn't enough woman for any man.

It would take him a hell of a long time to get over the guilt he stewed in because of his cold, speechless reaction to Meghan's confession about her sterility. He needed to make things right between them, not just for her own safety now, but for her future.

His own future would be long and painful and empty if he failed.

Even their friendship was doomed to become a thing of the past, once her stalker was caught and he'd fulfilled his promise to stay with her until the case was solved. And neither their love nor their friendship would make any damn difference if he couldn't catch the man who still wanted her dead.

The clock was ticking.

And he couldn't afford to waste a moment of it.

She closed the dishwasher and called him on his pensive mood. "You're staring."

"It's a nice view." One that he'd miss forever. She seemed startled by the unexpected compliment, but said nothing. He might be her ex-boyfriend, her former best friend, her soon-to-be-out-of-her-life lover.

But he wasn't dead.

And he didn't lie.

Dorie had gone outside to watch the little boys while

Alex and Eddie broke out the paint to finish priming the garage. He and Meghan were alone in the house and he wanted nothing more than to sweep her into his arms. To grab her by that lush little tush and set her up on the counter and kiss her and caress her until she understood what a perfect woman she was.

But that was a lesson that wasn't his to teach anymore.

However, there was one wounded heart they might still be able to heal. "I need your help. I read the Grimes file last night. I want to talk to Matthew."

Half an hour later Meghan was sitting on the sofa with Matthew securely tucked into her lap. Her fair head was bent low to snuggle against Matthew's dark one. It was a sweet, stunning contrast that tugged at Gideon's heartstrings.

That's how it should be. For her. For him.

But it wasn't. This was about Matthew's needs, not his.

He hadn't been sure quite how to handle this, but he'd tried to think of the serious talks he'd had with his father growing up. Nervous energy had him pacing the room as he tried to live up to Sid Taylor's standard. He began his report three different ways, apologizing at the end of each fruitless attempt. Finally, Meghan motioned him to sit so he wouldn't tower over the boy.

Matthew clung to Meghan, his chubby arms latched firmly around her neck. And while he didn't cower when Gideon sat beside them, he didn't turn around to look at him, either. Something close to the panic he'd felt when Meghan had disappeared in the fire tried to grab hold of him now. Matthew was just a little kid, barely thigh-high. And yet this was scary. This sitting and talking. Trying to reach the heart and mind of a troubled child.

The enormity of what Gideon was trying to do made choosing the right words difficult. "I know it sounds technical, but the fire at your house was caused by a plugged-up flue on your heating stove. The pipe was loaded with creosote that caught fire and burned through the main wall of the house before the alarms or anyone even noticed it."

Matthew slipped him a sideways glance and frowned as if Gideon had muttered a foreign incantation.

Try again. Meghan mouthed the words. Gideon nodded, needing her encouragement as much as the boy did, though he was envious of Matthew's needy clutch on Meghan. It was a very different sort of comfort than what she'd offered him that night in his apartment, but Gideon knew that Matthew felt safe and loved within the circle of her arms. He had.

He tried to think like a four-year-old to figure out the best way to make him understand the truth. "I work with scientists who can tell that the stove in your house got too hot and made the fire. I know matches are interesting, and maybe you play with them sometimes when you shouldn't. But *you* didn't burn down your house."

Meghan hugged the boy tight in her arms. "It's not your fault that your mom and dad died."

Gideon reached out to touch the silky mop of dark brown hair. He was so small, so delicate. "If that's what you've been thinking, don't. Sometimes bad things happen…" His gaze slipped over the boy's head and locked on Meghan's. The tears glistening in her honey-colored eyes made this that much more difficult, that much more important. "But it doesn't make you a bad person."

Matthew squinched his shoulders and scooted away from Gideon's touch. The rejection stung, but he didn't push it.

Planting himself on the far side of Meghan's lap, Matthew turned to look at Gideon. The bow-shaped circle of his lips opened. But no sound came out. Instead he sidled closer to Meghan. But Gideon recognized a boy-to-man willingness to listen. And it filled him with hope.

"Now it's important to understand that fire—even the

little ones that a match or lighter makes—is always dangerous. I don't want you to scare Meghan or Dorie or me again by playing with those things.'' Enough lecturing. He offered the boy a gentle smile. ''You did a very brave thing by taking your little brother to the neighbor's house when you heard the alarm. I can tell you practiced your safety drill.'' The brown eyes continued to watch him. ''I'll bet your mom and dad are very proud of you.''

Meghan pressed a kiss to Matthew's hair. ''I know they are.''

The therapist had said an official report from a real fireman might be the thing to help Matthew move past the guilt and fear that had rendered him silent. No matter how it was phrased, Matthew and Mark Grimes had been through an unspeakable ordeal. But hopefully the facts, and the calm reassurances of two caring adults, would give him the courage to come back to life and be a child again.

Since he didn't want a maudlin dwelling on the topic, Gideon had nothing else left to say beyond offering his support. ''Do you want to come outside and help Alex and Eddie and me work on the garage tonight?''

Matthew simply blinked.

Gideon tried again. ''I've got a paintbrush with your name on it.'' Matthew frowned in confusion. ''That's just a figure…'' He looked to Meg for help. ''How do I explain figure of speech to a four-year-old?''

She smiled with a serene Madonna-like expression on her softly freckled features. ''We can write his name on it.''

Gideon stood and extended his hand. ''You wanna come?''

Matthew hesitated. He looked up at Meghan, who simply nodded. Was every male a sucker for her sweet, sweet smile?

With that bit of encouragement, he climbed down from

her lap and took Gideon's hand. Again, he marveled at how small Matthew was. His hand barely fit into Gideon's palm. But he held on with an expectant trust that humbled him.

As he walked out the back door with the little boy at his side, he could hear Meghan sniffing back tears. Something warm and moist pricked at the corners of his own eyes. And he knew that she might be the only one who understood how much this meant to him.

This is what the best parts of fatherhood would be like— this is what losing Meghan had denied him.

Unexpected moments of love and pride and joy.

WITH THE RUMBLINGS of thunder in the distant sky to warn them, they'd packed up the paint supplies, cleaned up, and piled into Gideon's Suburban to go for ice cream. The wall of night was approaching, led by a line of dark clouds that charged the air and cooled the temperature to a balmy seventy-eight degrees. A storm was coming.

And it didn't promise a gentle quenching of the earth's thirst.

With Josh Taylor shadowing them in his cherry-red pickup, Meghan felt safe enough to relax her guard and to soak up every sweet moment of their evening. Alex downed twice as much ice cream as anyone else. Eddie picked out and sorted the marshmallows and chunks of chocolate from his Rocky Road and ate each delicacy one at a time. Matthew sat in her lap and quietly licked his vanilla cone. And Mark found new and wonderful places to smear his chocolate ice cream. With Dorie along to give their "family" outing a generational feel, Meghan looked across the table and found herself bathed in the rich, dark fire of Gideon's eyes.

This is what he longed for, she knew. With four Taylor boys of his own and a whole wife in her place. She looked away before the unfairness of it all caught hold of her.

This was heaven. Tonight it was hers. She wouldn't let yesterday's regrets or tomorrow's dangers spoil it. The memory of this night would have to feed her empty heart for a lifetime.

Mark was sound asleep in his car seat by the time they got home. Gideon carried the boy upstairs while Meghan brought in Matthew. Dorie hustled Alex and Eddie into their pajamas and gave them permission to stay up and play a video game in Eddie's room while the house quieted down to sleep. That was when the first raindrops began to fall.

It hit the parched ground with the thunder of stampeding hoofbeats. When the lightning opened up the sky and turned nighttime into daylight, Crispy gave her first yelp.

Meghan yelped herself as thunder cracked overhead and shook the old house. "I'm going to bring the dog in."

She dashed outside behind Gideon, who ran to the garage to carry in the ladder and drop cloths they'd stored outside. Rain pelted her face and plastered her shirt and shorts to her skin before she'd gotten off the patio.

Josh left his truck to help Gideon secure the garage while Meghan dashed across the backyard to Crispy's doghouse. She had to get down on her hands and knees and stick her head inside before the frightened pooch would even respond to her calls. "Come on, girl. If you survived fire, you can survive a little rain."

With her wide, round eyes flashing with panic, Crispy left her spot in the corner and leaped into Meghan's arms. Scrambling to her feet, Meghan tromped through the slick grass and carried the dog up the back steps into the house. With an armful of wet puppy, Meghan kicked off her soggy shoes and headed straight for the basement door.

At the bottom of the stairs, she set the dog down. Crispy darted off to the farthest corner of the basement, disappearing from sight. Meghan threw up her hands. "What is with you and being rescued, anyway?"

She shook her head and turned on the light in the basement bathroom. "Eek." She teased her drowned-rat reflection in the mirror, then searched for an old towel to dry off the dog so she could join the kids upstairs.

She'd stopped to wash the mud off her hands and smooth her wet hair back into its braid before Crispy's high-pitched whine registered. She knew a lot of dogs hated storms because of their sensitive hearing, but the finished basement was well-insulated and muffled the violent sounds of the storm.

"Crispy?" She whistled once to call the dog. No answer. Meghan stepped out of the bathroom and whistled again. The dog's whining cry sounded almost like a sob. "You big wimp," she whispered, aching for an innocent creature who could feel such fear. She whistled again and followed the frantic sound. "Crispy? Here girl."

A bright flash of lightning illuminated the entire basement an instant before she heard a loud pop. Meghan jumped, startled by the sound. Then the room went black. "Lovely. Lightning must have hit the transformer."

She pressed a hand over her racing heart and closed her eyes. Even in the absence of a flashlight, her vision should be able to adjust to the darkness so she could at least find her way to the stairs. "Crispy?" She whistled and opened her eyes. "Mommy's going back upstairs. Come with me, girl."

Wet and smelly or not, that dog didn't want to be down here in the muffled darkness during the storm any more than she did. Besides, the explosive noise might have awakened the boys. Dorie would be there to comfort them and console Eddie and Alex on losing the power for their game, but she'd like to check on them herself. Hopefully, Gideon and Josh would find the flashlights and candles in the kitchen.

"Now or never, Crispy." She called the dog one more time.

Crispy barked.

That *someone's in my yard* bark.

Meghan went perfectly still, pinpointing the source of the dog in distress. She hadn't heard from her fan today. And while that should have given her some comfort, she'd felt the tension building inside her all day. When? Where? Her heart beat faster, pounding so loudly against the quick, deep breaths of her expanding lungs it mimicked the thunder outside. She knew he'd contact her again. But here? Now?

There.

She turned toward the scratching claws and frantic pitch of Crispy's bark. Barefoot, and armed with nothing more than a towel, she followed the sound. She froze as lightning flashed again, temporarily blinding her in the darkness. "Damn."

She closed her eyes and shook her head clear, pressing her hand against the throbbing beat of pain beneath the stitches at her temple. If she could navigate her way through a fire, she could find her way through the disorienting darkness.

"I'm comin', baby," she promised, tuning in to sounds and instincts more than vision. They led her to the doorway leading to the unfinished half of the basement that housed the water heater and furnace and was used for storage. "Crispy?"

The dog launched herself at Meghan's shins, knocking her back a step. "Easy, girl." The dog charged her again, then disappeared into the darkness. "Ow. Stop that." Meghan knelt down. If the dog came again, she'd grab her.

"Crispy?"

The dog's whine was like a call for mommy. The pain of it tore at her heart and pushed her forward to help. "What is it, bab—"

Meghan stubbed her toe on something soft and tumbled. Throwing out her arms to protect her head, she landed with an oof on top of something solid. Her fingers curled into something scratchy, like wool. A pile of blankets?

The lightning flashed again and Meghan screamed. And swore. She scrabbled away into the darkness, waiting for the next lightning burst to verify what Crispy had already discovered. A man's body. In the basement.

Dead. Judging by the uneven shape of his skull and the pool of blood his face rested in.

"Damn, damn, damn." She snatched the dog into her arms, keeping her away from the body and seeking whatever comfort she could find in the basement's sudden chill. "Gideon!"

She shouted for help, but could only hear her own voice muffled by the depth of the basement and the thick walls of the old house. She was hidden away from the world, lost in the darkness of the storm. With a frightened dog and a dead man for company.

Lightning flashed again, giving her another view of the body. Enough light flickered across the man's face to illuminate his broken bug-eyed glasses and thinning hair. Jack Quinton.

Thunder punctuated her startled shock and left her heart pounding in her chest. Giving in to the dreadful curiosity that might finally give her the closure she needed, she set Crispy aside and crawled back to the body. Willing her eyes to focus in the strobelike effects of lightning flashes and blackouts, she pushed up the sleeves of his jacket and checked for marks on his arms and hands. An empty pill bottle rolled out of his stiff grasp. Had he taken something and passed out, hitting his head against the furnace?

Right now, she didn't care. Dead was dead. It was an uncharitable thought, but she was glad he couldn't frighten her again.

But there were no bruises.

Thoughts of relief vanished in a heartbeat. Meghan sat back on her haunches and let the numbing realization sink in. Jack Quinton hadn't attacked her. That meant…

Shock quickly gave way to that self-preserving adrenaline that shot through her system. Her attacker was still out there. Maybe still here. She had to warn Gideon and Josh, and get her boys someplace safe.

She rose to her feet and headed for the door, remembering the path and feeling her way. The concrete was cold beneath her bare feet, and the damp chill of the storage room raised goose bumps on her skin. *Or was that…?* A latent sixth sense tried to kick in and tell her something.

"Ow!" A sharp prick stabbed the bottom of her foot and she fell hard onto her hands and knees. She cursed as the impact jolted through her. "What now?"

She rolled onto her bottom and pulled her foot into her lap, trying to check the wound. She could feel the sticky flow from the tiny prick, taste the blood on her fingertip. At the next lightning strike she knew what had happened.

She'd stepped on a long-stemmed red rose. "You bastard," she cursed the dead body. "Even in death you want to hurt me."

She picked up the card beside the rose. A florist's card. Just like the others. Equally unnerving.

The lightning subsided from its violent fury, retreating up to the sky to create a laserwork display that flickered through the high basement windows like candlelight. If she held the card just right, there was enough light to read the message.

Goodbye, love.
I'm sorry.
I never meant to hurt you.
We'll be together soon.
Forever.

Goodbye? A suicide note? But did the pills or the blow to the head kill him?

"How do you kill yourself twice?"

The throbbing pain in her foot gave her the answer. Jack Quinton hadn't killed himself. He hadn't written the note and he hadn't left that flower for her.

A red rose?

His death had been staged to look like a suicide.

Now that sixth sense screamed at her. *Get out!*

Meghan scrambled to her feet. The sudden movement startled the dog and she barked. "Come on, girl. Let's get out of this place. We have to warn the others."

For once the dog did as she was told, rubbing herself around Meghan's ankles as she inched her way toward the door.

That's when she smelled the smoke.

Meghan's heart dropped into her stomach. "Not now. Not here." Panic welled up inside her. "Gideon!"

Crispy's bark punctuated the plea for help.

Now she was searching for smoke instead of escape. She used her nose instead of touch. Sound instead of vision.

The distinctive snap and sizzle of ignition stopped her in her tracks.

Fire.

"What have you done, you bastard?" The odors of sulphur and petroleum distillate slowly filled the air as she cursed her unseen tormentor. The fumes came from the finished part of the basement. Wait. How did a dead man start a fire? Someone was out there. Close enough to trigger a remote. "Sorry, Jack," she lamented to the dead man. "I think someone's trying to silence both of us."

"Now you get it." Meghan whirled around at the crisply articulated, beautifully modulated voice advancing through the darkness. "You were such an easy mark—so easy to spook, so determined to be brave. So heroic."

"Saundra?"

"But I need you to die this time."

With a menacing growl from Crispy, Meghan gauged the direction of the attack. A tall figure in black. A shadow from the shadows lunged toward her. Meghan put up her hands and deflected the first blow.

Something hard and metallic clanged against the concrete, shooting out sparks. The sudden shift of the heavy weight threw Saundra off balance. Meghan shoved at the solid shadow and knocked the woman to the floor.

She tried to run, but a hand snatched her by the ankle and jerked her off her feet. Meghan hit the floor hard, but she kicked out, dislodging the hand and earning a very unladylike curse.

As she tried to roll out of the way she hit a stack of boxes and crates that tumbled down on top of her, bruising and startling her, thwarting her escape. But they impeded Saundra's efforts to reach her, as well. While the redhead lifted and shoved the boxes aside, Meghan crawled backward on her heels and elbows, heading toward the flickering light from the open doorway.

Saundra saw the movement and scurried around to beat her to the opening. "No, you don't! You're not going to ruin the perfect ending to my story."

She raised that metallic cannister above her head again. In the glow of light from the main room Meghan could read the contents. Lighter fluid.

Saundra brought it down hard. Meghan rolled to the side,

dodging the blow, but hearing the crackle of sparks beside her ear.

"No. Not yet."

She turned her head at the panic in Saundra's voice. The sparks had hit the carpet and immediately ignited. Saundra stepped over Meghan and tried to stomp out the flames. But the can had spilled, sending a sea of instant flame flooding across the room.

A wall of flame shot up beside the door. Meghan swore and jumped to her feet. "That was too close. What have you done?" She shoved the other woman back into the storage room crates. She had plenty of light now to see the distinctive red hair poofing out from beneath Saundra's black stocking cap. There was no way to cross that basement now. Not without shoes. Not without protective gear. She turned and advanced on the incompetent pyromaniac. "We're trapped. Is that part of your plan, too?"

Meghan slammed the door between the storage area and the finished basement, locking herself in with a dead man and a murderer. Buying herself time to think of a way to survive.

A lick of flame flowed into the room at her feet and Meghan quickly retreated. She peeled off her tank top and tossed it onto the encroaching flame. The wet material slapped against the concrete and smothered the flame.

But more of the liquid seeped beneath the door. "Damn." Quickly, Meghan shed her damp shorts and scrunched them into the opening beneath the door. But they weren't enough to completely close the opening. She looked over her shoulder at Saundra, who was still mumbling to herself about blame and "doing it right." "Give me some of your clothes. That jumpsuit will do."

Saundra shot to her feet, as prissy and indignant as if she'd been refused an interview. "I don't think so."

"Do you want to live?" Saundra stared at her outstretched hand. "I'm sure you've got on one of those pretty silk suits underneath. Believe me, everything you're wearing is going to smell like smoke before we get out of here."

In a huffy burst of cooperation, Saundra unzipped her canvas coveralls and pulled them off. "This isn't how it's supposed to work. I'm supposed to be out of here right now, meeting my cameraman." She glared at the dead body behind her. "I followed his directions to the letter."

"Jack Quinton's?" Meghan grabbed the jumpsuit and stuffed it into the crack beneath the door. Even with the fire-retardant material, it was only a temporary fix. Eventually the clothes themselves would burn, filling the room with enough smoke to asphyxiate them if the flames didn't get them first.

"Panty hose next." She stood and motioned for the other woman to start stripping. She'd learned an old trick from Uncle Pete that might actually prove useful. "You may have borrowed Quinton's remote, but you got greedy. He's a man of patience. Let the fire burn slowly without detection. Eventually it will find plenty of fuel to feed on." She thumbed over her shoulder. "You saturated that room in there, looking for an instant conflagration. A slow burn you can escape. That out there already has us beat."

Saundra sat on a crate with one leg out of her hose, looking nothing like a beauty queen right now. "You don't think we can escape?"

Meghan couldn't resist the sarcasm that bubbled up. "I'm Kansas City's Sweetheart, remember? Everyone wants to know where I am and what I'm doing. I'm sure the cameras will come looking for me."

"I made you a celebrity."

"I didn't want the job." She took the panty hose and tied Saundra's wrists together, cinched them tight so the woman couldn't escape. She took note of the large, purplish bruise on her forearm. "Forgive me if I don't trust you. Apparently, Quinton did."

Bound and pouting in her peach silk suit, Saundra continued to talk while Meghan searched the storage room for another exit. "I needed to up the stakes. Jack wanted to quit. He said your love was a private thing. He didn't like sharing you with so many people." She shrugged her shoulders as if a point of view other than her own was impossible to fathom. "We were going national. I had networks calling me. This story was my big break, and he wanted to stop."

Meghan stacked boxes and climbed up to the small window near the basement ceiling. "So Quinton did set the other fires?"

"Yes. I'd interviewed him a couple of years ago when he was in prison. Getting the inmates' perspective on the need for building a new facility. When these fires started again, I knew it was his work. I called him. Told him I'd inform the police if he didn't tell me when and where the fires would be set."

Rusted from years of disuse, the window latch wouldn't budge. "That's why you were always first on the scene. You scooped the competition with inside information."

"I'm a reporter. I used my sources."

"You endangered lives." Meghan jumped down and pried loose a slat from a crate to use as a lever.

"No, we didn't. We chose abandoned locations. Daniel Kelleher can afford the losses. When I found out the two of you had a connection, he made the perfect patsy to throw anyone off our track. Jack wanted to blame the gangs, but the possibility of investigating a man like Kelleher made a much better story."

Story. The fight almost drained out of Meghan. She wasn't the only person who had suffered from this woman's quest for fame and success. Her lungs began to protest as she forced herself to breathe deeply. Gasses released by the fire on the opposite side of that wall were starting to drift into the room and gather near the ceiling where she was working. "Daniel Kelleher lost the woman he loved in that crash. Don't you care about anyone's feelings?"

"Of course, I do. That drama, that pain and joy, is what viewers tune in to see."

"What about the firefighters?" She wedged the board beneath the window latch and heaved with all her might. The wood snapped in two and she tumbled to the floor.

"Viewers love it. American heroes saving the day." Now Meghan could see the reporter wasn't just sitting there, bragging about her plan. She was working loose the knots. "And you, dear girl, were the icing on the cake. When Jack took an interest in you, I knew I had a ground-breaking story on my hands." She stood, wrapping each leg of the hose around her wrists and pulling it taut between her fists, arming herself with a strangulation device. "The perfect ending would be to find you and your stalker dead together in his last, fiery masterpiece."

Meghan picked up the larger of the two pieces of wood and wielded it like a baseball bat in her hands. "If you kill me, you'll die in here, too. Haven't you noticed? The smoke alarms aren't going off."

"I took out the batteries." Saundra advanced slowly. "And Dennis, my cameraman is already on his way to meet me here. If I don't show up, I'm sure he'll come looking. Imagine. Me happening upon this tragic murder-suicide, and then getting caught in the fire. How courageous I am to cover this story." She smiled a wicked smile. "My rescue will be the lead story, I'm sure."

"There are children sleeping upstairs." How could this woman ever justify endangering a child's life? "If they get caught in this fire, you'll have mass murder on your hands."

"Who are they? Orphans? Wards of the state? Who's going to miss them?" She was now circling around Meghan. "It'll make a tragic little sidebar for my story."

A fierce, red-hot rush of maternal emotion kindled every protective instinct inside Meghan. "You bitch."

She swung the wood. Saundra ducked and lunged, hitting Meghan in the gut and driving her back into the wall. But Saundra Ames was merely fighting for her own survival. Meghan was fighting for her children.

The wood made a satisfying whack against Saundra's back. It was enough to loosen her grip. Meghan shoved and Saundra stumbled backward and lost her balance. She hit her head on the side of the furnace and collapsed to the floor.

As much as she hated the woman, it was still part of Meghan's training to check her wound and to feel her neck for a pulse. Out cold, but living. "Good," said Meghan, damning charity for the moment. "I want you to pay."

But she still had one tiny, little problem. She looked up at the smoke gathering near the ceiling and slowly filling the room.

"Gideon." She whispered his name like a prayer, sinking down onto her knees and hugging herself, wishing his arms were around her now. "Come find me."

Chapter Fourteen

"Where the hell is she?"

Gideon wiped the moisture from his watch and checked it again. Twenty minutes ago they'd run outside to secure the house against the storm. He and Josh had been outside when the transformer had blown. Handing his keys to his brother, Gideon found a flashlight in the kitchen and ran upstairs to check on its occupants.

Mark had been startled awake, but Dorie was rocking him back and forth in a chair to soothe him back to sleep. Alex, standing guard in his big brother sort of way, stifled a yawn. And Eddie asked a question about how many fires were actually started by lightning.

"Go to sleep, Poindexter," Gideon teased him. By the time he'd explained that reference to the curious kid, several minutes had passed.

"You, too, big guy." He squeezed Alex's shoulder. After all his hard work, the young man was practically asleep on his feet. "Time to turn in." With the younger boys taken care of, Gideon and Alex came back downstairs.

And found no sign of Meghan.

"She can't have wandered off."

"She was outside in this?" asked Alex, perking up with concern.

"Maybe the dog got away from her." Josh slicked the water from his hair and wiped it on his pants leg.

"Maybe." But Gideon's radar was screaming at him. Meghan was alone. And "worried" didn't begin to describe what she was feeling. "You want to take the basement or outside?"

"There's a flashlight in my truck," offered Josh. "I'll brave the rain."

"I'll help," Alex volunteered.

Gideon spared a smile for both men. "Thanks."

"We'll find her." Josh nodded to Alex, and they headed out onto the patio.

The instant Gideon opened the basement door, Crispy shot out between his legs. The smoke billowed up seconds later. "Meghan!"

Gideon charged down the steps, but his path was blocked by the wall of flame that engulfed the basement. "Meg, answer me! Are you down here?"

Intense heat singed his skin and he lifted his arm to shield his eyes. He didn't even consider the possibility of one of Eddie's lightning-strike fires. The flames themselves provided enough light to see the damning pattern of arson. Whatever chemical had been splashed across the carpeting and walls was a quick burner and already hot enough to start melting the plastic fibers and blistering the paint.

This lady was alive. The fire extinguisher upstairs couldn't put it out. He pulled his cell phone from his pocket and called it in. Address. Description. Number of occupants in the house.

He leaped back a couple of steps as flames shot up like grabbing hands. "Meg!" he called again, feeling the sting of toxins unleashed by the heat burn his eyes and throat. His heart thumped an uneven rhythm, charged by adrenaline and weighted by fear.

If the response wasn't quick enough, and the fire contained down here, the whole house would go. Why the hell hadn't the smoke alarm gone off down here? He'd run a fire inspection himself after Matthew's mishap. It had been working fine. This fire was well established and the smoke would already be working its way upstairs.

No alarms.

The boys.

"Meghan?" He coughed and called her name again as he backed up the stairs. The one reassuring observation he could make was that the door to the furnace room was shut tight. If she was in there, and the fire out here, she could safely secure herself for several minutes before the smoke ate up all her oxygen. He'd find another way into that room if he had to. "I'll find you, sweetheart," he whispered, praying Josh or Alex already had.

Torn between responsibilities, Gideon ran up the stairs to wake the house and to find his brother. He'd better stumble across Meghan, too.

If not, the fire and the past and the future be damned. He'd cross through hell itself to save the woman he loved.

MEGHAN COUGHED. A hammer pounded inside her head with each jerking movement. The blackness around her swirled and flickered as she opened her eyes and breathed through the pain. When had she lost consciousness?

"Gideon?" She could barely mouth the word. But she'd sensed his presence a moment ago. She could feel his love and strength filling her heart and answering her prayers.

Smoke had filled the room, robbing her of precious air. Saundra Ames still lay unconscious beside her accomplice. Meghan had no intention of becoming the third body in that pile. She needed to do something. She rolled onto her hands and knees, staying close to the floor. "Help me!" She grabbed a chunk of wood and hurled it against the glass. "Help me!"

"Meg!"

She heard his voice like an answered prayer.

"Gideon?" She saw him at the window and her heart melted into a puddle of relief. "I can't get it open," she shouted through the glass. "We're trapped. There's no air."

"Stand back."

Obeying the order without question, she hunkered down behind a stack of boxes. She lost sight of Gideon a moment before she saw the soles of two big shoes brace against the glass. He kicked once. Again. The whole window shattered and flew out into the room. Meghan shielded her face from the rain of glass. The sudden influx of oxygen sucked the air from her lungs. With a flood of new air to consume, the fire licked itself into a tiny flame at the cracks of the door. It was coming.

Meghan didn't wait for Gideon's command to climb. Knocking aside the big shards of glass, she tiptoed onto the first crate, found a safe spot to step on the second. He spread a turnout coat at the base of the window to protect her from the ragged glass frame.

"There are two victims down here," she reported, her firefighter training temporarily overriding her fear. "One unconscious, one dead."

"EMT's are on their way," he assured her in his commander's voice. But then that hard tone softened. "You don't look in that great a shape yourself. I've got you, sweetheart." And then a long, strong arm reached in through the window, promising shelter, care, rescue. "Give me your hand, sweetheart. That's an order."

Latching on, hand to wrist, she met his offer strength for strength.

Holding tight, he pulled her free. Meghan tumbled into his chest as he fell onto his backside and gathered her into his arms. "Oh, God, baby." He bathed her face in hundreds of tiny kisses. "I thought I'd lost you. I thought—"

She framed his jaw between her hands and stopped up his mouth with a powerful kiss. "Thank you" was all she could think to say as he turned the kiss into a powerful affirmation of life and love. "And the boys?"

"They're safe. I want to work things out, sweetheart." He kissed her once. "I have an idea to run past you." He kissed her again. "I want to—"

"Get a room, guys." Josh Taylor cleared his throat to politely snag their attention. He towered over them as the rain pelted down around them. "Good to see you, Meghan. This guy's been driving me nuts looking for you."

"Shut up, Josh. I'm trying to propose."

"What?" Had she heard him right?

"There's more." Gideon kissed her once more and stood, pulling her up beside him without explanation as he ordered Josh to report their status on his radio. "Tell the chief I found her and give the EMT's this location. But we're not out of this yet."

"Got it."

"Josh, wait." She grabbed his sleeve and stopped him. "I've got your arsonist. And my stalker. Jack Quinton. He's the dead man. Saundra Ames is in the basement, too."

"Hell of a time for an interview."

"She killed Quinton." Meghan knew she had a lot of explaining to do. So did Gideon. She nodded toward the basement. "If you want justice, talk to her. She's got quite a story to report."

Josh crouched beside the opening and shone a light inside. He swore when he saw the body. Gideon hugged her tight and she gladly huddled close to his warmth. But she couldn't bring herself to question what he'd meant a moment ago. There was too much going on right now.

Josh pulled out his cell phone and punched in a number.

"A.J." Whatever his partner was saying, he ignored it to ask her a question. "Which of them gave you those bruises?"

"Saundra. She was blackmailing Quinton. Getting herself the story of a lifetime." She shivered as the rain hit her skin. Shivered as she realized how close she'd come to death. "This was supposed to be the grand finale. I didn't want to be part of the story anymore."

As Josh left to fill in his partner, Gideon untucked his wet shirt and peeled it off. "Interesting outfit. You *are* okay, aren't you?"

Meghan's blush heated her skin from the inside out. Her bra and panties were hardly the right uniform for fighting fires, but she still had the presence of mind to ask about the situation. "Can the fire be contained? And what did you mean by proposing while I'm in my underwear in the pouring rain while the house is on fire?"

He grinned suspiciously. "I never claimed to be a romantic. Let's take care of business first, then I promise I'll do better." He slipped his shirt over her head and pulled it down while she pushed her arms through the sleeves. "The rain's helping suppress the fire. But it looks like Dorie will lose the basement and the dining room and den above it. The south end of the house and the upstairs might be all right." The EMT's and police were arriving on the scene as he pulled her back to his side and she hugged herself close to the warmth and scent of his rain-sleek skin. "Let's go out front to the command center."

"Gideon!" They turned as one as Josh jogged up to meet them.

"What's wrong?" Gideon asked.

"Dorie's blood pressure spiked and she passed out. She's gonna be okay. But in the confusion of getting her into the ambulance and stabilizing her, she lost track of Matthew."

Meghan clutched Gideon's arm and felt it tremble. He

sensed it, too. An awful, empty dread clutched at her empty belly. "Please don't tell me this."

"I'm sorry. He didn't know you'd been found." Josh's grim apology took in both Meghan and Gideon. "We think he went back into the house."

"I'LL GO." Meghan's weary resignation reverberated in the recesses of Gideon's soul. "Matthew won't be afraid of me."

He quickly assessed the way she shivered beneath the blanket the EMTs had draped around her shoulders, the stitched-up wound that was seeping blood, and the uncustomary fear that dulled her pretty eyes. He felt that same fear deep in his own heart. He put a hand on her shoulder and halted her march toward the nearest fire engine. "You're not in any shape to go into that fire." A sense of destiny thrummed along with the jitters of adrenaline flowing through his veins. "I'll go."

Meghan looked up into his eyes with such hope, such faith, he knew he couldn't fail. She made him stronger. She'd given him the precious gift of believing in himself again. And whether she knew it or not, she'd offered him the family he'd always wanted.

"I'll be okay with whatever happens to us, Gideon." She sounded as if she was making some sort of sacrifice. But he didn't have time to make her see, to understand. He released her only to pull on the pants and turnout coat one of the firefighters had brought him. "Just please...please keep Matthew safe."

"I heard the kid doesn't talk." One of the firefighters placed a helmet on his head, another handed him protective gloves. "How will you know where to find him?"

"I'll know."

Luke Redding's face popped into his mind. But it wasn't

a guilty reminder. He felt the strength and trust of his former partner instead.

Meghan squeezed his left hand when he hesitated. Tip-
ping back his helmet, he bent and kissed her soundly. "I'll
be back."

MEGHAN NEVER TOOK her eyes off the front door where
Gideon had gone in. He was such a noble man. Tall and
dark and strong. Gentle and patient. And good. He had such
a good heart.

She loved him so much.

Mark squirmed in her arms, sensing her tension if not
quite understanding the danger his brother was in.

"How long has it been?" she asked.

"Six minutes." Josh stood by her side, watching for his
brother just as diligently.

Other firefighters had retrieved the bodies from the basement. Saundra Ames was in an ambulance, handcuffed to
her gurney while A. J. Rodriguez questioned her. The fire
now engulfed the first floor of the house on the north end.
Smoke would have filled the upstairs by now. She hoped
Matthew was hiding in another closet, if not, the fumes...

"He'll be okay, Meghan." Alex had his arm around her
shoulders, acting far more confident and comforting than
his sixteen years. "Gid takes good care of us."

"Yes, he does." Tears stung her dry eyes. She'd been
around too much smoke. She'd been staring too long. She
blinked them away, trying to be strong. "You boys love
him, don't you?"

Eddie snorted in front of her. "Well, yeah. In a manly
man kind of way."

Meghan leaned over and kissed the crown of his head.
That was quite an admission for the tough guy. "He'll be
all right."

Another minute passed. And while the fire was no longer

spreading, she could see smoke streaming from the upstairs windows. She prayed.

The scene commander approached, his white turnout coat reflecting the lights from the trucks and the spotlights that shone on the house to direct the spray of water. "I'm sending in another team," he announced. "He's been in there eight minutes."

"No, wait." Meghan latched on to his sleeve before he could give the order. "Matthew will be terrified. He knows Gideon."

"But to save his life?"

She wasn't above begging. "Please, Chief. One more minute."

"One minute." He nodded and walked away.

"Come on, Gideon. You can save him." He'd saved her. Her heart, her soul, her self-esteem, her life—Gideon had saved them all. She wouldn't believe he'd lost his way in the fire. She wouldn't believe he'd give up without a fight. She wouldn't believe he wasn't coming back. "Gideon."

A minute passed and a tear streamed down her face. She hugged Mark tight in her arms as a new team of firefighters prepped for the rescue.

"Come on, sweetheart," she breathed. "I believe in you."

She jumped as one of the front windows exploded. "No!"

They couldn't have flashover. The whole house would be engulfed. "Gideon!"

A heartbeat past hopeless she saw the ax strike the window again. "Gideon!"

Unthinkable terror became heart-pounding joy as a black-clad firefighter crawled through the window, carrying a bundled-up blanket in his arms. And then she was running. Running to meet the hero who carried a precious little boy in his arms.

"Meg?" He pushed off his helmet and tugged the mask from his face. "Meg! He's all right. Matthew's all right."

She threw her arm around his neck and thanked him and rewarded his soot-streaked mouth with a kiss. "Thank you." She was weeping openly now. "Thank you." Gideon pushed the blanket away from Matthew, but kept him in his arms. She hugged the boy and the man and kissed Matthew's chubby face. "You scared me, sweetheart. I love you so much. I don't know what we'd do if you got hurt."

Alex and Eddie were there. And Josh. And little Mark. Crispy, too. There were handshakes and hugs and tears and smiles. And in the middle of all the chaos, a soft little voice was finally heard.

"I want you to be my daddy." Meghan gasped in open-mouthed shock. But it didn't come close to matching the pride and humility and absolute love that shone in Gideon's wide, startled eyes. Matthew blinked at her. "And you can be my mommy."

Gideon hugged the boy tight in his big, sheltering arms. Despite the tears that glistened in his eyes, he was laughing. And while Meghan tried to absorb the miracle, Gideon turned those beautiful eyes to her.

"Sounds like a plan to me." He reached out and stroked the tears from her cheeks with the backs of his fingers, holding the child safe and confidently in his left hand. "What do you say, Meg? I asked this once before. Will you marry me?"

Meghan sniffed. Her heart was breaking. Her heart was hoping. "But, Gideon, you know I can't give you children. No matter how much we love each other, that will never change."

He looked around the circle at each expectant expression. Alex. Eddie. Matthew. Mark. "We have four boys already. How many kids do you want?"

She was stunned, but no more so than the boys. "Are you talking about adoption?"

"I can't see my life without you. And I can't see my life without them. Make us happy."

The chorus of proposals was sweet and loud and impossible to resist.

"Yeah!"

"Come on, Meghan!"

"You gotta marry us."

"Mommy."

She'd had more than her share of hard knocks in her life. She'd been denied happiness time and again. But she was no dummy. She simply smiled and said, "Yes. I'll marry all of you."

Meghan was reduced to that euphoric combination of tears and laughter by the time Gideon had swept her into his embrace and she was well and thoroughly kissed. She kissed each boy. She kissed Josh. Then Gideon handed Matthew over to Alex, took her into his arms and kissed her again.

Eddie voiced one of his typical questions. "Are you guys going to be doing that all the time?"

Meg tried to put some space between them and come up with an age-appropriate answer, but Gideon beat her to it. "Yes."

She blushed. "Well, not—"

"Yes," he corrected her, and hugged her close again. He looked at Eddie and shared a grin that was more like a kid's than a thirty-six-year-old man's. "In a few years, you'll meet a girl and you'll be wanting to do this all the time, too."

Eddie's answer was emphatic. "Ooh. Gross." Having had his fill of romance, he walked away toward one of the ambulances, with Crispy trotting merrily at his heels. "I'll tell Dorie what you guys are up to."

Gideon laughed, but Meghan knew how to remind him of his place. "In a few years he'll be a teenager, and we won't want him to be doing that all the time."

Gideon looked stricken. Fatherhood had responsibilities as well as joys. "Can I take that back?"

But Meghan laughed and circled her arms around his neck. "You wanted to be a dad."

He nodded. "Yeah. But more than that, I want to be your husband."

"These boys belong to my heart." She touched his cheek and thanked God for her miracle. "Just like you."

HARLEQUIN®
INTRIGUE®

presents another outstanding installment
in our bestselling series

COLORADO
CONFIDENTIAL

By day these agents are cowboys; by night they are
specialized government operatives. Men bound by love,
loyalty and the law—they've vowed to keep their
missions and identities confidential...

August 2003
ROCKY MOUNTAIN MAVERICK
BY GAYLE WILSON

September 2003
SPECIAL AGENT NANNY
BY LINDA O. JOHNSTON

In **October**, look for an exciting short-story collection
featuring *USA TODAY* bestselling author
JASMINE CRESSWELL

November 2003
COVERT COWBOY
BY HARPER ALLEN

December 2003
A WARRIOR'S MISSION
BY RITA HERRON

PLUS
FIND OUT HOW IT ALL BEGAN
with three tie-in books from Harlequin Historicals,
starting January 2004

Available at your favorite retail outlet.

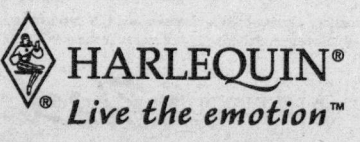

HARLEQUIN®
Live the emotion™

Visit us at www.eHarlequin.com

HICCAST

Is your man too good to be true?

Hot, gorgeous AND romantic?
If so, he could be a Harlequin® Blaze™ series cover model!

Our grand-prize winners will receive a trip for two to New York City to
shoot the cover of a Blaze novel, and will stay at the luxurious Plaza Hotel.

Plus, they'll receive $500 U.S. spending money!

The runner-up winners will receive $200 U.S.
to spend on a romantic dinner for two.

It's easy to enter!

In 100 words or less, tell us what makes your boyfriend or spouse a true romantic
and the perfect candidate for the cover of a Blaze novel, and include in your submission
two photos of this potential cover model.

All entries must include the written submission of the contest entrant, two photographs of the model
candidate and the Official Entry Form and Publicity Release forms completed in full and signed by
both the model candidate and the contest entrant. Harlequin, along with the experts at
Elite Model Management, will select a winner.

For photo and complete Contest details, please refer to the Official Rules on the next page. All entries
will become the property of Harlequin Enterprises Ltd. and are not returnable.

**Please visit www.blazecovermodel.com to download a copy of the Official Entry Form and
Publicity Release Form or send a request to one of the addresses below.**

Please mail your entry to: **Harlequin Blaze Cover Model Search**

In U.S.A.	In Canada
P.O. Box 9069	P.O. Box 637
Buffalo, NY	Fort Erie, ON
14269-9069	L2A 5X3

No purchase necessary. Contest open to Canadian and U.S. residents who are 18 and over.
Void where prohibited. Contest closes September 30, 2003.

HBCVRMODEL1

From the bestselling author
of *The Deepest Water*

KATE WILHELM

SKELETONS

Lee Donne is an appendix in a family of overachievers. Her mother has three doctorates,
her father is an economics genius and her grandfather is a world-renowned Shakespearean
scholar. After four years of college and three majors, Lee is nowhere closer to a degree.
With little better to do, she agrees to house-sit for her grandfather.

But the quiet stay she envisioned ends abruptly when she begins to hear strange noises
at night. Something is hidden in the house…and someone is determined to find it.
Suddenly Lee finds herself caught in a game of cat and mouse, the reasons for which she
doesn't understand. But when the FBI arrives on the doorstep, she realizes that the house
may hold dark secrets that go beyond her own family. And that sometimes, long-buried
skeletons rise up from the grave.